Praise for the Novels of Ralph Cotton

"Disarming realism . . . solidly crafted."

—*Publishers Weekly*

"The sort of story we all hope to find within us: the bloodstained, gun-smoked, grease-stained yarn that yanks a reader right out of today." —Terry Johnston

"Cotton writes with the authentic ring of a silver dollar, a storyteller in the best tradition of the Old West."

—Matt Braun

"Evokes a sense of outlawry . . . distinctive."

—*Lexington Herald-Leader*

"Cotton's blend of history and imagination works because authentic Old West detail and dialogue fill his books." —*Wild West Magazine*

RIDE TO HELL'S GATE

Ralph Cotton

A SIGNET BOOK

SIGNET
Published by New American Library, a division of
Penguin Group (USA) Inc., 375 Hudson Street,
New York, New York 10014, USA
Penguin Group (Canada), 90 Eglinton Avenue East, Suite 700, Toronto,
Ontario M4P 2Y3, Canada (a division of Pearson Penguin Canada Inc.)
Penguin Books Ltd., 80 Strand, London WC2R 0RL, England
Penguin Ireland, 25 St. Stephen's Green, Dublin 2,
Ireland (a division of Penguin Books Ltd.)
Penguin Group (Australia), 250 Camberwell Road, Camberwell, Victoria 3124,
Australia (a division of Pearson Australia Group Pty. Ltd.)
Penguin Books India Pvt. Ltd., 11 Community Centre, Panchsheel Park,
New Delhi - 110 017, India
Penguin Group (NZ), 67 Apollo Drive, Rosedale, North Shore 0632,
New Zealand (a division of Pearson New Zealand Ltd.)
Penguin Books (South Africa) (Pty.) Ltd., 24 Sturdee Avenue,
Rosebank, Johannesburg 2196, South Africa

Penguin Books Ltd., Registered Offices:
80 Strand, London WC2R 0RL, England

First published by Signet, an imprint of New American Library,
a division of Penguin Group (USA) Inc.

First Printing, September 2008
10 9 8 7 6 5 4 3 2 1

Printed in the United States of America

PUBLISHER'S NOTE
This is a work of fiction. Names, characters, places, and incidents either are the product of the author's imagination or are used fictitiously, and any resemblance to actual persons, living or dead, business establishments, events, or locales is entirely coincidental.

The publisher does not have any control over and does not assume any responsibility for author or third-party Web sites or their content.

For Mary Lynn . . . of course

PART 1

Chapter 1

Matamoros, Mexico

Lawrence Shaw, aka Fast Larry, aka the Fastest Gun Alive, aka the Mad Gunman, aka Chever Reed, had been too drunk for too long to be standing in a dirt street about to do battle. Yet here he stood, squinting through a whiskey haze. He held his right hand poised at the butt of the big Colt holstered on his hip. He stood with his feet spread shoulder-width apart, not so much in preparation for a gunfight, but rather to settle the unsteady world beneath him and keep himself from falling.

"I know who you are," Titus Boland, stone sober, called out from thirty feet away, advancing slowly toward Shaw as he spoke.

So do I, Shaw answered to himself, not sure what he meant, or if he could have formed any intelligent reply even if he'd intended to. Instead he only nodded; he dared not attempt a step forward, not until the world stopped spinning and wobbling before his bloodshot eyes.

"You're sure as hell not Chever Reed, the attorney from Brownsville, the man you've tricked everybody here into thinking you are. You're Lawrence Shaw, the murdering coward from Somo Santos, Texas," Boland called out. "I aim to take from you what you took from my poor brother, Ned, in Eagle Pass . . . *your life!*"

All right, now on with it. Shaw nodded again; he didn't care. He stared at Boland, feeling his bleary eyes begin to focus. He wasn't the least bit concerned with Titus Boland's angry threats, even though he knew Boland meant every word he'd said and had every intention of killing him, right here, right now, drunk or sober. It made no difference to Boland. *Me neither, as far as that goes,* Shaw thought, taking a deep, drunken breath.

Lawrence Shaw had long forgotten how many men had shouted the same threats at him from countless dirt streets, from hastily abandoned saloon bars, from overturned card tables, from hotels, restaurants, houses of ill repute. . . . Death threats all sounded the same; they had for a long time.

"Let's get it done," Shaw managed to say without his thick tongue betraying him. He almost attempted a step forward now that his senses seemed to be returning. But unsure, he stopped himself at the last second and remained standing perfectly still.

"I've been killing you in my sleep for more than three years, Fast Larry!" Boland bellowed. "Today I'm bringing everybody's chickens home to roost."

A few feet behind him, to his left, one of Boland's

gunmen pals, Albert McClinton, looked sidelong at Vincent Tomes and whispered, "What the hell is he talking about, *chickens roosting*?"

"I don't know. Hush up," Tomes replied nervously without taking his eyes off Shaw. "This Shaw fellow is faster than a rattlesnake. We do not want to be caught unawares by him."

"Yeah, but *chickens roosting*?" Albert persisted, still in a whisper. "I don't see what *chickens roosting* has got to do with any—"

"It's just a figure of speech, *damn it*!" Tomes growled. "Now spread out, so's one shot don't kill us both! I wish I'd never got talked into this."

"That goes double for me," McClinton murmured.

Okay, there's three of them. Shaw grinned to himself. *Good.* Maybe these three were the ones who would do it. Maybe this would be the day the undertaker closed the lid over his face and lowered him into the ground forever. *Mexico, eh . . . ?* So this was where it would happen. He cut a glance across the wide street, seeing colorful banners and streamers fluttering on a breeze in front of the American consulate building a block away.

Mexico would do, he told himself. He'd always liked Mexico. Rosa was from Mexico, not far from here. That was good enough for him. *Ah, Rosa, dear precious Rosa,* he said silently to his deceased wife, partly closing his eyes. For a numb, drunken moment he felt a deep joy sweep over him. Was she here? Could she see him? He hoped so; God, he hoped so. *I'm coming to you at last, Rosa,* he spoke silently to her, even as the three gunmen settled into position.

"Here it is, Shaw!" Boland shouted, his fingers opening and closing restlessly. "Anything you want to say before I send you straight to hell?"

Shaw shook his head slowly, a dreamy smile on his lips as he thought of Rosa, seeing her loving face, her dark eyes. He could feel her arms warm around him. "Get it done," he said, his hand poised and relaxed near his holster as if he might or might not decide to draw it when the time came.

"My God, look at him!" Tomes whispered to McClinton in a shaken voice as the two stood a few feet apart. "He's as calm and cold-blooded as any man I've seen! He has no doubt what's about to happen here."

"Because he knows for cocksure that he's going to kill us all," McClinton replied, his voice strained and shaky.

"Go for your gun, Shaw!" Boland raged, seeing Shaw's indifferent attitude. "Else I'll kill you anyway. It makes me no never-mind if you fight back or not!"

Still wearing his drunken, reposed smile, Shaw slapped his hand to his gun butt.

Instantly Boland made the same move, his Colt coming up cocked and firing as Shaw's hand seemed to stick to his holstered gun. McClinton and Tomes stood stunned, not believing their eyes, as Boland's bullet punched Shaw in the right shoulder. The drunken man pitched forward, unfazed by the gunshot wound, and landed passed out cold, facedown in the dirt.

"Watch it, Boland!" Tomes warned, sidestepping

away with his gun drawn and ready to fire. "It's just a ploy!"

"A ploy?" Titus Boland cut Tomes a disgusted look as he advanced toward Shaw, who was lying limply in the street. "This is no *ploy.* He's hit. I nailed him fair and square." He stopped a few feet from Shaw and aimed the gun down at the back of his head. "This one here is for my poor deceased brother."

But before Boland could pull the trigger, he and the other two froze at the sound of a shotgun cocking behind them. "Drop your guns, hombres," a voice said with urgent determination.

Without turning or dropping his gun, Boland said over his shoulder, "Oh? And just who is making this request?"

"It is no request. It is an order," the voice said. "I am Gerardo Luna, constable of Matamoros. But it will not matter to you who I am if you do not do as I say."

"Gerardo Luna? The one all the local vaqueros and rounders call *Moon*?" Recognizing the name, Boland lowered his gun and let his aim move away from Shaw's head.

"*Senor* Moon to you," said the Mexican lawman. He stepped forward, in between Tomes and McClinton, and nudged first one, then the other with his shotgun barrel. Their guns fell to the dirt.

"With all respect, *Senor* Moon," Boland said, his gun still in hand, "but you're meddling in a fair fight. He drew first."

"His gun is still holstered," said Luna with an accent. "He is drunk. He passed out and fell. I saw it on my way here. Lucky for you I was not in range, or *mi pequeño ángel* here would have shot you into the sky. Now, *you* drop *it*, or *I* drop *you*."

Boland sighed. He uncocked his Colt and let it fall to the dirt. He relaxed a little and looked at the shotgun in Luna's hands. "Your *little angel,* eh?"

"*Si,* my little angel," Luna repeated. He gestured down at the ornate eight-gauge shotgun with its brass-trimmed, fluted barrel and its tall hammers, which were drawn back.

"Well, ain't that just sweet as can be," Boland said stiffly. "Maybe we'll meet someday while your *little angel* ain't handy. We'll reflect back on this thing from a whole other outlook. You just might find I'm a man you do not want to anger—"

Almost before the words left his mouth, Tomes and McClinton winced at the sound of the shotgun butt snapping up into his chin. Blood and broken teeth spilled from his lips as he fell to the ground beside Shaw.

"Whoa!" Tomes said instinctively. "You had no cause to bust the man up that way."

"Oh, you think not?" Luna took a step toward him.

Tomes and McClinton both backed away. Tomes raised a hand in a show of peace and said quickly, "Although I can certainly understand how you might have thought it was justified. . . . Titus has a way of getting testy if he goes unchecked."

"Which, in all honesty, he is prone to do from time

to time," McClinton joined in, also raising his hands chest high in submission.

"I see," said Luna, the short shotgun still clenched in his fists. "I am happy that you both agree with my decision." He jerked a nod toward the knocked-out gunman. "Now get him up and out of here. It looks bad, hombres lying in the middle of my street."

Poco Río, Mexico

Cray Dawson stepped from behind the stone wall circling the village well, raised his Colt and took aim at the fleeing horseman through a rise of dust from the horse's hooves. But at the last second he held his fire, seeing the faces of frightened women and children, seeking cover, dart back and forth.

"Don't let him get away," warned his partner, Jedson Caldwell, standing across the narrow street from him with a hand pressed to his bleeding side.

"I couldn't risk it." Dawson lowered his Colt and let it hang at his side. "Too many villagers in the way." Blood from a bullet graze ran down his left forearm and dripped from the cuff of his shirtsleeve. Inside one of the small adobe and plank homes a baby cried loudly.

"That was Black Jake Patterson," Caldwell said, stepping forward and standing beside Dawson. The two watched the fleeing gunman sink down out of sight over a rise of sand. "There's still one more somewhere around here," he added cautiously, scanning the street as he spoke, his eyes going to four sweat-streaked horses at a hitch rail.

"Yes, it's Leo Fairday," said Dawson. He looked at the three bodies strewn along the narrow street. Then he looked at the darkened doorway of a dingy cantina and called out, "Leo, I know you're in there. Throw out your gun and show yourself. We'll take you in alive."

"Now that is damned generous of you, Dawson," said a voice from inside the cantina. The voice was followed by a dark chuckle. "But I've another idea you might want to think about."

A burly older gunman, Leo Fairday, stepped forward from the cantina. He held his left arm wrapped around the neck of a young girl who wore nothing but a ragged blanket she held against her breasts.

"Turn her loose, Fairday," Dawson said. "Holding her hostage won't buy you a thing." Yet even as Dawson spoke he knew this changed everything.

"Oh, I say you're wrong, lawdog," said Fairday with the same dark chuckle, the tip of his big Remington shoved up tight under the young woman's cheek. "I say it buys me the way to my horse and a good head start out of here . . . less you want to spend the evening picking her brains off your hats."

"Senors, *por favor*, do not let me die, I beg of you!" the girl sobbed in broken English. "I have a small baby! She needs her mother—!"

"Shut up, whore," Fairday warned, poking her harder with the gun barrel. "I'll say whether you live or die. All these bummers can do is what I tell them to do."

"Easy, Fairday," Dawson said calmly. "You'll get what you're asking for." He lowered his gun barrel but left the big Colt cocked and ready in case he needed it. Looking at Caldwell he said, "Let him go, Jed. He gets off free this time." He turned a cold stare back to Fairday. "But only if he turns her loose, *unharmed*."

"I'll let her go, Dawson, once I get my knees in the wind and catch up to my pard there." Fairday nodded toward the dust from the other fleeing gunman. He stepped backward to the hitch rail where he'd tied his horse earlier. "But until then this girl stays alive only if everybody acts right, *comprende*?" He poked the gun barrel enough to cause the girl to gasp in pain. She stared wide-eyed and fearfully at Dawson.

"Yeah, I understand," Dawson said. There was no point in trying to reason or threaten. He could only grit his teeth and stand by helplessly watching as the gunman stepped between two horses and swung up into his saddle in a way that gave neither Dawson nor Caldwell a chance to take a shot at him.

"Give me your word!" Fairday demanded.

"All right, you've got my word," said Dawson. "Don't hurt her."

" 'Don't hurt her,' " Fairday mimicked with a chuckle, backing the horse out into the street with the naked girl on his lap. With the cocked gun still beneath her chin, he said with mock mannerism, "Do have yourselves a *mescal*, gentlemen." Then his false manners changed quickly. "If I see your dust on my trail before I reach the hills, you'll find this little chili pepper staked down Apache style, gutted like a deer."

Dawson and Caldwell stood watching the young woman tremble in terror at the sound of Fairday's words. When the horse had backed and sidestepped itself ten yards away from them, Fairday turned the animal quickly and rode away, looking back over his shoulder.

"Now what?" Caldwell asked, his hand still pressed to his bleeding side. He wore black gloves with the fingers cut short at his first knuckle.

"Now we wait until he reaches the hills, just like I said we would," said Dawson with disgust and anger at himself. He stared after Fairday and the young woman.

Riding away from Poco Río at a fast pace, Fairday reached a gloved hand down into the young woman's naked lap and pinched her playfully. "You did good, honey, real good."

Slapping his gloved hand away, the young woman said in a pouting voice, "I should be angry with you, poking me with that gun barrel . . . calling me a *puta*."

"Aw, now, little darling, I had to make it look real, didn't I?" Fairday said, grinning. "Besides, you are a *puta*, and a dang good one at that." He reached up and jiggled her breast. The girl giggled and slapped halfheartedly at his hand.

Chapter 2

Gathering their horses from the streets of Poco Río, Dawson and Caldwell led the tired animals toward a lean-to livery shed. "We've got to have more men riding with us," Caldwell said, pushing up the brim of his stylish, flat-crowned black hat. "You've got to tell them."

"We won't get any more men," replied Dawson, watching the dust rise from Fairday's horse's hooves. "You heard Messenger. It's up to you and me, nobody else."

Caldwell shook his head. "We threw down on *five* men. *Two* of them got away from us. It shouldn't have happened. It *wouldn't* have happened if we'd had more men. We need *more men*," he repeated firmly. "We're both worn to a frazzle. We need to rest." A black string tie lay loosely around his neck. His white shirt had turned the color of sand, suet and dried sweat.

"Then we'll have to manage to get ourselves some

rest," said Dawson. "But that's all we'll get. Don't expect anything from Messenger and his *federal government* boys."

"Then we're in big trouble." Caldwell gestured toward the two fleeing gunmen's rise of dust. "Once the Barrows and Sepreano join forces, we won't stand a chance against them. Maybe Messenger needs to ask himself how he's going to feel facing the president, telling him this border operation didn't work."

Hearing the exhausted tone of Caldwell's voice and noting the wound in his side, Dawson said, "Why don't you stay here, get a hot meal and some rest. Get your wound looked after. I'll ride on out and bring the girl back."

"I'm riding with you to bring the girl back, in case Fairday has a trap waiting for you," Caldwell replied firmly. "But maybe afterward it's time we both turned back, returned this dog to its pen."

"I'm not turning back." Dawson stopped and allowed his horse to lower its muzzle into a trough of water beneath the shade of the lean-to overhang.

"In that case, neither am I," said Caldwell, letting his horse drink beside Dawson's. "But if the U.S. government doesn't give us the help we need, we might want to consider taking the matter into our own hands, bring in some guns without them knowing about it."

"Yeah?" Dawson said wryly. "Look around us, Jed. These hill-country folks are too poor to afford corn, let alone guns and bullets. Anybody who knows how to use a gun around here has either been killed by Sepreano and his gang, or thrown in with them."

On the street behind them, villagers ventured forward. Some of them stripped the deceased's pockets inside out in search of money before dragging the bodies away. At a hitch rail the two dead men's horses had already disappeared, as if by magic.

When Leo Fairday reached a trail at the base of the hills, he followed it up into the cover of broken rock, scrub pine and juniper. There he stopped the horse, let the girl down from his lap and stepped down behind her. "Well, little darling," he said, handing her the blanket that had come undone during the ride, "looks like this is where we say adios, for now anyway."

The girl wrapped herself in the blanket and pulled her long, disheveled hair back and wrapped it deftly in a way that held it in place. "*Si*, and now for my money," she said with a smile, extending her hand.

"Money? What money?" Fairday shrugged. "I already paid you for everything we did back at Poco Río."

She kept her hand out, wiggling her fingers. "You said if I would act like you were stealing me away, you would give me *more* money."

"Did I? I swear I can't recall. . . ." Fairday appeared to think hard about the matter.

"*Si*, you did, and you know you did," the girl insisted, keeping her hand out.

Fairday gave a strained, perplexed grin. "In the heat of excitement it must have slipped my mind. How's about let's say you just did this because you like ole Leo so much, you know, for the way I always take good care of you when I ride through these parts? Sort of a token of your fondness?" He took a step toward her, his arms outspread.

But the girl would have none of it. She stepped back saying, "No, no, no," and shook her head. "I give myself to you only for the money, nothing else."

"Now that is awfully cold-hearted of you, little darling," Fairday said, appearing taken aback by her words and actions.

"Don't put me off, Leo," the girl said, her attitude growing more emboldened. "You said you would give me something extra, and I want it."

Leo shook his head as he reached inside his shirt pocket and took out a sweat-dampened roll of cash. "All right then. I suppose I shouldn't have expected anything different from you. Your mama was the same way, always grubbing for every dollar she could squeeze out of a fellow."

"Leave my mother out of this, Leo," she said in a strong tone, her hand extended toward him.

"Here." Fairday peeled off two one-dollar bills from the roll and flung them at her. She snatched the bills from the air and gripped them tightly as she looked at them.

"Is this all? Two dollars for helping you escape the law?" she asked, more angry than disappointed.

Leo looked embarrassed. "Don't push me, honey," he warned. "The law is no big deal to me. They're always after me for something or other." He tried to turn away and step back into his stirrup.

"And now what?" the girl asked. "You are going

to leave me out here? I must walk all the way back to Poco Río?"

"Yep, that's what I had in mind. But you ain't hurting. Play your cards right and those lawdogs will be fighting one another to see which one carries your plump little bottom back to town on their lap." Leo chuckled and started to step up into the saddle. But he stopped with his hand on the saddle horn when the girl slapped his shoulder.

"You stinking old pig!" she shouted, swinging at him with both hands. "It is no wonder the other girls have nothing to do with you! It was only I who took pity on you and let you do what you wanted to inside me! You are old and dirty, and you smell like—"

Her words stopped short. Leo backhanded her away from him; her blanket flew away. She landed on her naked rear end in the dirt. He turned toward her in a fiery rage, but then he stopped and took a deep breath and kept control of himself. Raising a finger for emphasis he said, "Your mama never acted like that. She knew how far to go and when to stop."

"My mother died a penniless whore!" the young girl shrieked, throwing the two wadded-up bills at him. "Killed by a pig like you!"

"Too bad she never taught you when to keep your mouth shut," Leo said. He turned back to his horse and stepped up into the saddle. "I don't have time, or I'd teach you myself. I'd paddle you with a plank." He winked at her, trying to keep control of himself, and turned his horse to the trail. "Try to settle yourself down some before those lawdogs get here."

"I hope they get here soon!" she shouted. "I want them to ride me back to Poco Río instead of you!" She threw a hand onto her naked hip. "I will give them whatever they want for *free*! Over and over I will give it to them!"

Leo Fairday made no response.

Seeing her words were having no effect, she shouted at him, "And I tell them what a tiny *pene* you have!" As she taunted him she looked all around, spotted a good throwing-sized rock, picked it up and hurled it at him. It struck him on the shoulder. "I will tell them what my mother told me about us . . . who you are and why you always choose me! I will tell them where you hide when you are not killing and robbing!"

Leo grunted and turned the horse around toward her, rubbing his shoulder. "What did you say?" he asked in a low and even voice.

She saw she had gone too far. She threw a hand to her mouth and said, "I didn't mean it. I would never tell where you hide."

"Before that," he said, his face red, his eyes wide, filled with rage and humiliation.

"Nothing," she said, backing up a step as he nudged his horse closer. "I don't know what I said! But you better stay away from me, or I *will* tell everybody!"

She saw his boot lift up from the stirrup and his hand go down to it. She saw his hand streak up and around in a high loop. But she did not see the big knife until she felt the blinding pain of sharp steel sink deep into her naked breast, the impact of the knife's hilt hitting her solidly and knocking her backward.

She struggled up onto her knees, gasping for breath, her hands trembling near the knife's hilt, yet not touching it. "*Santa . . . Madre—*," she pleaded for help brokenly in her native tongue.

"Now look at you," Fairday said, stepping down from his saddle. He took his time searching through his saddlebags and pulled out a rolled-up length of rawhide. Shaking out the long length of rawhide he walked calmly over to her. "You've let your mouth get you killed, you foolish girl."

"*Por favor,*" she begged, although she had no idea what she was asking from him, no idea what he could do for her now.

Fairday stooped down eye level and looked at her closely, cupping a hand to his ear. "What's that? Oh, you're sorry? Sorry for all those bad and cutting things you said to ole Leo?" He gave a cruel grin and gestured at the knife sticking from between her breasts, a growing web of blood spreading beneath it. "See, your mama could have told you not to ride me so hard. She knew how I was. But no, she was busy filling your head with things you shouldn't even know about. Now you've done it, and after me telling that lawman I wouldn't kill you."

"Please," she gasped in English, her voice growing weaker.

"You still won't shut up, will you?" Fairday grabbed her roughly by her wrist, wrapping the end of the rawhide around it and tying it tight. "Just so's you know," he said, his voice taking on an urgent sound, his breath quickening, "I'm going to stake you down and stir your guts up, Apache style, just like I said back in Poco Río."

Two miles farther up the hill trail, Black Jake Patterson held a bloody bandanna to the bullet graze along the side of his head. He'd watched Fairday's dust on the flatlands below until it dissipated up onto the winding hill trail. He'd waited another half hour before seeing the rider appear in and out of sight through the maze of rock, brush and scrub pine. When he recognized Leo Fairday he murmured to himself, "Leo, you old cur, if anybody else made it out of there I'd bet it'd be you."

Lying low in his saddle, Fairday searched the hard ground for any sign of Black Jake's hoofprints. As his horse rounded an upward turn and stepped into a clearing, a rifle shot exploded above him, kicking bits of dirt and rock against the spooked animal's forelegs.

"Halt. Who goes there?" Black Jake shouted down, stepping up from behind a large boulder and looking down with a dark laugh as Fairday struggled to settle his horse.

"Damn it, Jake!" Fairday replied, wobbling in the saddle, one hand planted atop his head to keep from losing his battered Stetson. "It's me! You see clear as day, it's me!"

"A man can't be too careful these days. For all I knew you could have been U.S. Federal Marshal Crayton Dawson dogging my trail." Black Jake laughed again at his little joke and levered another round into his rifle chamber as he looked back along the trail behind Fairday. "Did we kill them? Are they following us?"

"No, we didn't *kill* them," said Fairday, "but they're shot up same as us." Settling his nervous horse, he looked back himself. "I'll wager they heard that rifle shot and honed right in on us."

"Then they *are* following you?" said Black Jake, visoring a hand above his eyes for a better look.

"Yes, you can bet your mama's old corset they're following us," said Fairday. "What did you expect? Dawson ain't no easy piece of work."

Black Jake shook his head in disappointment. "I figured you boys would have killed them deader than hell, else I never would have left the way I did."

"Well, we didn't." Fairday crossed his wrists on his saddle horn. "I took the young whore with me, threatened to kill her. It got me a head start. But they'll still be coming."

"You mean the little half Mex? The one that's supposed to be kin to you?" asked Black Jake. As he spoke he backed away out of sight, picked up his horse's reins and led the animal the few yards down the trail toward Fairday.

"She's no kin of mine, Jake," Fairday called out to the rocks and brush. "It'll serve you well to know that saying she's my kin is the very thing that got Rodney Turner's throat cut and gullet sliced." He spit a stream of brown trail dust and wiped a hand across his dry lips, waiting until Black Jake stepped into sight.

"Then excuse the hell out of me," said Black Jake, walking out of a stand of trailside brush and leading his sweat-streaked dun. "I only mentioned it because that's what I heard."

Fairday stared at him for a moment, then said, "I was with her mama off and on for a year or two. That don't make us kin."

"It might," Black Jake said knowingly. Realizing he was pushing Fairday a bit more than he should, he kept his rifle handy as he led the dun onto the trail.

"And it *might not*," Fairday added quickly. His face reddened. "Anyway, she's dead. The lawdogs caught up to us. I had to leave her behind. I looked back and saw them kill her." He looked down at his saddle horn, shaking his head. "The poor girl . . . not much more than a child."

Black Jake studied him curiously, noting blood on his gloves and shirtsleeves. "*You* killed her, didn't you, Leo?"

Fairday bit his lower lip as if to keep himself from admitting what he'd done. But finally he said, "All right, damn it, maybe I did kill her. But we was no kin."

"I don't care who's kin or who's not," said Black Jake, "and I don't care that you killed her. I just like knowing what's going on around me."

"She wouldn't shut her mouth," said Fairday. "She kept on running me down, calling me names. She hit me with a rock." He rubbed his shoulder as he mentioned it.

"Well . . . so long, Poco Río." Black Jake stepped

up into his saddle. "Unless you want to lie up here and ambush Dawson and his pal."

"I don't want nothing to do with Dawson, unless there's more of us than you and me," said Fairday. "I don't think it's sporting of him and his dude-dressed deputy to be down here below the border stirring up trouble with us."

"Let's get to the Barrows and let them know he's coming," said Black Jake. "There's enough of us, we won't have to worry about Dawson for long."

"We was supposed to be rounding up some horses for when we meet up with Sepreano," Fairday reminded him.

"Yes, but we didn't, now did we," Black Jake said, nudging his dun forward.

Fairday nudged his tired horse along beside him. "I don't want you telling anybody I killed that girl," he said.

"I won't," said Black Jake. He smiled. "I'll just tell them what you told me. Dawson and his deputy killed her. How does that suit you?"

"Suits me fine." Fairday let out a breath of relief and nudged his horse along the trail. "It was Dawson's fault we didn't bring back any horses, eh?"

"Yep." Patterson grinned. "He's the reason we're heading back empty-handed, sure enough, the sonsabitch."

Chapter 3

The two lawmen first saw the girl's body draped backward across a rock as they rode up and around a turn in the trail. The gruesome sight stopped Dawson cold in his tracks. Behind him, Caldwell reined his horse down to keep from running into him.

"My God, he did it," Dawson whispered, his hand going instinctively to the rifle across his lap. "He killed her, just like he threatened to if we dogged him."

"Yes," said Caldwell, "except we didn't dog him any." He drew his Colt and cocked it quietly. "We kept our word." He nudged his horse a step forward, beside Dawson. The two then urged their horses forward together, both with guns in hand, wary of a trap.

When they had eased their horses closer without incident, Dawson winced at the sight of flies already swarming above the dead girl's open chest cavity and said in a lowered voice, "What kind of fiend does something like this, Jedson?" He asked as if Caldwell's past profession as an undertaker might offer an explanation.

"Don't ask me," Caldwell replied, his voice also lowered as if in respect to the deceased. "I've seen murder at its most depraved, but I've never seen anything worse than this."

"It makes no sense." Dawson shook his head and looked away from the terrible sight. "He had no reason to do this. It was in his best interest to keep her alive. If we'd found her here afoot, we'd have to take her back to Poco Río. By the time we'd have gotten back onto his trail it would have given him twice the head-start time."

"Nobody can figure why a man like Leo Fairday does what he does," said Caldwell, holstering his Colt and swinging down from his saddle. He stepped forward, fanning away the gathering flies with his gloved hand. "There's not time to take her back to town now, not if we want to catch her killer."

"All we can do for her now is cut her loose and get her buried," Dawson agreed. He stepped down from his saddle and led both their horses to the side and hitched them to a short stand of brush. "We'll mark her grave so anybody from Poco Río who comes looking can find her easy enough."

"I'll be surprised if anybody from town comes looking for her," said Caldwell. As he spoke he took a jackknife from his pocket, opened it and cut through the rawhide strips tied tight around her wrists. "Nobody there seemed to care that Fairday left town with a gun shoved beneath her chin. They were too busy picking over the dead in the street."

"They're poor, Jedson," Dawson offered in the people of Poco Río's defense. "Whatever they do, they're doing to stay alive."

"I didn't mean to judge them," said Caldwell. He picked up the bloody blanket lying in the dirt, shook it out and laid it over the dead girl. "There, you poor thing," he said under his breath, tucking the blanket under her enough to pick her up and walk toward the edge of the trail with her.

Having no shovel with which to dig a grave, the two scrapped out a low bed in the hard earth, laid the blanket-wrapped girl in it and carried rocks and piled them over her. When they finished, they stood over the grave, hats in hand, and stared down as if in meditation.

"It's all my fault what happened to you," Dawson said at length, speaking to the dead girl beneath the stony mound.

"No, it's not, ma'am," Caldwell interceded, his head bowed but his eyes tilted stubbornly up at Dawson. "Leo Fairday is to blame for killing you, and nobody else. We did what we said we would . . . but he killed you anyway."

After a pause, Dawson said, still speaking down to the rocks, "But if we hadn't come to Poco Río looking for Fairday and the others, none of the rest of this would have happened. You'd still be alive."

"Still," Caldwell replied toward the ground, his eyes again turned up to Dawson, "if we don't stop men like Fairday and his kind, how will the world ever get—"

"All right, that's enough," Dawson said, cutting him off, realizing that they were both talking to each other, yet using the dead girl's gravestone as some silent mediator. He gave Caldwell a look of disbelief. But before placing his hat back atop his head, he looked back down at the ground and said, "We will bring this man to justice for what he did to you. You have my word."

"Mine too," Caldwell added, closing his eyes for a second as if in prayer, then murmuring, "Amen."

"Amen," said Dawson. He stooped down and laid a folded note he'd written between two rocks, leaving enough of the paper sticking out to be noticed by anyone passing by. "There," he said. He looked back and forth, noting the well-worn trail. "Somebody will come along and see the grave. This will have to do for now."

The two walked toward their horses, looking down at the hoofprints leading up the winding hill trail. The tracks of Fairday's horse overlapped with those of Black Jake Patterson's. "If these two haven't already met up, they will before long," said Dawson.

"Where's the nearest place for them to get fresh horses and supplies?" Caldwell asked, not being familiar with this region of harsh Mexican countryside.

"There's a trading post outside of Matamoros," Dawson said without having to stop and think about it. "If we were them, that's where we'd be headed."

Without another word on the matter the two mounted their horses and rode on.

* * *

Somewhere in the sweet, cool darkness of sleep and alcohol, Rosa had come to him. He had felt the touch of her hands upon his chest, his forehead; he had smelled her familiar scent. He had heard her voice. She had talked as if nothing had ever happened to her. She was alive! Yes alive!

Yet, no sooner had he allowed himself to hope this was not a dream than Rosa had disappeared, simply vanished, and Shaw's eyes opened at the sound of a shotgun cocking near his ear. Without moving his head, he cut a sidelong glace toward Gerardo Luna who stepped back with a grin as he lowered the shotgun's hammer.

"I knew *pequeño angel* would awaken you. She has awakened many men whose dreams are haunted by their past. Haven't you, little angel?" He spoke to the shotgun and patted it as if it were a living thing.

"Who says . . . I have haunted dreams—?" Shaw's broken voice turned into a deep cough, followed by a groan as a pain shot through his wounded shoulder. Reality had set in upon him. He clasped a hand down to the bandage on his bare chest. "How long . . . have I been asleep?"

"*Asleep*, I don't know," Luna replied with a shrug. "You have been *passed out* for three days."

"Three days?" Shaw looked stunned and confused. "I've never been knocked out that long from a gunshot wound."

"You were so drunk I don't think you knew you were shot," said Luna. He examined the shotgun in his hands and said matter-of-factly, "I can tell much about a man by the way he awakens to the sound of my little angel's hammer." He stepped back out of the small cell, laid the shotgun across a battered desk and picked up a coffee mug with a sliver of steam rising from its brim.

"Oh?" Shaw said, not caring.

"Si," said Luna. "If a man's eyes fly open and his ears perk up like a rabbit's, he is a man who has spent much of his life in fear. He is a runner, not a fighter."

Shaw's pain eased enough for him to collapse back on the cot. "That's real interesting, Mr. Moon," he said with a dry, cynical tone.

"Do you want to know what kind of man wakes up the way you did?" Luna asked.

"No, I don't." Shaw closed his eyes for a moment and hoped everything around him would be gone when he reopened them.

"I'll tell you what kind," Luna said, undaunted. "The kind of man who wants to die—the kind of man who wants to embrace death like some dark, mysterious lover, but whose instincts to live are too strong and stubborn to allow him to do so."

"All right, now I know," Shaw said, trying to dismiss the matter. "You're saying I'm too *ornery* to die."

Luna considered Shaw's take on the matter, then said with a raised finger for emphasis, "Yes, too *ornery,* up until now perhaps. But today is a brand-new day. Who knows, perhaps there is some younger, faster gunman on his way here right now who will go out of his way to oblige you. It will be what both of you are looking for."

"Lucky him, lucky me," Shaw said wryly. "Speaking of gunmen"—he raised his head enough to look at the bandage above his right breast—"who put the bullet in me?"

"Which one?" Luna asked with a slight grin, seeing the scar tissue of several old bullet wounds.

Shaw stared at him with a no-nonsense look. "You know which one I mean."

"Titus Boland shot you," Luna said flatly, his tone turning more serious when he realized he had said nothing that Shaw had not already considered a thousand times in his drunken, tormented mind. "The shot broke some bone in your shoulder joint. It will take time to heal properly."

"Titus Boland . . . ," said Shaw, paying little attention to Luna's assessment of his wound. He struggled with no success to recall anything at all about the incident. "I must have been awfully drunk." He ran his left fingers back through his hair.

"Oh, you think so?" Luna asked wryly. "You passed out in the middle of a gunfight."

Shaw ignored his remark. He shook his head slowly, digging deep for recollection. "I killed a man named Ned Boland up in Eagle Pass, must have been two or three years back. I remember that."

"*Si*, Titus Boland remembers it too," said Luna. "He said Ned was his brother."

"Is he still in Matamoros?" Shaw asked with no concern.

"No," said Luna, "my little angel sent him and his amigos on their way. But I have no doubt he's nearby, looking for a chance to kill you."

"His chin? Did I . . . ?" Shaw pondered the incident, still drawing a blank.

"No," said Luna, "I told you it was my little angel. She cracked his chin real good for him."

"Then I suppose he's got a mad-on at you, too," said Shaw. "If he's anything like his brother, Ned, he won't stop until a bullet stops him." He paused for a moment, realizing that Gerardo Luna must've saved his life out on the street. Whether he'd wanted his life saved or not didn't matter. What did matter was the fact that Luna put his own life on the line for him. "I'm obliged, Mr. Moon," Shaw said with sincerity.

"You can thank me by sobering up and staying away from anyone else who wants to kill you," Luna said. "Whatever it is that makes you want to die is not going to be of any help if—"

"All right," said Shaw, cutting him off, "I've had enough sermons this morning." He pushed himself up onto the side of the cot and reached out a shaky hand toward the coffee mug.

Luna held the mug steady by its stem until Shaw got his hands around it. Shaw took a deep sip in spite of the coffee's hotness. "I don't suppose you'd want to reach into your desk, get out your bottle of whiskey?"

"No whiskey, not at this time of day," Luna said firmly. "I did not save you in order to watch you drink yourself to death."

"Yeah?" Shaw said, looking up at him. "Then why did you save me?"

"Because I am a lawman," said Luna. "It is my job, to stand up for those who cannot take care of themselves."

Shaw felt the sting of the Mexican constable's words. "I can take care of myself," he said in a lowered voice. "Titus Boland and his friends just caught me on a bad day."

"I see," Luna said coolly, "and when was your next *good* day going to be?"

Shaw only stared at him in silence and sipped the hot coffee. Finally he said quietly, "Mr. Moon, I appreciate what you did for me. But the fact is, I'm not looking for a *good day*. Not looking, not expecting. If I had ended up lying dead in the street, it would have been no loss—not to me, not to anybody else."

"In that case you are a sorry piece of work, Lawrence Shaw," Luna said, his expression turning grim, "but it makes no difference if you are worth saving or not, or whether or not you want to live or die. As long as you are in my town, I am responsible for you." He thumbed himself on the chest.

"Then I will get out of your town just as soon as I can get a shirt on," Shaw said, looking around for his shirt and boots. He tried lifting his right arm but could not manage to do so. He winced in pain, and gave up trying to stand up by himself. "Give me a hand, and I'll get out of here."

"How do you know you are not under arrest?" Luna asked.

"Under arrest for what?" Shaw snapped.

"For being too loco or stupid for your own good," Luna snapped right back. "A man who walks the street unable to use his gun hand when men are out to kill him must be either loco or an imbecile. I will not allow you to leave here until you are sober and better able to defend yourself."

Shaw cooled down and let out a breath. After a moment of silence he said in a humble tone, "*Gracias*, Mr. Moon. I don't deserve your friendship."

"*Si*, I agree with you on that," Luna said. He backed away, out of the cell. Then he closed the iron-barred door and locked it. "If you wonder who bandaged your wound, it is a woman you insulted on the street the other day."

"I insulted a woman?" Shaw looked bewildered. "That's not something I make a practice of doing."

"I know, but you did insult her," said Luna. "Her name is Anna Reyes Bengreen. She is the widow of Judge Logan Bengreen from Texas. When you are able, you must go see her and apologize for what you said."

"Yes, I suppose I should," said Shaw, rubbing his beard stubble. "What did I say to her anyway?"

"It is better that she tell you when you go see her," said Luna. "You would be too ashamed to face her if I told you beforehand."

"That bad, huh?" said Shaw. He hung his head and cursed himself under his breath.

Luna stared blankly at him. "I am leaving you locked in there, but only until I return with some food for you."

Shaw nodded his bowed head in submission and

stared down at the stone floor until he heard the front door close. Once he knew he was alone he murmured under his breath, "Well, Rosa, it looks like I messed it up again." He squeezed his eyes shut in anguish. *Too damned miserable to live; too damned ornery to die . . .*

Chapter 4

The shot from Cray Dawson's big Colt rolled away across the flat, hard land and lost itself in the distant hill line. In those hills, the two fleeing gunmen brought their horses to a halt and looked back. Black Jake took a dusty field lens from his saddlebags and raised it to his eye.

Squinting against the sun's glare and fine swirling dust, Leo Fairday asked impatiently, "Well? Tell me something, Jake."

"About what?" Black Jake said, staring through the lens with a reserved grin. He liked teasing and agitating Fairday.

"About *what*?" Leo bristled, but kept himself in check. "About what the hell he's shooting at?"

Black Jake took his time. He lowered the lens and rubbed his eye, then said coolly, "His horse."

"His horse?" Fairday growled. "What the hell are you talking about? *He's shooting at his horse.*"

Fairday shrugged. "You asked what he was shooting at. I told you."

Fairday cursed and nudged his horse closer. "Let me look," he demanded, reaching a hand out for the dusty field lens.

But Black Jake backed up his horse a step and held the lens out of reach. "Don't you believe me, Leo? I thought we were pards," he said teasingly. But then, seeing the rage in Fairday's eyes, he said, "His horse must've broken a leg or something. He shot it." As he spoke, he handed over the lens.

Growling under his breath, Fairday took the lens, wiped it on his sleeve and looked out across the rolling sand. Focusing on Clay Dawson standing with his smoking Colt hanging down his side, Fairday eased down and said to Black Jake, "Why didn't you just say so?" He kept his eye to the lens.

Black Jake looked him up and down with a grin of contempt, shrugged again and said, "I just did. Wasn't you listening?"

Leo knew the man was intentionally goading him, treating him in a less than respectful manner. But he held on to his temper and let it pass. Black Jake Patterson had been with the Barrows Brothers Gang a lot longer than he himself had. Rumor had it that Black Jake had once saved Wild Eddie Barrows' life. Fairday wasn't about to risk having Wild Eddie down his shirt, he reminded himself. *No sir . . .*

Fairday didn't answer the question. Instead he managed a smile as he lowered the lens and passed it back to Black Jake. "This is just the stroke of luck we need. It's still fifteen miles to Matamoros. They're down to one horse between them. I'd say we've seen the last of them."

"Yep," said Black Jake, putting the lens back under the flap of his saddlebags. He took off his crumpled hat, dusted it against his leg and put it back on, adjusting the dents in the crown with his thumb and fingers. "We can slow down now, rest these animals some and ride into town at our own pace." He paused and studied Fairday for a moment, then said, "Or, we can pick a good spot across the hilltops, lay up and shoot their eyes out when they come along. What best suits you?"

"You know what best suits me," said Fairday. He ran a gloved hand across the rifle in his saddle boot. "I owe Dawson for causing me to kill that young whore."

"Dawson caused it, huh, Leo?" Black Jake mused, looking intently at the aging gunman.

"Damned right he caused it," said Leo, his view on the matter changing now that he sensed they were getting the upper hand, "and I'll kill him for it, like the dog that he is."

Black Jake chuckled and shook his head slightly as the two turned their horses back to the narrow trail and nudged them forward at a walk.

On the sandy lowland, Crayton Dawson squinted off toward the hills as he shoved his Colt back into its holster. "I expect they heard the shot," he said to Caldwell who sat slumped in his saddle, the shoulders of his black coat, hat and his dark beard stubble covered with a dusting of fine silver sand.

"They've seen us too, unless they've already topped

the hills and gone on," Caldwell replied, disheartened. "Either way, we just made them real happy."

Dawson looked down at the dead horse lying stretched out in the sand, a strong desert breeze having already gusted enough to begin spreading a thin silver sheen over the animal's sides.

"I figure we'll lose them sure enough," he said. He stooped down and hefted his saddle and bridle onto his shoulder. "Either they've seen us and already cut out, or else they'll pick a good spot and try to ambush us up in the hills."

"Yeah, I say they'll go for an ambush," said Caldwell, reaching down and taking the saddle and tack and laying it up over his horse's rump.

"I think they'll cut out," Dawson said. "But just to be on the safe side, when we get to the hills we'll swing wide to the north and follow the low trails."

"It'll take us longer," Caldwell said, swinging down from his saddle beside Dawson.

"But it'll be easier walking," Dawson replied, "and less chance of getting caught in a trap. We'll take shade as soon as we reach the hills, rest until late evening and walk all night."

"There's just no defense for bad luck," Caldwell said, looking down at the dead horse as he walked alongside Dawson.

"I expect not," Dawson said grimly, staring ahead toward the hills.

The two walked on, haggard, wounded, needing medical attention, food and rest. "I still say we need more men," Caldwell said, offering a tired, wry smile.

"I still say, don't expect any," Dawson replied dryly.

For three days Titus Boland and his comrades lurked around the outskirts of Matamoros. Tomes and McClinton waited and watched restlessly while Boland nursed his swollen chin and split lips and drank bottle after bottle of rye whiskey to ease his pain. The more he drank, the more he talked about catching the Mexican sheriff on some dark street and gunning him down.

"It's time we got out of here before he does something foolish and gets all three of us hanged," Tomes said quietly to McClinton as the two watched Boland sit with his drunken head bowed, a bloody wet cloth pressed to his large, purple chin. "These Mexicans don't take it lightly, some gringos like us just up and killing their town lawman."

"But we can't just leave him," said McClinton. "He's the one who can get us into the Barrows Gang. He's the one who knows Crazy Ed, don't forget."

Tomes gave him a look. "It's not *Crazy Ed,*" he said correcting him. "It's *Wild Eddie*. You wouldn't want Eddie Barrows hearing you call him *Crazy Ed.* It would most likely get your tongue cut out."

"See what I mean?" said McClinton. "Not knowing the Barrows, I might have made such a slip purely out of ignorance."

Tomes looked at him for a moment longer, considering things, then said, "Yeah, I expect we might need him with us at that." He looked away, to where Titus sat swaying back and forth in the dirt. "He'll be facedown again in a few minutes. Why don't you go get our horses ready. We'll load him up and get out of here."

McClinton nodded, watching Boland weave back and forth. "Yeah, he'll thank us for it once he gets his senses back."

"He should," said Tomes. "We'll probably be saving his life, getting him away from here before Lawrence Shaw gets up and around."

McClinton turned and walked away toward a field of sparse wild grass where they'd picketed their horses. When he'd returned with the mounts saddled and ready for the trail, before Titus Boland knew what was happening the two had raised him up into his saddle and ridden away. By the time the pain in his chin began clearing his whiskey-dulled mind, the three had ridden ten miles farther from town and halfway up the hill trail where Black Jake Patterson and Leo Fairday sat perched in the cover of rock awaiting Dawson and Caldwell.

"Well now, look at this," Black Jake said, looking to the west at the three horsemen riding upward at a walk along the winding trail below. "That's Titus Boland in front."

Fairday turned from watching the trail in the other direction and looked down at the horsemen. "It sure is," he confirmed. "Who's the other two?"

"I have no idea," said Black Jake, raising his rifle to his shoulder.

"You're not going to shoot them, are you?" Fairday asked.

"Naw," said Black Jake, cocking his rifle, "I'm just

going to have some fun with them." He took close aim along the rifle sights.

Realizing this was the same nasty stupid joke Black Jake had done to him when he'd ridden up on him, Fairday growled under his breath, "This rotten snake."

On the winding trail, Titus Boland toppled sidelong from his saddle when the rifle shot spooked his horse and caused it to rear up. Tomes and McClinton kept their horses settled and spurred them off the trail into the shelter of rock and brush. But Boland let out a painful scream and rolled back and forth in the dirt in agony, cupping his chin with both hands. Fresh blood oozed from his swollen lips. Tomes and McClinton winced at the sight as they drew their guns and searched the towering hillside.

Above them, Black Jake stared down with a bewildered expression and said to Fairday, "Damn, Leo, I never saw a grown man carry on that way."

Leo just stared at him, his temper ready to boil over and explode any second.

"Hello, the trail," Black Jake called down at length when Boland quieted down, stopped rolling and struggled up onto a knee. "Hey, Titus, is that you?" he asked.

Unable to speak, Titus only whimpered and nodded his head. From their cover, Tomes called up to the ledge where Black Jake stood, rifle in hand, "Hell, yes, it's Titus Boland. If you thought it might be him, why'd you shoot at us in the first place?"

"That was just a warning shot," Black Jake called out, keeping himself from chuckling at his joke. "You can't be too careful these days." He looked at Fairday with a grin. But Fairday didn't share in his humor. He stared coldly back at him.

"Who's up there?" McClinton called out.

Turning back to the lower trail, Jake called down to the two men behind cover, "It's Black Jake Patterson and Leo Fairday. What's wrong with Titus anyway? Cat got his tongue? What's he squalling about?"

"The constable back in Matamoros cracked him in the chin with a shotgun butt, broke a bunch of his teeth. He's a mess."

"It sounded like it, the way he carried on," Black Jake chuckled. "Stay where you are. We're riding down."

"What about Dawson and his pal?" Fairday asked, giving Jake a hard stare.

"Don't worry about them," said Black Jake. "If they heard that shot they won't be coming along this trail. I think they took a different trail anyway."

Fairday stared at him, seething.

By the time the two had ridden down to the lower trail, Tomes and McClinton had helped Boland to his feet. He stood with his boots spread, the wet cloth back against his bleeding mouth. "Just a *warning shot*?" Boland asked, his voice sounding thick and stiff, and angry through his swollen lips. His Colt hung in his hand.

As they stepped down from their horses, Fairday pointed out quickly to Boland and his comrades, "It was Black Jake's doing, not mine. He knew it was you down here. He did me the same way. He's a horse's ass, you want to know my thoughts on the matter."

Black Jake chuckled and said to Boland, "Hell, I wouldn't have done it if I'd known you was hurt. How'd you let a Mexican constable get the drop on you anyway? I always figured you better than that."

Boland stared at him, seething in rage. "A *warning shot*?"

"Yeah, a warning shot," Black Jake said, seeing the look in Boland's eyes. "Why don't you let it go, before one of us ends up doing something we'll be sor—"

Boland swung his six-shooter up and emptied it into Black Jake's chest before he could finish his words.

Blood streaked the air as bullets ripped through Black Jake. In the ringing silence afterward, Boland, Tomes and McClinton all turned and stared at Fairday. Above them the noise had sent birds of all sizes and colors streaking away in every direction. The explosions rolled and echoed out across the land.

"There's your warning shot," Boland growled.

Fairday raised his hands chest high in a show of peace and said, "Fellows, draw your horns in. You only did what I've been wanting to do all day."

Boland eased his smoking gun toward the ground, keeping his eyes on Fairday. He opened the chamber and dropped the empty brass cartridges to the dirt and replaced them with fresh rounds from his gun belt while the other two kept Fairday covered. "What were you two doing up there?" Boland asked in his strained, distorted voice.

Fairday said quickly, "Waiting to surprise a couple of lawdogs from over the border. But I expect the *surprise* part is gone now."

"Are you still riding with the Barrows brothers?" Boland asked stiffly. He closed his gun chamber with a flick of the wrist.

"Yeah, why?" Fairday eyed the loaded gun warily.

"Just asking," said Boland, twirling his gun once backward and dropping it into its holster. "We're looking for the Barrows ourselves. We heard that since they've thrown in with Luis Sepreano and his Army of Liberación, they're all living high on the hog. We want to ride with them ourselves."

Before Fairday could reply, Tomes, who had stepped forward and looked down at Black Jake's body, said, "It appears that you just killed the one sonsabitch who could've taken us straight to the Barrows."

Seeing an opportunity to better his position with the three gunmen, Fairday said, "You're half right. But you're now looking at the one other man who can do it." He thumbed himself on the chest and grinned. "That's where I'm headed right now."

Boland considered it as he motioned for McClinton to hand him a canteen. Canteen in hand, he poured a trickle of water onto a bloody damp cloth he pulled from his vest pocket. "You've ridden with the Barrows brothers a long time—that's a fact," he said. He touched the wet cloth gently to his bleeding lips and purple chin.

"A fact indeed," Fairday grinned, looking from one to the other.

"One problem," said Boland, giving Fairday a dark stare. "What's Eddie Barrows going to say about this?" He nodded at Patterson's bullet-riddled body lying on the ground.

"Oh, he's going to be mad as hell," Fairday said, weighing his words. As he spoke he took a testing step toward his and Patterson's horses. "I expect he'll want to kill those two lawdogs that did it."

"I like the way you think, Leo." Boland tried to smile, but his swollen lips only twisted into a crooked, pained grimace. Turning to Tomes and McClinton, he said as he pressed the wet cloth back to his split and bleeding lips, "Holster your cannons, boys. Looks like we're all of the same mind here."

Relieved, Fairday stepped into his saddle and walked his horse toward Boland and the others, leading Patterson's horse by its reins.

Chapter 5

Shaw stood with his right arm in a sling that Luna had fashioned for him out of the clean white cloth he'd said Widow Bengreen left there for that very purpose. "You must wear this for more than just a few days if you want your arm to recover quickly and have your skills come back to you as strong as they were before," Luna had advised him.

My skills, Shaw thought bitterly, kneading his wounded shoulder gently, testing the soreness. There had been a time when his skills would have been riding, sticking atop a wild cow pony, roping, rounding strays, taking a herd across a swollen stream without losing a head. He realized that those were not the skills Luna spoke of. Those skills had slowly been overtaken by his skills with a gun—his knack for killing. But he said nothing. Luna meant well.

Instead he said, "*Gracias*, my friend," then turned and walked away toward the town livery stables.

Watching him walk out of sight, Luna said under

his breath, "I hope this works out for you, *mi amigo*." Then he turned back into his small office and shut the door behind him.

Inside the livery stables Shaw stood aside and watched a Mexican stable boy bridle and saddle his horse for him. When the boy finished and led the horse to him and extended his palm, Shaw put a small gold Mexican coin in his hand and thanked him. But instead of backing away, the boy gestured at Shaw's arm in the sling and asked him in broken English, "Can I get you a stool to climb up on?"

"I'm good," Shaw replied. He took the saddle horn with his left hand and stepped stiffly up into his saddle, the effort of it causing his right shoulder to throb in pain for a moment, until he settled and took up his reins and put the horse forward at a walk.

With a warm meal in his belly and Luna's hot coffee washing away much of the lingering alcohol haze that had clouded his senses, Shaw rode away from Matamoros. Following Luna's directions, he rode northwest toward the late Judge Logan Bengreen's spread. He stopped in the afternoon and gazed along a narrow trail leading into a Bengreen hillside strewn with bear grass, cactus and clumps of juniper. A small herd of cattle drifted aimlessly, grazing on tobosa grass in narrow flats between lower lying hillsides.

"This must be it," he said to his horse, patting the big buckskin's neck with a gloved hand. "Let's get this over with and get back to town." He noted the agitation that crept into his voice; he sighed, realizing it wouldn't be long before he needed a drink to calm both his hand and his state of mind. Laying the reins on his saddle horn, he reached back with his left hand, lifted the flap to his saddlebags and rummaged around, searching for the feel of a bottle but finding none.

"What kind of fool drunkard rides this far without a bottle of rye for emergencies?" he asked himself aloud. He raised his hat enough to wipe the back of his glove across his sweaty forehead. Then he adjusted his hat back into place and nudged the horse forward.

Moments later as he rounded a turn, Shaw saw the Logan Bengreen hacienda seem to rise up from the earth a thousand yards ahead of him. At the sight of the majestic stone, timber and adobe structure standing behind a long meandering stone wall, he slowed the buckskin's walk. For a few seconds he allowed the horse to step back and forth while he took in a tall stone archway with iron gates swung open.

Beyond the gateway at the center of a large front yard filled with flowers, trees and vines, he saw a low, ornate stone wall circling a well. Red clay roof tiles mantled both the sprawling hacienda and the separate buildings standing behind and on either side. "Well now," Shaw said quietly to the horse, "what was a woman who lives in a place like this doing riding all the way to town, to take care of a wounded drunk like me?"

As he drew closer to the front yard he saw a curtain sway, then close at one of the front windows. When his horse stepped off the dirt trail and onto a wide stone-paved walkway, he looked all around, a bit surprised that none of the Bengreens' hired help had met him at the open gates.

As he stepped down and led his horse around the well, he saw the large front door open. He reached up and removed his hat as a tall, raven-haired woman stepped out onto the porch, a shotgun cradled in her arms.

My God, Rosa, he thought at the sight of her. Yet upon noting the shotgun in her arms, he stopped short instinctively and stared, giving the big double-barrel all the respect it deserved. "Ma'am, it's me, Lawrence Shaw," he said, his own voice sounding strained and shallow to him.

Recognizing him, the woman called out with a trace of a Spanish accent, "Yes . . . welcome, Mr. Shaw. You must be feeling better, to take such a long ride as this?"

Shaw was immediately taken aback at the sound of her voice, a voice that sounded too much like his late wife Rosa's to be ignored. "Ma'am, I—I—" He stopped and stood speechless, staring, wondering if this was one of his drunken visions coming upon him unexpectedly, the kind where Rosa walked right up to him as if she'd only just returned from a long journey, rather than from the grave.

"Mr. Shaw? Are you all right?" the woman asked, looking concerned upon seeing him sway unsteadily. She lowered the big shotgun from her arm and leaned it against the front of the house.

Easy now. Shaw tried to steady himself, realizing that this was neither Rosa nor one of his haunted, drunken visions of her. He was sober. Well, at least reasonably so, he reminded himself. He wasn't imagining this; he wasn't going to roll over and wake up and find this all a dream. All he could do was play this out, see where it took him.

"Uh, yes, ma'am," he managed to say at length. He forced himself to look closer and more calmly at her as she stepped down from the porch and walked toward him.

"Mrs. Bengreen . . . ?" he asked shakily, with uncertainty. *Of course it's Mrs. Bengreen. Who else would it be?*

"Yes, Mr. Shaw, I'm Anna Reyes Bengreen," she replied. "Are you certain you are all right?"

Shaw let out a breath. Her voice sounded so much like Rosa's that it had staggered him. But there were differences he noted now that he managed to collect himself a little and get his whiskey-jangled nerves settled back into place.

"Yes, ma'am, I'm all right, just a little worn-out from the trail. I'll be fine in a . . ."

His words died as he looked into her eyes, thinking once again in spite of himself that this was Rosa reaching out to him, taking him by his forearm and leading him to the shade of the wide front porch. "Here, you must let me help you to the porch," said Anna Bengreen.

Shaw stepped onto the porch, her hand on his arm guiding, assisting him. "Ma'am, what you must think of me," he said apologetically, turning and lowering himself onto a cushioned wooden bench hewn from the trunk of a Chinaberry tree.

"Nonsense, Mr. Shaw," said Anna Bengreen. "Do not forget, I have cleaned and dressed your wounded shoulder. I am aware of your condition." She stepped back and smiled down at him. "Let me get you something . . . some cool water perhaps?" She looked around and gestured toward an old Mexican who stood lurking inside a door at the far end of the porch.

Shaw couldn't answer her. He sweated; he wondered if she could smell him, knowing how much whiskey and mescal he had poured through his system in the past month. He struggled for something to say, something polite, sociable. But the haunting sight of her, the *too* familiar sound of her voice, the scent, the feel of her hand on his arm. *My God.* What a cruel terrible joke for fate to play upon him, he thought, staring blankly at her.

"Yes, some cool water, I think," she answered herself, as if seeing how uncomfortable she made him. She backed away another step, turned and said, "I'll only be a moment."

Don't do this to yourself, Shaw thought. This was not Rosa, and he knew it. *Settle down. Don't look like a drunken fool!*

By the time the old Mexican arrived with a tray, carrying a clay pitcher filled with water and a clay drinking cup, Shaw had gotten himself in hand. He watched Anna Bengreen fill the cup herself and hold it out to him. "*Gracias,* ma'am," Shaw said, taking the cup of water, his hat on the bench beside him. His bandanna was dark with sweat where he had raised it and wiped his forehead. "I rode out here to thank you for all you did for me, not to impose on your hospitality."

"It is not an imposition, Mr. Shaw." She smiled, gesturing for the old man to set the tray down on a table beside the bench. "I am pleased to learn you are up and around so quickly after what happened to you." She pulled a small chair up and sat down facing him and motioned for Ernesto to leave. Shaw sipped the cool water and felt himself grow more comfortable.

"All the same, ma'am," he said, "I am much obliged for all you did for me those three days before I came to." He paused, looked down at his boots and added, "I also want to tell you how truly sorry I am for having offended you on the street the other day. I'm ashamed of myself."

The woman's expression perked up. She gave him a curious look. "Perhaps you are confused, Mr. Shaw. It is true I attended to you when you were brought to Sheriff Luna's jail. I cleaned and dressed your shoulder wound, but only the one time." She raised a finger for emphasis. "The rest of the time, it must have been Luna himself who took care of you."

"It was Mr. Moon, not you . . . ?" Shaw let the information sink in.

Anna Bengreen smiled. "Luna knows that when I was little more than a child I worked as a nurse at the Castillo de los Santos in Barcelona, Mr. Shaw," she said. "I was in town searching for a vaquero, someone to work for me. The vaqueros who worked here left when they heard Cedros Altos would be sold. Only Ernesto, his wife and two sons remain. When you were shot, Luna sent for me. You were unconscious when I arrived, and you remained so when I left. But it was only one time that I attended to you."

Shaw pondered everything she'd said. "The Castillo de los Santos?" he said. "Then you must have been a . . ." He let his words trail, not certain how she would take them.

"A nun?" she asked with a soft, patient smile, finishing his words for him. "No," she said, "but that was to have become my avocation when I went there." She sighed slightly and looked away for a moment. "But it was not to be. I left the Castillo de los Santos in my second year and traveled to the United States."

"I see," said Shaw, although he wondered why Luna had said she'd been the one to attend to him those days when his senses were more dead than alive. "I'm still obliged to you," he added, "and I still want to apolo—"

She cut him off, saying, "Do not apologize to me, Mr. Shaw. You said nothing to offend me. I do not even recall seeing you on the streets of Matamoros. I'm afraid Sheriff Luna is mistaken."

"I didn't say anything untoward to you in Matamoros?" Shaw asked to make certain.

"The first time I saw you was when you were lying on a cot inside the jail," Anna assured him.

Shaw murmured under his breath, "That sneaking dog, Luna." He looked down and shook his head slowly, catching on to what Luna had in mind.

"Is something wrong, Mr. Shaw?" she asked, watching him closely.

"Oh, it's nothing you did, ma'am," Shaw pointed out quickly. "But I think Luna made a few things up just to bring the two of us together, face-to-face."

"Oh? And why would he do a thing like that?" Anna asked.

"Because he's a meddling dog," Shaw said before stopping himself. Then he took a deep, calming breath and said, "Ma'am, you said you were searching for someone to work for you. I bet you didn't find anyone, did you?"

"No," said Anna. "Each time I inquired about someone in particular, Sheriff Luna said they were not the kind of man I should trust out here where I am all alone."

"That's what I thought," said Shaw. "Ma'am, Luna knows I used to be a cowhand. But he knows I'm not anymore. He knew I wouldn't ride out here looking for work. But he knew I would go out of my way to apologize for anything wrong I might have said to you." Shaw set the water glass on the table beside the pitcher. "So, he made that part up, and sent me out here hat in hand, figuring once I got here I'd go to work for you."

"I don't understand," said Anna. "How did he know you would want to work for me?"

Shaw thought about Rosa as he watched Anna brush a strand of hair from her cheek, of how much Anna Reyes Bengreen looked like her. "Oh, it's just something he knew," Shaw said, not wanting to explain that to her right then. He reached his free hand up and kneaded his healing shoulder. "Luna knows I need work. He knows I've been sort of down-and-out of late."

"Oh?" She looked him up and down. "But what made him think you are the person I would choose to have work for me?"

Shaw read the look in her eyes; her expression was kind, but knowing. She wasn't naïve, he thought. She knew a down-and-out drunk when she saw one. It was hard to miss. "Ma'am," he said, picking his words as he went, "I think Luna wanted you to see that a man who would ride this far just to apologize for something he doesn't even remember doing would have something to his credit."

She considered it for a moment, then nodded and said with a warm and genuine smile, "If that is what he thought, he was correct. Only an honorable man *would* do such a thing. It is a long ride from Matamoros, especially with a wounded shoulder."

Again he felt her eyes take him in, as if able to see through him, the same way Rosa always could. He realized it would be hard for him to ever hide anything from this woman. "Ma'am, I want you to know that I haven't always been this way. I'm not a drunk. It's just that lately I've had lots of things not go the way I—"

"Please call me Anna, Mr. Shaw?" she asked, cutting in, not allowing him to go any further in either denouncement or defense of his low condition.

"Yes, ma'am—*Anna*," Shaw said, catching and correcting himself.

Before he could finish what he'd started to say

about his sore condition, she went on to ask, "And may I call you Lawrence?"

"Yes, Anna, I hope you will," Shaw said. He leveled his shoulders, summoning up what dignity he could on such short notice. He realized she didn't want to discuss his drinking problems, or any of his other problems. He made an effort to stand up from the bench; but she stopped him with a look, saying, "Now that we know what to call each other, are you looking for work, Lawrence?"

"Well, I need work. . . ." Shaw let his answer linger as he rubbed his chin and looked around the open land surrounding the outer stone wall. "But if you don't mind me saying so, it looks like you've already sold off most of your cattle."

"Yes, that is true," said Anna. "I have only a few head of cattle and twenty-two head of horses left—my late husband's personal herd of riding horses. But now that some less reputable vaqueros from the neighboring ranches know I am selling out, they steal from me nightly. I had hoped that if they knew there is a man around, especially one who is a good shot with a rifle, it would keep them scared away until I am finished with my business here." She gave him a questioning look. "Is this the kind of work you would be comfortable doing?"

Shaw gave her a level gaze. "I'm comfortable scaring thieves away," he said. "It shouldn't take long for word to get around that there's a rifle standing guard. Then they'll leave things alone."

"You are a good shot with your left hand?" she

asked, then added quickly, "I would not want you to accidentally shoot someone."

"Don't worry, ma'am," said Shaw, "I'm best at drawing and shooting right-handed. But with a rifle I hit what I shoot at with either hand."

"But only to scare them away," she pointed out.

"Yes, ma'am," said Shaw, "I understand."

She considered for a second. "Of course if they should become too bold, and try to harm either of us . . ." She paused for a moment in dark contemplation. "Then I suppose it would become necessary, you would be *capable* of . . ." She glanced toward his wounded shoulder.

"Don't worry, Anna," Shaw said, "I am *capable.* My thinking was off the day this happened. If I'm protecting you and your ranch, nobody is going to harm you."

Chapter 6

No sooner had Dawson and Caldwell led Caldwell's horses to the town stables and begun watering them at the public trough than Gerardo Luna walked up to them with his ornate shotgun draped over his forearm. "Marshal Crayton Dawson, *mi amigo*!" Luna said, having recognized him immediately as the two walked into Matamoros off the flat, dusty trail. "What brings you to my town?" As he spoke he gestured an arm, taking in all of the sprawling village.

"Good day to you, Mr. Moon," said Dawson, stepping forward to meet his old friend. "Since when do I need a reason to come visit my friend?"

"You will never need a reason." Luna smiled. "But I will wager you are on the trail of some felon." He shifted a glance to Caldwell.

"Mr. Moon," said Dawson, "I'd like you to meet my deputy, Jedson Caldwell." Gesturing a hand toward Luna he said, "Jedson, this is Gerardo Luna, the man I have been telling you about—the law in Matamoros."

"It is a pleasure meeting you, Sheriff Luna. I've heard a lot about you," said Caldwell, stepping forward with his right hand extended.

Shaking hands, Luna said, "And I have heard much about you, Senor Caldwell."

"Oh?" said Caldwell. Both he and Dawson gave the sheriff a questioning look.

"Si," said Luna, "Lawrence Shaw has told me much about you." Luna's smile waned a bit as he added, "Before he got started staying too drunk to carry on a conversation, that is."

"Shaw is here in Matamoros?" Dawson asked.

Luna sighed. "He was here. I sent him away."

"You ran him out of town?" Dawson asked.

"You know I would not do that, no matter how drunk and rank he became," said Luna. "I sent him to a place where I hope he will sober up and get back to his old self."

"I see," said Dawson. "That's good." He and Caldwell gave each other a look, both of them knowing how much help a big gun like Shaw would have been, had he been there sober, ready to ride. "Well, let's hope it gets him straightened out," Dawson added, sounding just a little disappointed.

"Yes, let us hope so." Luna eyed the two lawmen, having understood the look they'd exchanged. "But now, what about you?" he asked Dawson. "You still have not told me what brings you here to my town."

"The Barrows Brothers Gang." Dawson's expression turned grim, down to business. "Word has it they have thrown in with Luis Sepreano and his Army of Liberation."

"Army of Liberación . . ." Luna spit in distaste. "Luis Sepreano has gathered for himself an army of murderers and thieves, nothing more."

"Yep, and now he's taken in the Barrows Gang. With them riding with him, he gets the run of both sides of the border. Your government agrees with the American consulate that this bunch has to be stopped."

Luna gave Dawson a look of bemused disbelief. "So, the two governments have decided to send out *one* U.S. marshal and *one* deputy?"

Dawson gave a wry smile. "It took me three days to convince them I needed a deputy."

Luna looked back and forth between the two lawmen and shook his head. "You need more men."

"I've mentioned that myself," Caldwell said, giving Dawson a thin smile of satisfaction.

Ignoring the remark, Dawson said to Luna, "We shot it out with some of Barrows' men in Poco Río and chased two of them toward here. But my horses went down on me and we had to pull away. We heard shooting yesterday on our way around the hills. But I figure they know we're heading here and have cut out in another direction by now."

"Do I know these two desperados?" Luna asked, his hand deftly stroking along the butt of his shotgun.

"Probably," said Dawson. "It's Leo Fairday and Black Jake Patterson. They've been riding both sides of the border for a long time, even before they threw in the Barrows."

"Yes, I know these two," said Luna, "and they are both bad and dangerous men. They are both wanted throughout Mexico, but no one man has been able to stand up against the gangs they ride with. Patterson is best friends with the Barrows brothers. Leo Fairday has long been wanted for killing a woman he once lived with near Poco Río. It is said she was the mother of his child."

"We don't doubt it, after what we've seen," said Caldwell, giving Dawson a look.

"Oh?" Luna inquired.

Dawson's expression turned darker. "Fairday took a young whore hostage in Poco Río. He said he'd let her go if we gave him a head start to the hills. I figured he'd leave her for us to have to take back to town. But instead, we found her gutted like an animal."

"Senseless," Luna commented. "But rest at ease knowing that I will introduce them to *mi pequeño ángel,* if they show up in my town." He patted the shotgun.

"We'd both appreciate any help your *little angel* might give us, Luna," said Dawson. "But like I said, they've most like cut out by now. We'll be pushing on as soon as I can get a fresh cayuses under me and we take on some trail supplies."

"Pushing on to where?" Luna asked.

"We'll backtrack and try picking up their trail at the hills where we heard all the shooting," said Dawson. "I hope it wasn't Fairday and Patterson waylaying some innocent travelers."

"I am riding with you." Luna's hand tightened on his shotgun.

"What about Matamoros?" Dawson asked. "What if I'm wrong about them cutting out? What if they decide to come here anyway?"

Luna let out a tense breath. "You are right, my friend," he said. "It is at times like this I must remind myself that my first duty is to protect my town."

"Not that we wouldn't welcome you with us," said Dawson, "you and your little angel." He nodded at Luna's ornate shotgun.

"I am honored," Luna said seriously. Then he looked off toward the American consulate building that towered above the rooflines from two squares away. "I wonder if your leaders or mine even realize how bad things could get along the border with Sepreano and the Barrows joining forces."

"Of course they realize," Caldwell said with a dark chuckle. "That's why *we're* here."

Dawson considered things for a moment, gazing off with Luna toward the looming American consulate building where an American flag flew alongside a Mexican flag. "How long do you suppose Shaw has been drunk?"

"How long?" Luna looked at him. "Long enough that he passed out in a gunfight. Long enough that he did not even remember being in the gunfight until he awakened three days later and saw a bullet hole in his shoulder. Even then I had to tell him about it."

"He's turned into a falling-down drunk," Dawson said with remorse. "I hate hearing that."

"Perhaps he will change," Luna said. "But for now he and his fast gun are of no help to you. Riding with you to face the Barrows and Sepreano, he would get himself killed." Luna considered it, then added, "Although it would appear that getting himself killed is what he is trying to do these days."

"I'm glad you're here looking out for him, Mr. Moon," Dawson said. "We've been friends since we were kids in Somo Santos. Losing Rosa has just about caused him to lose his mind." He wasn't about to mention how much he himself had loved Rosa Shaw, or how many nights they had spent together those times while her husband, Lawrence Shaw, was off somewhere building his reputation with a gun.

"She was a beautiful woman, Rosa Shaw," said Luna, seeing the sadness move into Dawson's eyes but not being able to fathom the depth of it. "We grew up near here, she and I. Sometimes I think that being here makes Lawrence feel closer to her spirit."

"Yeah, I see how it could," Dawson said. Not wanting to bring up her memory at a time like this, he did not want to talk about anything to do with Rosa Shaw. Changing the subject he asked, "What kind of horse can I expect to buy here for forty dollars?"

"A dead one, perhaps," Luna said earnestly.

Dawson stared at him. "How much more for one that's breathing?"

"A hundred will buy one that is not only breathing, but perhaps even able to carry a rider," said Luna, his smile widening. "Horses have become gold here." He pointed toward the American consulate. "Your wealthy *políticos americanos* buy the best of them for themselves, their children and their mistresses. The *federales* buy them up for the soldiers in

Mexico City. A *rurale* lawman like myself rides a mule if he can afford one, or a donkey if he cannot."

"I've got to buy one, and a good one at that," said Dawson. "Who do I need to see?"

"There are a few horses left at the stables that came from the late Judge Bengreen's Cedros Altos spread," said Luna without mentioning that was the place where he'd sent Shaw. "They are not from the judge's private stable, but they will be good, hard-boned Spanish Barbs from his working string."

"*Gracias*," said Dawson. "A good cattle horse will suit me fine. While Jedson waters his horse, what say you walk over to the stables with me and introduce me to your local horse dealer?" As he turned with Luna to walk away toward the stables, he said to Caldwell over his shoulder, "As soon as I get back, we'll go round up some supplies and have ourselves a meal."

"I'll be waiting," said Caldwell, watching the two walk away.

When Dawson and Luna turned the corner of an adobe building and started toward the open doorway of the town livery stables, Luna asked, "Do you want to know where I sent our friend Shaw?"

"If you want to tell me," Dawson replied, gazing straight ahead.

"Yes, I want to tell you," said Luna. "I sent him to work for a woman who looks enough like Rosa she could have been her sister."

"Why would you do a thing like that?" Dawson asked, giving him a look. "He has a hard enough time keeping Rosa off his mind as it is." Dawson winced a bit, realizing that he himself still had difficulty keeping his memory of Rosa Shaw from overshadowing his thoughts.

"This woman is the widow of the judge whose horses we will be seeing in the corral." He gestured a nod toward a corral beside the livery stables. "I sent Shaw to work for her hoping that it would at least sober him up . . . perhaps even give him something he feels is worth living for."

"Good luck," said Dawson, turning his gaze back to the livery stable, toward the corral. He had lived with Rosa's sister, Carmelita, after Rosa's death, but it hadn't helped. Carmelita had seen through him. In the end it had only made both him and Carmelita miserable.

"The widow has had trouble with sneak thieves," said Luna. "Shaw can keep them scared away while his wound heals. If he stayed here with a wounded shoulder, the word would soon get out. Every gunman along the border would be upon him like wolves."

"You're a regular matchmaker, Mr. Moon," Dawson said as they walked to the side of the stables where three sturdy Spanish Barb horses stood under a thatched overhang, out of the hot sunlight.

Catching a slight bitterness in Dawson's tone, Luna stopped and shrugged. "Did I do something wrong, my friend? If I did, you must tell me what it is."

Dawson stood looking at the three horses for a moment as if appraising them. Finally he let out a tight breath. Realizing he'd been a bit testy with his longtime friend, he turned to him and said quietly,

"Pay me no mind, Luna. You did the right thing. I would have likely done the same, given the situation, the circumstances." Dawson rubbed his neck irritably. "I've just been too long on the trail. It's making me cross for no reason."

"*Si*, I understand," said Luna, studying Dawson's expression, seeing the same cloud of sadness he'd detected earlier upon mentioning Rosa Shaw's name. Dismissing the matter he stepped closer to the corral rails and gestured toward the three horses. "Here are the last three of the judge's Spanish Barbs. These fellows are handsome animals, eh?"

"Yes, they are," said Dawson, opening the corral gate and stepping inside, Luna right beside him. "How many were here to start with?" He ran a gloved hand along the flank of a cream-colored roan with black stockings. The big Barb gelding tossed his strong head and puffed at Dawson.

"There were many, perhaps a hundred or more," Luna estimated. "Most were taken across the border and purchased by the army. But the army does not accept branded animals if they can keep from doing so. A few branded ones were culled and left behind, sold to the dealer here in Matamoros at a cheap price. Since he bought them cheaply, perhaps you will be able to do the same, from him."

"Yes, that would be good," said Dawson, beginning to understand that these horses were not the lesser of the lot. They were all fine animals. "Who bought the rest that were left behind?"

"A Mexican rancher from over near Reynosa bought five or six." He shrugged. "There are still many branded horses waiting at the Cedros Altos ranchero to be sold."

"I see," said Dawson, running his hand across the Cedros Altos brand, the letter C with a tall A standing inside it. "If they bear the brand, they must've been part of the judge's personal riding stock."

"*Si*, this is what I think," said Luna. He stood back, watching Dawson walk around the cream Barb, inspecting it before lifting each of its hooves in turn. "They are the best horses we have seen in my town for a long time." He grinned. "But we must not let the horse dealer know that we think so when you see him, eh?"

"Right." Dawson set the Barb's forehoof down and dusted his hands together. "Where will we find the dealer?"

"At the cantina, where else?" said Luna.

Dawson looked at the three horses again as he stepped back toward the corral gate. "The late Judge Bengreen had good taste in horseflesh," he said. "I take it he left his widow well provided for?"

"Beautiful women always find themselves provided for. It is the way of the world," he pointed out. "She is very wealthy, this one," he added, shaking his fingers as if money had stuck to them.

"That figures," Dawson said with a tired smile. "Shaw is the only man I know who can get blind drunk, pass out in a gunfight, get himself shot and wind up working for a beautiful wealthy widow . . . protecting her."

"It is true," Luna laughed, not having thought of it that way before. "Always it is the way things happen for Lawrence Shaw! Always he is like a cat. He lands on his feet!"

"Well, good for Shaw," Dawson said, meaning it. Luna noted the sadness in his eyes go away as he latched the corral gate and turned in the direction of the cantina. "I hope it all works out for him. I guess I'll have to just settle for a good dependable horse."

Chapter 7

After riding all night around rocky hillsides, through sandy draws filled with brush and prickly cactus beds, Leo Fairday led the other three riders down a shadowy canyon trail where they stopped at first light to water the horses. In a thin stream that pooled beneath a natural abutment wall of earth and stone, the men stepped down and stretched as the horses drew water. Above the earth and stone standing before them stood another wall, this one made of weathered stone, chiseled, shaped and erected by ancient hands, a monument to some vanished civilization.

"This is as far as I can take you fellows," Leo said, "until I hear Eddie or Redlow Barrows tell me otherwise."

Boland stood beside his horse, having dipped the bloody mouth cloth into the cool water, rinsed it and wrung it out. "But Redlow knows me, Leo," he said.

"He won't mind if you bring us all the way in. I need some whiskey to ease my pain."

"Whether you know Redlow or not, I've got orders about how to do things," said Leo. "I ain't letting you get me killed over a mouth of rotgut whiskey."

"Go on, then," Boland grumbled, and looked away, the cloth back against his lips. "Get to the Barrows and bring us in. My chin is killing me."

Leo finished watering his horse and the spare left by Patterson's death. Then he stepped into his saddle, the reins to Patterson's horse in hand, and started to give his horse a tap of his spurs. But before doing so, he stopped at the sight of a band of riders moving toward them at a fast pace across the sandy terrain. "Well, I expect I won't be leaving you here after all. Here come the Barrows now. They're riding like hell's on their heels." He stepped back down from his saddle and stood beside the two horses.

"Good," said Boland, staring out at the swirling sand and galloping horses coming toward them in a fiery morning light. "Don't forget, it was the two lawmen who killed Patterson."

"I ain't forgot," said Fairday. "You just remember that you three found us pinned down in an ambush and just couldn't get there in time to save ole Black Jake's life. But you saw them kill him."

They stood in silence, watching the horsemen gallop toward them. When the horses slowed and half circled and came in closer, Fairday took off his hat and waved it back and forth. "*Hola,* Redlow and Eddie," he called out. "It's Leo."

The Barrows brothers stopped their horses twelve

feet away. Redlow looked back, searching to see if anyone had followed the four men. Then he said to Leo, "I seen it was you. Put your hat on unless you come to court one of us."

The five riders who had spread out behind the Barrows gave a short laugh at Redlow's joke. Beside Redlow, Eddie Barrows only sat staring at Fairday with his wrists crossed on his saddle. "If he come looking to court me," he said, "there better be a long string of horses standing over the rise somewhere." He eyed Patterson's horse standing beside Fairday. "Where's Black Jake?" he asked.

Pretending not to hear him, Fairday dropped his hat back onto his head and stood in a tense silence for a moment until Redlow asked, "Well, Leo, what say you? Did you bring my brother, Eddie, a string of horses, like you was supposed to?"

"I said, 'Where is Black Jake?'" Eddie asked in a stronger tone.

Still not answering him, Leo shook his head and said to Redlow Barrows, "Red, things went awfully wrong for us this trip—"

"Wait a minute," said Redlow, cutting him off. He rose in his saddle. Looking all around behind Fairday and the other three he asked, "Where *is* Black Jake?"

"That's what I've been asking," said Eddie, giving Fairday a harsh look.

"And where're Roy, Little Dick and Shala?" Redlow added.

"Dead, every last one of them," said Leo, knowing he could put it off no longer.

"Dead?" said Redlow. "There better be a damned

good reason—" He eyed Patterson's horse up and down.

"Who is this bloody-mouthed sonsabitch? These other two bummers?" Eddie cut in, staring coldly at Boland.

"Shut up, Eddie," said Redlow, turning his eyes away from the spare horse. "I know this man. He's Titus Boland. His brother, Ned, and I sweated out a year in a California prison braiding hemp lines for naval vessels."

"So?" said Eddie, staring hard at Boland.

"So, shut your mouth for a minute and show some manners," said Redlow. "I want to hear what Leo's got to say." He turned his attention back to Leo.

"We got ambushed by lawmen in Poco Río," Leo said, widening his eyes as if reliving a horrible event. "We had to leave Roy Owens, Little Dick Johnson and Bud Shala lying dead in the street!" He shook his head. "It was awful." Adding something heroic for himself he said, "I saved Patterson's life. He was hit, but I went back for him, bullets flaying, dragged him into his saddle and we made a run for it."

"That was damned bold of you, Leo," said Redlow. He and Eddie slipped one another a dubious glance and continued listening.

"Well, that's just what good pards do for one another," said Leo, bowing his head humbly for just a second. "I only wished it helped. The lawmen dogged us all the way into the hills past Azúcar flats." He paused and touched his gloved fingers to his bowed forehead. "It was there that they killed him."

"Um-umm," Eddie said skeptically, "just how many

lawmen are we talking about here, Leo, a dozen, two dozen, *three*?"

The question stung Fairday, but he snapped back, saying with raised fingers, "*Two*."

"Oh, *two* dozen," Eddie nodded. "No wonder it went so bad for yas." Redlow watched Fairday closely, seeing a bead of sweat break on his forehead and run down the beard stubble on his cheek.

Fairday's face reddened. "No, not *two dozen*. There were *two* lawmen." He continued, his two raised fingers becoming a raised palm as if to hold back any oncoming criticism. "Fellows, I know that doesn't sound like a lot, especially against men like us. But this is Crayton Dawson we're talking about . . . and a deputy that's just as cold-blooded as he is. A couple of hardened murderers, if you've seen any."

"Federal Marshal Crayton Dawson . . . ," Redlow said in a lowered tone. Letting out a breath, he said, "What the hell is he doing down here? Can't he find enough trouble in Texas to keep him busy?"

"I'm not the one to ask about that," Fairday replied. "I can only tell you what he did to us. Trapped us, butchered us like animals—even killed a young whore for trying to help me and Black Jake get away. They're animals, these two. Straight out wild animals!"

Eddie was having none of it. "Let me make sure I understand this," he said, pushing his hat up in contemplation. "*Two* lawmen from over the border, trapped five of yas . . . killed three, and scattered all the horses you'd gathered all over the desert floor?"

"Hold on, Eddie," Leo said, catching Eddie's attempt at putting words in his mouth. "I never said anything about Dawson scattering any horses." He'd meant to mention a string of horses getting scattered, but he'd forgotten to. Now he hoped that simple omission hadn't been a mistake. It had.

"I know that," said Eddie, "but you should have." As he spoke he calmly drew a big Walker Colt from the holster slung around his saddle cantle. Before Leo realized what was at hand, the gun lay cocked on Eddie's thigh. "You boys were gone more than a week. You didn't round up any horses, not a single one in all that time?"

Leo sweated, seeing the horse pistol lying there, ready to be raised and fired by a man known for his explosive nature. "All right, I admit we hadn't stolen any horses yet. But it wasn't my fault. I tried to get them to leave Poco Río. But, as much as I admired every one of them men like brothers, you have to know they were a stubborn bunch when it come to—"

"You're lying, Leo," Eddie said, cutting him short.

"Lying . . . ?" Leo spread his hands and shrugged innocently. "Lying about what?"

"Probably everything," said Eddie, staring coldly at him. "But to start with, here's what I see happened. The five of yas went straight to Poco Río and started drinking and bouncing on whores instead of doing what you was told to."

Fairday stood silent, his hands still spread, listening to Eddie call things exactly the way they had happened, up to a point.

"I figure when the lawmen rode in, all of yas was drunk on bad liquor and dope. One little schoolboy with a good slingshot could've overpowered yas. Am I right so far?"

Behind Eddie, the rest of the men didn't laugh at his remark. They sat silent as stone; this was no laughing matter. Leo didn't dare reply. Eddie was too unpredictable for him to know how to respond.

After a moment of tense silence, Eddie took Fairday's lack of a reply to be an admission of guilt. "That's what I thought," he said quietly. Raising his big horse pistol at arm's length, he took aim and said, "So long, Leo."

Leo wasn't going to go down without a fight. He had started to make a move for his Colt when Redlow called out to his brother, "Wait! Damn it, Eddie!"

"For what?" Eddie answered, ready to fire. "I never liked him much anyway."

"You can't go around killing everybody just because you don't like them!" said Redlow.

"Oh? Why not?" Eddie stared at his brother for a satisfactory explanation.

"Because you just *can't*," Redlow said in a stronger tone. "For one thing I'm not finished talking to him. Don't you want to know how your pal Black Jake Patterson got slain?"

"He killed him," Eddie said matter-of-factly, still aiming the big horse pistol, and feeling it grow heavier in his hand, "by not lifting a finger to help him."

"Eddie, don't make me barrel-smack you," Redlow said in a low, even tone. "Lower that cannon before your arm clamps up and locks on you."

Eddie lowered the big gun reluctantly, but only an inch, enough to relieve the weight of it for a moment.

Seeing the gun lowered, Fairday eased down and let out a tense breath. To Redlow he said, "I'm ashamed to say it, but maybe he's right. Maybe I could've done more, and failed to. If that's true, I'll have to live with the burden of it from now on."

He gestured a gloved hand toward Boland who had been watching tensely, wondering if he could trust Fairday to not break down and tell them who had really killed Black Jake. "These fellows saw it, the tail end of it anyway. You could say they come along in time to save my hide." He threw the *saved-hide* part in to make certain Boland gave a good account of him.

Redlow and Eddie both turned their gaze toward Boland and the other two. "What happened, Titus?"

This was going to work out all right, Boland thought, lowering the wet cloth from his lips. "What I saw was Leo here and Patterson fighting off the lawmen. They was both doing their part. Then Patterson went down." He gave Leo a look and went on to say, "By the time we hightailed it in there and chased the lawdogs away, Patterson's eyes were rolled up. He was dead, sure enough."

Redlow looked at his brother and nodded at the big pistol. "Well . . . ?" he asked.

"Well what?" said Eddie.

"Well, are you going to put that heavy-assed gun away or sit there holding it up like an idiot until it wrestles you to the ground?"

"It's not that heavy for me," Eddie said, struggling to keep his hand from starting to tremble and buckle under the gun's weight.

"Yeah, right," Redlow said skeptically. "Put the damned thing away and let's get down to business."

Both Boland and Fairday felt relieved seeing Eddie lower the big horse pistol, uncock it and slip it back into its saddle holster.

"What business is that?" Eddie asked, his wrist throbbing and stiff. But he wasn't about to rub away its stiffness in front of the rest of the men.

"Horse business, Brother," said Redlow. As he spoke he gave Fairday a scalding stare. "These men didn't bring any. We'll have to go find some ourselves. I told Sepreano we'd bring a big string next time we meet. I won't be made a fool of. Will you?"

Eddie didn't answer. Instead he turned a hard frown to Fairday, then to Boland and the other two men. "Send these jakes out to steal horses, is what I say."

"That's real smart, Eddie," said Redlow, "after what happened last time. How do you figure it would go any better? With Dawson prowling around below the border, we'd be wise to stay together in strength. You know the story about the bundle of sticks?"

"No. What story?" Eddie asked.

"Never mind," said Redlow. "This time, we're all going after horses." He looked at Boland, Tomes and McClinton. "I take it you men came to join up with us, like every other *smart* gunman on the run down here."

"You got it, Redlow," Boland said in his distorted voice. "I always wanted to ride with the Barrows brothers. My brother, Ned, always spoke highly of you."

"I hated hearing about Ned getting it from Fast Larry Shaw," said Redlow. He shrugged. "But I have to say, tease a hornet, you will get stung."

"Shaw is a dead piece of meat as soon as I lay eyes on him again," said Boland, taking the wet cloth from his lips. "Any chance I can get a shot or two of whiskey? I'm hurting something awful here."

"*Again?*" Redlow looked at him curiously, not seeming to hear his plea for whiskey. "You mean you've seen him lately, and he's still alive?"

Boland looked ashamed. "I shot him real good, but the fool didn't die."

"You shot Fast Larry Shaw? Damn!" said Redlow, looking impressed. Over his shoulder he said to the men, "Anybody got a bottle handy? Give this man a few shots. He's hurting." To Boland he said, "Your brother, Ned, always told me you was the bold one in the family. I suppose he wasn't just blowing air."

Boland felt his chest swell with pride. "I shot Fast Larry Shaw, straight up, face-to-face. But Gerardo Luna stepped in, shotgun-butted me before I could put a righteous bullet through Shaw's head. I still owe Shaw a killing—Luna too for that matter." A bottle of rye made it from hand to hand, then to Redlow, who handed it down to Boland. "Luna's bad about sticking that shotgun butt wherever he pleases," said Redlow.

Taking the bottle, Boland pulled the cork. "I'll kill him for it, mark my word," said Boland. He took a long swig of rye and let out a satisfied hiss. "I'll kill them both—"

"All right, men, you heard Redlow," Eddie cut in, saying in a wry tone, "Right now, we're not killing Fast Larry Shaw or Gerardo Luna. We're going after horses." He stared down at Boland. "Think you can handle that?"

Boland only stared at him. When Eddie turned away, he raised the bottle of rye and took another long swig. Then he patted the wet, bloody cloth to his burning lips.

"Pay my brother Eddie no attention, Titus," said Redlow. "I always said Pa should have beat him more with a branding iron." As he backed up his horse a step and turned it, he added, "Everybody listen up. There's a big spread a couple of days' ride from here—the late Judge Bengreen's spread. We're going to ride over there, slip in at night and steal ourselves some fine horses there."

"What about them two lawdogs?" Fairday asked. "We're not going to let them get away with killing four of our own, are we?"

"What do you think, Leo?" Redlow asked pointedly. As he spoke he reached forward and took the reins to Patterson's horse from his hand and gestured for a man nearby to take them. "Take this horse back, Sweeney. Then catch up to us." He returned his gaze to Fairday. "Well, have we, Leo?" he asked again.

"No, we never have," Leo said. "I was just asking is all."

"We never *have* and we never *will*, Leo," Redlow

said in a firmer tone of voice. "If they're still on your trail and catch up to us, we'll make short work of them. If they show up at the ruins, Delby and the ones we left guarding the place will kill them deader than hell. Does that make you feel better?"

"Damned right it does." Leo grinned. "A whole lot better!" He stepped up into his saddle and tightened his hat down onto his forehead. *"Montamos esta noche!"* he called out in Spanish. "Tonight we ride!"

Chapter 8

Dawson and Caldwell lost a full day having to back-track to the place where they had heard the sound of pistol fire in the distance. But once they reached that spot and saw buzzards looming in a wide circle above the hills, they gave each other a knowing look and nudged their horses off the trail across the sandy flats. "At least they're easy to track," Caldwell said.

"Yep, just follow the bullets, the buzzards and the bodies," Dawson replied.

An hour later the two had climbed a hill trail in the evening sunlight and stopped with their rifles lying readily across their laps. Along the edge of the trail they saw a flock of the grisly scavenger birds squawking and batting their wings as they fussed back and forth over Black Jake Patterson's bloody remains.

Not wanting to risk the sound of a gunshot, the two lawmen raced their horses in close and slid them to a halt. Shouting and waving their arms, the lawmen watched the big birds rise reluctantly into the air. A string of intestines hung from the last one's blood-smeared beak. "Filthy buzzards," Caldwell growled. He took off his hat and waved it against the terrible smell of death simmering in the hot desert air.

Looking down at the half-eaten corpse, Dawson winced and said, "It's Black Jake." He looked away from the gruesome scene and located the gathering of hoofprints on the trail. In the dirt lay the six spent cartridge shells Boland had dropped from his pistol.

Staring at the eyeless, earless, picked-over remains, Caldwell said wryly, "It looks like him and Fairday had themselves a disagreement."

"Maybe not," said Dawson, directing his attention to the other hoofprints. "They must've met up with somebody here."

The two turned their horses and stepped them over to the tracks in the trail. Looking down Dawson said, "Three riders here." He looked off toward Matamoros.

"Some more of Barrows' men," Caldwell said in speculation.

"Possibly," said Dawson, scanning the land back and forth, as if trying to discern something from the endless rocky, brushy, sandy terrain. "Right here would have been a perfect place for them to ambush us." He gestured a nod up toward the rocky ledge above them where Patterson and Fairday had been waiting.

"But instead, one of them decided to shoot Black

Jake six times," said Caldwell. He shook his head, puzzled by such reasoning.

"It wouldn't have mattered," said Dawson. "We weren't coming up this trail anyway. We can thank my poor dead horse for causing that."

As Dawson spoke he'd idly patted the neck of the cream-colored Barb beneath him and stepped the animal slowly along the narrow trail. Leaning in his saddle looking down, he took note of three sets of tracks of three horses coming up the trail, and five going down. One set of tracks cut the earth less deep than the other four, the riderless horse belonging to Black Jake Patterson, he surmised.

With Caldwell behind him, Dawson followed the tracks to a place where the trail sloped down and wound out of sight through a tangle of cedar, scrub pine and wild sage. At a clearing the two looked out across a long rolling stretch of cactus and desert sand. The five horses had left a trail of upturned sand that snaked off into a blur of grainy light and darkening shadows and disappeared from sight.

"Once we ride down from here, we've got nothing but desert the next thirty miles," Dawson said. He turned a tired gaze to Caldwell. "The less we stop, the closer we'll be to them by morning."

Without reply, Caldwell nudged his horse forward down the narrow trail.

They rode on. . . .

In the chilled desert air they stopped only once in the pale moonlight, long enough to water their horses sparsely from their canteens. For themselves, they took only a small sip of water, enough to wet their dry mouths. In order to stave off their own thirst they picked small flat stones from amid the sand and placed them under their tongues. They rode in silence beneath a silver-purple dome, conserving their energy and fluids.

At midnight the two lawmen began taking turns, one dozing for an hour or more in his saddle while the other kept watch. By the time dawn wreathed the eastern horizon, Dawson had kept the horses following the narrow path of upturned sand through a narrow canyon. Riding out of the canyon he picked the tracks up again and stopped at the pool of water at the base of the abutment wall of earth and stone. "Caldwell, wake up," he said quietly, yet loud enough to stir the dozing lawman.

"I'm awake," Caldwell said abruptly, shaking off sleep and straightening himself in his saddle. He looked all around, batting his eyes. "What is it?"

"Maybe nothing," said Dawson. He gestured down at all the hoofprints around the water's edge. His eyes followed them a short distance away. "It looks like these three met with some others right here."

"Whoa," said Caldwell, getting interested. He stepped his horse forward and looked out along the trail leading south, away from the water. "Have we come upon the whole Barrows Gang?"

"I don't know," said Dawson, studying the ground, seeing where a single rider had turned and led the spare horse back alongside the trail. "But we're going to find out, soon as we get ourselves watered." He stepped down from his saddle and let the cream-colored Barb lower its muzzle to the water.

As Caldwell stepped down, he froze for a second, looking off into the distance, opposite the large number of tracks headed northwest. "What was that?" he asked, seeing a tiny glow of firelight rise and fall in the distant early-morning gloom.

Dawson had also noticed the flicker of firelight. In a lowered voice he said, "That was a sign from heaven." He levered a round into his rifle chamber, keeping quiet in spite of the distance between them and the flicker of light. "Before we go tracking these riders, maybe we best ride back along their trail and see where they're coming from."

"Yep, I believe you're right," said Caldwell. He reached over, slid his rifle into his saddle boot and jerked the sawed-off double-barreled shotgun from beneath his bedroll.

Behind a half-collapsed wall of old Indian ruins, a gunman named Herco Delby said, "Who struck that match?" But he didn't have to ask. He knew. Walking stiffly over to where the man on guard, Blue Joe Selbert, sat puffing on a fresh cigar, he looked down coldly at him, and said, "Put it out, you stupid son of a bitch."

Blue Joe calmly turned his face up to Delby and blew a thin stream of smoke. "Like hell I will." He looked all around at other grim faces as the six men began to gather to see what the heated talk was all about. "The brothers left you in charge, Delby," he said. "Don't let your new hat size get you killed." He gave a short chuckle as if to pass it all off as a joke.

But Delby wasn't laughing. "You know better than to light a damned cigar this time of morning. Somebody could see it all the way from the hill trails."

"There's nobody out there," said Selbert. "If there was, he'd have already been trampled over by Eddie, Redlow and the gang."

Giles Sweeney had brought Patterson's horse back and lingered overnight before riding out to catch up with the gang. He stepped forward and said, "Delby's right, Blue Joe. We've got Cray Dawson and a deputy on our trail. We can't be taking stupid chances."

Selbert kept the cigar clamped between his teeth and said, "Who are you calling stupid, Giles? I hope it's not me. I hate name-calling."

Sweeney backed off.

But not Delby. Stepping even closer, his fists clenched at his sides, he said down to Selbert, "Put it out, or I'll put it out for you."

A tense silence fell across the ruins as the men watched expectantly.

With the cigar clamped firmly in his teeth, Selbert laid his hand on his holstered Remington and said, "It would be a great source of amusement to see you try, wouldn't it, boys—?"

The words had hardly passed his lips when Delby's boot shot out and kicked him solidly in the face. Selbert flew backward on the ground in a spray of cigar sparks. Pieces of the flattened cigar stuck to his beard and eyebrows. Hair sizzled as the half-conscious gunman slapped at his burned face, spitting the stub of the cigar from his lips.

"Damn you, Delby! I'll kill you!" he shouted, his hand grabbing the handle of his Remington.

But Delby's boot clamped down on his wrist before he could snatch the gun up and put it to use. Delby's Colt came down into his face, cocked and ready to fire, an inch from his blackened nose. "You're not killing anybody, Blue Joe. It's over," Delby growled. "Ain't it?" He stood poised and ready.

Selbert saw the dark determination in his eyes. He eased down and let his wrist drop. Nodding, he cut a quick glance all around at the other men but saw no support for himself. "Damn it. Yeah, it's over, Delby," he said, again trying to play it off as a joke. "You said you'd put it out for me . . . and you did. What more do you want?" He tried a stiff grin. "I was just funning with you some. Don't go getting so damned serious. Right boys?" He looked all around again, still seeing nothing but grim faces; no support.

A scar-faced gunman named Wally Click said in a no-nonsense tone, "Firing up that cigar could have gave us away and got us killed. You're lucky we don't all kill you."

"Hey! Come on pards," said Selbert. "We're all pals here. I made a little mistake. Nobody else here ever done that? It was almost daylight."

"Almost the daylight is not the daylight," said a Mexican outlaw named Paco Bonapey, in stiff English. He wagged a finger back and forth. "You knew that it was wrong, what you did."

Before Selbert could reply, Delby said, "It's over,

Paco. Let it go. Everybody go on about your business." He looked at Sweeney and said, "Giles, you need to get saddled and get out of here, catch back up to the others."

"I'm on my way," said Sweeney, walking briskly to where his horse stood in a small makeshift corral constructed of downfallen tree limbs and brush tied together with lariats and scraps of string, wire and rawhide. In moments he'd slung his saddle up onto his horse, cinched it, climbed up and ridden away.

A hundred yards away, Dawson and Caldwell stopped their horses in a low sandy draw and stepped down. They kept the animals quiet, hearing hooves move away across the desert floor in the grainy morning light. As the sound of the hooves faded out of hearing, the two lawmen climbed to the edge of the draw and bided their time. They waited until they had enough light to identify three of the six men in the ruins lying ahead.

Finally Dawson said, "It's them. Let's go." If they waited too long, sunlight would leave them exposed on an open stretch of ground.

Inside the ruins, Paco asked Delby, "Can I gather some wood, to make for us some coffee?"

Delby looked all around, judging daylight, seeing the purplish veil lift slowly from the desert floor. "Go ahead and gather it. But wait a little longer before starting a fire."

"*Si*, I will gather it and wait," said Paco.

From the edge of the sandy draw, as soon as Dawson and Caldwell could see well enough to count six figures moving about within the crumbled walls of the ruins, they both stood in a crouch and moved forward.

Inside the ruins, a gunman named Bob *Tall Pockets* Stevens stood with his saddle raised, ready to throw in over his horse's back. But upon seeing the two shadowy figures move into sight and spread out, he said, "Uh-oh! Trouble coming, Delby!" He let the saddle fall from his hands and grabbed for his holstered Colt.

But Delby had already seen the two approaching figures himself. "It's the law!" he said, drawing his Colt and cocking it as he backed away behind part of a crumbling stone wall. "Damn it, Selbert! You're supposed to be on guard!"

"What the hell do you want from me?" Selbert shouted at Delby. He stood up, his Remington in hand. But before he could raise it toward the advancing lawmen, a bullet from Dawson's Colt picked him up and hurled him backward onto the ground.

"Kill them!" shouted Tall Pockets Stevens. But as he fired wildly, Caldwell had raced in closer and taken cover behind the low stone wall. A blast from his ten-gauge shotgun silenced Stevens and left him lying dead in a spreading pool of blood.

Firing toward the sound of the shotgun blast and the rise of smoke, Wally Click raced toward the horses. A few buckshots from the second blast of the double-barrel hit him but only wounded him. He went down to his knee but managed to come back up firing, racing toward the spot where Caldwell had taken cover, knowing the lawman had to reload or come up with a pistol. Either way, Click saw his opportunity and he took it.

But Dawson also saw what was going to happen; he stepped out into the open from behind a wood pile to draw Click's attention, and shouted, "Over here!"

It worked. Click jerked around toward him. Delby and Paco also turned toward him from their position beside the horses. Seeing Dawson's Colt pointed at him, Click turned his fire away from Caldwell. But as his shot whirred past Dawson's head, Dawson took aim and fired. His shot lifted Click and flipped him backward.

Caldwell had reloaded quickly. He rose up from the stone wall in time to see Delby and Paco firing at Dawson. The first blast on the shotgun hammered Delby backward. Delby tried to catch himself but only managed to stagger sidelong into the frightened horses. A gunman named Indian Jack Toeburg sprang from his cover behind a rock and raced in a crouch, firing at Dawson as he hurried to join Paco at the horses.

Dawson's Colt nailed him. The first shot hit him in the side of his neck as he ran; the second shot struck him full in the chest as he turned and tried to take aim at Dawson.

Jumping into his saddle, Paco dug his spurs into the horse's sides and raced across the ruins. As the horse made a leap over the three-foot-high stone wall, Caldwell's shotgun exploded and blasted him sideways from the saddle. He hit the ground limply and rolled to a halt.

As the echo of gunfire rolled up against the distant hills, the two lawmen stood up cautiously; a low cloud of gun smoke loomed on the still air. "Are—are you hit?" Caldwell asked Dawson.

Dawson resisted the urge to feel his chest and make sure. Instead he said quietly, almost in disbelief, "No, are you?"

"No," said Caldwell. Touching his fingerless glove to his cheek he said, "A piece of rock nicked me, but I'm all right." He swallowed a tense knot in his throat, looking all around at the carnage. "Is that all six?"

"Yep, all six," Dawson said. They stood in silence for a moment, feeling a cool morning breeze blow steadily across the ruins. "We got lucky, Jedson," Dawson said at length. "It's not likely to happen again."

From a thousand yards out, Giles Sweeney had heard the sudden gunfire erupt, followed by the dead silence only a few seconds later. He circled and rode back just close enough to see that the only two men left standing were not of the Barrows Gang. Then he turned his horse and gave it spurs. There was nothing he could do, unless he wanted to ride back to the ruins and die himself. *Uh-uh,* he thought, racing away across the sand. This was something Redlow and Eddie needed to hear about.

In the ruins, the two lawmen saw the rising dust of the fleeing horseman. "He's headed out now to tell the Barrows all about it," said Caldwell. He'd taken a bandanna from around his neck and pressed it to his bleeding cheek.

"Yes, he is," said Dawson, reloading his Colt. "But the Barrows brothers were already expecting us." He dropped his Colt into his holster.

They stood in silence for another moment, Dawson watching the rider's dust move farther out of sight, Caldwell looking around at the dead on the ground. "Do you feel right about what we're doing, gunning them down this way?"

"No, I don't," Dawson said bluntly. He thought about Fairday and the young girl they'd found lying staked out dead along the trail. "If you know any other way to deal with these men, I'm listening."

"No, I don't," said Caldwell. He broke open the shotgun, pulled out the two spent shells, dropped them to the ground and replaced them. Clicking the shotgun shut he said, "I'm starting to understand Shaw, feel the way he always appears to be."

"How's that?" Dawson asked.

"Just empty," said Caldwell, "empty and dark, like I need to make something right with myself."

"That's Shaw all right," said Dawson, "empty and dark." He took a deep breath and let it out, allowing the tightness to uncoil inside his chest. "Whatever he's doing at the Bengreen spread, I hope it's making him *right with himself*."

PART 2

Chapter 9

Lawrence Shaw needed a drink. *No,* he thought, looking out across the shallow valley below, watching the four Apache make quick work of the dead steer, he didn't *need* a drink. But he sure *wanted* one. He licked his dry lips. *Wanting* a drink wasn't exactly accurate, he told himself. It wasn't so much that he *needed* a drink or even *wanted* a drink. All right, he could *use* a drink right then, he told himself with a nod, hoping that would settle whatever argument was going on inside him. But it didn't.

Use a drink for what? the arguing voice inside him quickly shot back. *Damn.* He didn't know. He let out a breath, tired of thinking about it, tired of quarreling over it with himself. He was sober, at present anyway, and the *present* was all he felt able to deal with right now. Besides, it wasn't as if he'd stopped drinking from now on. He'd stopped long enough to sober up, to get his senses back. After that . . . well, it was hard to say. But for now, he wasn't drinking. *Good enough . . .*

How many days had it been? He wasn't going to start counting—run the risk of opening up a whole argument with himself. "No thanks," he murmured beneath his lowered hat brim. He remained hidden behind a mesquite bush, the rifle cradled in his left arm. His hands weren't shaking as bad. That's how long it had been.

He waited until the two spindly-legged Apache elders and two young boys not yet near their teens had cleaned the steer to the bone and packed the last of the bloody meat out of sight. Then he raised the rifle to his left shoulder, took aim and fired just as one of the elders disappeared into a stand of rock, scrub trees and brush. The first rifle shot had sent the old man scurrying along like some stiff ancient wolf. Two more shots kicked up dirt along the path after the old man had taken cover.

That'll do it. Shaw stood up and looked out across the harsh terrain. He saw no movement inside the brush and trees, but with the Apache he hadn't expected to. They had taken the meat and vanished. His shots had been meant only to warn them. Dusting his trouser leg, Shaw walked to his horse, slid the rifle into its boot, mounted and rode away, back toward the hacienda.

Ten minutes later, before the Bengreen hacienda rose into sight, he saw the fresh plume of trail dust coming toward him. Batting his boot heels to his horse's sides, he brought the animal into a comfortable gallop and hurried forward. He didn't slow down until he could make out Anna Bengreen riding at the head of the dust.

Moments later, when she rode up at a slower gallop, she circled her horse to a halt a few feet away. "I heard shots," she said. "Are you all right, Lawrence?"

Shaw stopped and rested his left wrist on his saddle horn, his right arm still in the sling. "I'm fine, Anna," Shaw replied. "Riding toward rifle shots is not a good idea," he added.

"I—I know," she replied, nudging her horse up closer to him. "But I became worried." She pushed her riding hat back from her head and let it hang by its strings behind her shoulders.

"Then you should have sent Ernesto," Shaw said, but in an easy tone, reminding her only for her own good.

"Yes, you are right," she said. "I will remember your advice, if it should happen again."

"Yes, ma'am," Shaw said, using *ma'am* to let her know he knew who was the boss here. "Anyway it was nothing," he said. "A band of Apache dressing out a dead steer. They looked awfully lean in the shanks. I figure they needed it."

"They killed one of my cattle?" she asked, not seeming upset, only curious.

"A wild one, I figured," said Shaw. "Not a part of any herd. I doubt if they killed it. Most likely they found it already dead, or dying. If they were killing it for food, they would have taken it with them on the hoof, killed it and dressed it somewhere else."

"Oh . . . Then the shots I heard . . . ?"

"They were just warning shots," Shaw said, "letting them know to keep moving. Your hacienda is seven miles from here. These old-blanket warriors can smell a horse that distance."

"I see." She considered it, then asked, "Do you know a lot about the Apache?"

"I wouldn't say I know a lot," said Shaw. "But I've learned a little . . . mostly I've learned to give them wide breadth. They were here a long while before the rest of us showed up." He raised his left hand and kneaded his mending shoulder.

Anna studied him as he looked out across the broad, harsh terrain. *Fast Larry Shaw,* she said to herself, liking what she'd learned so far of the infamous Texan gunman. Of course she had heard of Lawrence Shaw, the Fastest Gun Alive, and it went without saying that he realized it. Although neither of them had brought the matter up, they had both carefully directed their brief conversations around or away from it.

While she had heard of him, she knew little about him, other than the fact that he was rumored to have killed many men . . . men who had come seeking to kill him. Did that justify his actions? Certainly it did, she answered herself without hesitation, gazing out across the wild desert land with him for a moment. Then she returned to his weathered face, his confident, flint-sharp eyes.

Suddenly, to her own surprise, she heard herself ask him, "Why did you give the name of the *Tejas* lawyer for yourself?"

Without turning his eyes to her, Shaw sighed, almost in relief that the subject of himself had come up. He had nothing to hide, not from Anna Reyes Bengreen. "Chever Reed was my lawyer, and a friend," he said bluntly, finally turning to her as he spoke. "Before he died, he made me promise him I'd use his name." Shaw shrugged his left shoulder. "So I did."

"May I—" She halted, then continued, "May I ask why?"

"Yes, of course you may," Shaw said, feeling even more relieved. "He knew my circumstances, how many men were out to kill me, just to claim my reputation. He knew he was dying, so he asked me to use his name—sort of his way of leaving behind a little mystery about himself."

"But why was such a thing important to him?" she asked, not about to even try and fathom why men would kill one another just to prove themselves faster with a gun.

Shaw thought about how to explain it for a moment. Then finding no way, he said, "I suppose you would have to have known Chever Reed to understand why that was important to him."

"Oh, I did not mean to pry," she said quickly, thinking she had stepped too deep into Shaw's world.

"No, Anna," Shaw said quietly, nudging his horse closer to hers, "I didn't take it that way. It's just that some things don't explain out as easily as others. This is one of them." He looked into her eyes, not wanting her to remind him so much of Rosa, yet feeling powerless to keep her from it. "Let's—let's keep talking though, about anything you want . . . that is, if it's all the same to you."

She studied his eyes in return and asked, "I want to talk about you. But I do not know what I should or should not ask."

"Ask me anything, Anna," Shaw said, his voice growing softer. His horse was sidled up against hers, so close he could smell the scent of her hair, a scent so achingly familiar to him.

"It is said you faked your own death," she said, averting her eyes down to her gloved hands for a moment, but then back to his.

"Yes, that's true—I did," Shaw replied. "But little good it did me." He paused, took off his hat and laid it on his saddle horn. "It worked for a while. . . . I'm still rumored to be dead in some places, I suppose. But it's wearing thin. People are catching on to it, even all the way here in Mexico."

Anna considered his words for a moment. "So, a person cannot hide from themselves forever," she mused, shaking her head slowly. "What a terrible way to live, always wondering each day if someone will know the lie you are living and destroy the new life you have created for yourself. This *is* how you must live, yes?"

"Well . . . Yes, I suppose you could say so." His life seemed even more sad and seedy to him, hearing her describe it, and at the same time catching glances of his life and how much darker and more hopeless it had become since his wife's death.

She reached out a hand and brushed a lock of

damp hair from his forehead. Shaw sat stunned by the act; but he liked it. "I think I understand."

"You do?" Shaw wasn't sure what it was she understood, or what it had to do with anything. But he knew by the change in her voice, the touch of her hand, that she had resolved those questions a woman has about a man before giving herself to him.

"Yes, I do," she whispered.

They looked deep into each other's eyes, each knowing, each asking and replying to one another without needing words. At length, she whispered breathlessly, "Not here . . . follow me."

Shaw watched her turn her horse expertly and gallop off toward a line of trees at the base of the rock hillside. Without a second thought he booted his horse along behind her.

When they'd finished making love on the bedroll Shaw had hastily thrown to the ground from behind his saddle, he lay watching her as she poured water from a canteen onto his bandanna and touched it to her naked breasts. When she had bathed herself all over with the canteen water, she stood facing an afternoon breeze coming off the hills. Her arms spread, her eyes closed, she let the breeze both cool and dry her skin.

"I have been too long in mourning," she said quietly, her face comfortable and relaxed. Wringing the bandanna, she tied it loosely around her throat and walked back to the bedroll. "Do you suppose Gerardo Luna foresaw this happening between us when he planned our meeting one another?" She smiled as she reached down, picked up Shaw's shirt, slipped it on and stretched out beside him.

Her action gave him pause. It was the same thing he'd watched Rosa do countless times when they had finished their lovemaking and lay together closely for a while.

"Well, do you?" she asked when he didn't answer right away.

He caught himself before she'd seen the dark cloud move across his brow. "I wouldn't be surprised," he said, forcing himself to let the other thought go. Even in the midst of their passion he'd made up his mind that this was no ordinary woman. He knew that Anna Reyes Bengreen was not Rosa Shaw; but he also knew this was a woman he did not want to lose.

She pressed herself against him and spoke softly, close to his face, "I am not angry with him if he did. I am glad."

"I'm glad too . . . Anna," he said, realizing how close he had come to calling her Rosa. He held her tight against him, the taste of her mouth still fresh on his lips. "It's been a long time since I felt this way with a woman." He closed his eyes and lay with her, letting her scent engulf him. This was not Rosa; this . . . was . . . not . . . Rosa! He didn't want to think about Rosa. Yet he knew, even as he held this warm, beautiful woman and felt the need in her respond to him, *this was not Rosa* . . . and his heart ached.

He felt her pull away from him and heard her say, "What is wrong, Lawrence?"

Damn it, even her voice, he told himself, growing angry at himself. "Nothing, Anna," he said. "But it's getting late. I need to get you back to the hacienda before it gets too dark."

At first she looked puzzled, seeing him pull back from her and stand up. But she liked his smile as he reached down, helped her to her feet and held her for a moment longer. "I don't want anything to happen to you. I only saw two old men and two children. But I don't know how many Apache were waiting in the trees."

"I understand." She looked around as he turned her loose. True, it was getting dark; they were seven miles from the hacienda. "Anyway, Ernesto is preparing a nice dinner for us." She turned from him and dressed. Shaw did the same.

When he'd finished buckling his gun belt and buttoning his shirt, he slipped his arm back into the sling, rolled up the bedroll and carried it to his horse. In moments the two had mounted and ridden the horses onto the trail leading back to the hacienda.

Chapter 10

When they had returned to the hacienda, Shaw and Anna sat down to the dinner Ernesto had prepared for them. Afterward, Anna dismissed the elderly houseman, and the two watched him walk away in the glow of a tall candle he carried. When he'd turned out of sight, toward the far end of a long hallway leading to the back door of the sprawling house, Anna smiled. She picked up her glass of wine and moved around to the head of the long table to the chair next to Shaw, where he sat sipping coffee, his hat and gun belt hanging on the chair back, within reach. His rifle stood leaning against the wall behind him.

As if in secrecy she said, "I don't know if it is the wine going to my head." Through an open window Ernesto's horse's hooves rode toward the small house near the horse stables a hundred yards away. "But tonight I feel so free, more free than I have felt since I was a child." She reached a hand over to Shaw.

"And how do you feel, *Mr.* Shaw?" she asked playfully.

Shaw took her outreached hand in his. "Mr. Shaw has never felt better, *ma'am,*" he said, unable to feel as playful as her, yet going along with her. There was something wrong with her reminding him so much of his deceased wife, Rosa. He felt as if he were betraying someone, either *her,* or Rosa's memory; he wasn't sure which. *Maybe both,* he thought.

In spite of his thin smile, the look in his eyes said something different. "Are you happy?" she asked, seeing through him.

Shaw looked at her. She was still the same, strong beautiful woman surrounded by her wealth and all that came with it. Yet now she was a woman like every other woman, he thought, and she needed to hear from the man she'd given herself to.

Was he happy . . . ? Hell, he'd forgotten there was such a thing as happiness. He managed to prop up his thin smile for her sake. "I'm *very* happy," he lied, raising her hand to his lips and kissing it.

"Good," she whispered, having to take his words at face value. She reached over and brushed a strand of hair from his forehead. "I know that what happened today happened suddenly, and it has caught us both unprepared. But it is time I come out of mourning." She paused in reflection, then said quickly as if to keep from wrestling with her decision, "I want you to move your things into my room tonight, that is, if you feel the same—That is, if you would like to . . . ?" Her question trailed.

Looking at the glass of wine in Anna's hand, he

swallowed against a tightness in his throat that the coffee had not been able to loosen. He needed to tell her about Rosa, didn't he . . . ? "Yes, Anna," he said sincerely, "I would like to do that. I would like to very much."

She studied him closely, then said, "Something troubles you, Lawrence. Please tell me what it is so I can make it go away."

Here goes. . . . "Anna," he said, "I know this sounds strange, coming from a man. But I too have been mourning the loss of someone I love . . . and it's been much longer than—"

"Shhh," she said, stopping him. "You do not have to tell me this."

"I feel like I should," Shaw said, ready to tell her everything, how she reminded him so much of Rosa Shaw that he had felt guilty—had almost called her by his wife's name when they'd made love earlier in the shade of the desert hillsides.

"Gerardo Luna told me about what happened to your wife," she said before he could continue. "He told me how much she and I look like one another."

Shaw sat in silence, not knowing what to say next. Did she already realize how he felt? How when he looked into her eyes or touched her or breathed her fragrance, it was not her but another woman?

"He told me that you lived with her sister, Carmelita, after Rosa's death," she said, as if she had thought the whole thing out and drawn her own conclusions before ever giving herself to him today.

"I just don't want to be dishonest with you, Anna,"

he said. "I don't want to be dishonest with anyone anymore. I'm weary of dishonesty, of lying to a woman to get what I want from her, of trying to put up a false front and pretend things I don't feel." He shook his head.

"I understand," she replied quietly, "and I feel the same." Her eyes changed slightly; Shaw saw there were secrets lying there. "Time is too short for dishonesty, for deceit between two people who care for one another."

"Yes," Shaw agreed, "I learned that the hard way."

"As did I," she said. She closed her eyes as if in reflection of regret. But when she opened her eyes her expression brightened. "But that is the past, and we must not let the sadness of the past hold our future for a ransom we can never pay, must we?"

"That's a good way of putting it, Anna," Shaw said, he himself feeling the regret and sadness lift from him. "If I can just keep that thought in mind."

"You must keep it in mind, Lawrence," she said. "You cannot feel guilty and responsible for that which you can no longer change, but only for those things that can still be changed by you. Once something is done, all you can do is learn from it. It is all God asks of us, and all we can ask of ourselves."

Shaw stared at her. "You're right" he said, realizing it was just the sort of thing Rosa would have said to him. *But knock it off,* he warned himself; it was also something anyone with good reasoning and a sense of human compassion would say. He squeezed her hand gently and pressed it to his cheek. "I—I want to feel that way about things. It's just so hard sometimes."

"I know," she whispered, responding warmly to his touch, "and at those times when it is so hard to live with the past, please let me be there, to remind you of the present."

"Yes, I want you here in the present, Anna—" Shaw's words cut short at the sound of gunfire coming from the direction of the stables.

"Ernesto!" Anna cried out. She leaped up from her chair as more gunfire erupted. She had turned toward the door when Shaw grabbed her and pulled her back.

"Stay here, Anna!" he said firmly.

"But Ernesto! His family!"

"Stay put! I'll get to them!" Shaw demanded, standing quickly, snatching up his rifle and heading out the door. In his haste he left his hat and gun belt behind; but he knew he had fifteen shots in his rifle chamber. "There's my Colt. If you need me, fire a shot!" he said over his shoulder. But Anna only glanced at the big gun with fear in her eyes.

Outside the small adobe house where Ernesto, his wife and his two sons lived, Titus Boland, Leo Fairday, Tomes and McClinton pulled out of the circling riders and rode wide into the darkness. The four men pushed six of the Cedros Altos horses ahead of them from the broken gates of the corral. The Barrows brothers and three other men continued circling and firing at the small adobe house while four others shooed the horses out of the corral, and from the stalls inside the large barn.

A gunman named Billy Elkins jumped down from his saddle, grabbed up a dusty saddle blanket from a rail and set fire to it with a wooden sulfur match. "This will get out any stragglers," he said. He lit a thin cigar butt he pulled from behind his ear, giving the flames a few seconds to grow and lick up along the blanket.

"What the hell are you doing, Billy?" a gunman named Teddy Barksdale shouted as he raced his horse up close and slid it to a halt. "These horses are no good to us *roasted*!"

Billy laughed. "Then you best hurry and get them out of there. I'm firing this place to hell on earth!" Across the yard from the barn, the gang kept a constant barrage of gunfire on the house. A shot through the broken window struck an oil lamp, overturned it and sent a streak of fire across the floor. Ernesto's eldest son, Tecco, ran out screaming through the front door, flames blazing the length and width of his back.

"Damn, Billy-boy, you might have the right idea after all," said Barksdale, watching as bullets sliced through the young man and left him facedown, burning in the dirt. He quickly reached down, snatched the burning saddle blanket from Elkin's hand and rode away, his horse starting to spook at the sight of the flames dancing so near its side.

"Give it back, damn you to hell!" Elkins shouted above the raging gunfire and screams from inside the burning house. But Barksdale raced his horse inside the barn where other riders were shooing horses out the open rear door. Without a moment of hesitation he hurled the burning blanket up into a hayloft filled with fresh, dried wild grass.

"What the hell, Teddy?" said an older gunman named Fred Townsend. "You want to burn us all alive?"

"No, but I damned sure got you busy, didn't I, ole Freddy?" Barksdale shouted, turning his horse and racing out of the barn among the spooked and fleeing Cedros Altos horses.

"Smart sonsabitch," Townsend growled under his breath, gigging his horse along and twirling a three-foot length of lariat to keep the horses moving.

"Get going, Freddy. That damned fool set the loft on fire!" shouted a gunman named Drop the Dog Jones as he pressed close behind Townsend, having shooed three ranchero horses out of their stalls and toward the rear barn door.

"I know," said Townsend, "I saw him do it!"

Out front of the burning house, Redlow and Eddie Barrows rode back and forth in front of the other men, all of them gathering together now that they heard no more gun shots coming from within the raging fire. "Hold your fire," Eddie called out, waving a hand back and forth. "They're all done for inside!"

"Everybody get behind the horses. Keep them moving close and tight until we can get somewhere to split them up and string them!" Redlow called out as he dropped six spent cartridges from his Colt and reloaded. He grinned at his brother in the flickering firelight. "This wasn't half bad, was it?"

"Easy as you please," Eddie replied. He gave a quick look toward the shadowy horde of horses and riders disappearing at a fast run across the sandy ground. Turning his horse toward two nearby riders named Lying Earl Sunday and Phil Gaddis, he said, "You two ride over and make sure the corral is empty. Then ride like hell and catch up to the others."

"You got it, Eddie," said Phil Gaddis. But as he and Lying Earl turned to heel their horses away toward the corral, a rifle shot lifted him from his saddle and slung him backward to the ground.

"What the—?" Eddie and the others ducked in their saddles and looked toward the muzzle flash just in time to see the blossom of blue-red fire as Shaw's next shot hit a gunman named Brady Lawton full in the chest and rolled him backward to the ground. "Get out of the firelight!" Eddie shouted as the men raised their weapons and shot round upon round into the darkness.

Fifty yards away, bareheaded, down on one knee, Shaw took aim as the men dispersed and rode out of the flickering light. He knew he could get off one more shot as bullets whizzed past him like angry hornets. But upon seeing the house ready to fall beneath the flames, the blazing barn not far behind it, he held his shot. In a second, the guns fell silent; he heard hooves pounding away across the sand.

In the shelter of darkness he hurried forward, in a

crouch, his eyes searching into the flames as he hoped beyond hope that someone had made it out alive. He risked calling out, "Ernesto," into the darkness surrounding the house and barn. When he heard no reply he tried again. "Anybody!" But the only sound was the crackling of burning barn timbers and the roar of flames.

He had not taken the time to run to the small barn beside the hacienda and get his horse. In his urgency he had run the hundred yards on foot, firing at the riders from half that distance when he'd seen what they were up to. Now he stood helplessly looking all around, knowing the horses were gone, knowing Ernesto and his family were dead and knowing there was nothing he could do about any of it right then.

He opened and closed his right fist, feeling the stiffness in the length of his right arm. He breathed deep, catching his breath. Whoever the men were, they were gone now, he thought, taking stock of the situation. He turned and started walking back toward the hacienda. He needed to get to the small barn, get his horse saddled and get onto their trail. Luckily for him they were headed in a direction that would allow him to swing off their trail long enough to ride into Matamoros, where he knew he could rely on Gerardo Luna to join him.

But before he had walked ten feet, he heard the sound of three rapid-fire gunshots come from the hacienda. "Oh no! Anna!" he shouted, breaking into a hard run, his voice muffled by two more shots.

Out front of the hacienda, Titus Boland grinned toward the glow of candlelight from the open door and holstered his pistol. Seeing what he thought was the body of Lawrence Shaw lying slumped dead in the doorway he said, "I got you this time, Fast Larry. Now rot in hell." He jerked his horse around and rode off fast, in order to catch up with the other three men and the six stolen horses.

Lagging back, waiting for him fifty yards up the trail in the pale moonlight, Leo Fairday called out, "Did you get him, Boland? Did you kill that drunken sonsabitch?"

"Oh, yes," Boland said, barely slowing his horse as Fairday sidled up alongside him. "I killed him this time. Make no mistake, he's dead and in hell."

"You faced him right down—did the job on him, did you?" Fairday asked eagerly, wanting details.

"Yep," Boland lied. "I faced off from him about ten feet and put three in his liver before he could get a single shot off. He never cleared leather." He gave a smug grin.

"But I heard five shots," Fairday said.

"Yeah," Boland said, realizing he had fired wild and relied on luck and the cover of darkness, rather than taking a chance and getting up close, making sure his victim was dead. "I stepped in and put two in his head, just to make sure he'd never breathe again."

"Good work!" said Fairday, excited by the prospect of any man killing Fast Larry Shaw, let alone out-drawing him and killing him up close. "Hot damn! I'm riding beside the hombre who killed the Fastest Gun Alive!" The two hurried their horses along in the darkness until they saw the outline of

Tomes and McClinton in front of them. "I call it a feather in my cap, bringing you boys to join up with us."

"Yeah, I suppose it is at that," said Boland, feeling more than just a little pleased with himself. He batted his heels to his horse's sides. "You still carrying that pigsticker I saw you with the other day?" he asked.

"I always keep it handy," said Fairday.

"Good, I want to borrow it for a spell," said Boland, reaching his hand out toward Fairday.

Fairday gave him a leery stare and asked, "You ain't fixing to stick me with it are you?"

"No," said Boland, getting impatient. "Now hand it over."

"I always like to ask first," Fairday said, drawing the knife from his boot well and laying it in Boland's hand. "Who you wanting to stick with it?"

Boland didn't answer. Instead he said, "You want to take a ride with me as soon as we take these horses to Redlow and Eddie?"

Fairday gave him a suspicious look. "I guess so," he said hesitantly.

"Good," said Boland, gigging his horse up into a run, getting into a hurry. He had one more stop to make along the trail. . . .

Back at the hacienda Shaw kneeled in the doorway with Anna Reyes Bengreen in his arms. His hands trembled as he brushed a strand of hair from her face. "Oh no, God no!" he sobbed, seeing her struggle for every shallow, waning breath. "Please don't die, *please* don't die," he said, resisting the urge to shake her, as if to awaken her from sleep. But this was not sleep, he knew, seeing the trickle of blood run down from the corner of her lips.

"I—I tricked them?" she said in a broken voice, trying to smile. "You're . . . safe? I saved you?" Shaw looked at his hat lying a few feet away, where it had fallen from atop her head when the bullets hit her. In the dirt beside her lay his Colt.

"Yes, you tricked them, Anna," Shaw said, holding her tightly, seeing life fade from her eyes. "I'm safe. You saved me."

Anna gave a faint smile and relaxed in his arms, as if death were no more than a long, peaceful sleep.

Chapter 11

In Matamoros, Gerardo Luna stood up from the cot in the empty cell. Outside, the first promise of morning lay stretched along the hills to the east like a thin silver wreath. At his bare feet a skinny cat appeared as if from nowhere. The hungry animal purred and meowed as it rubbed itself back and forth against his ankle. "Paciencia, my friend," he said. "You are always hungry, eh?"

He moved the cat aside with a gentle nudge of his foot. He dressed, pulled his boots on and walked over to the potbellied stove in the front corner of the small, dusty office. He put a pot of coffee on top of the stove and fed the cat a few crumbled pieces of jerked beef from a canvas bag. "Now go outside, and let me awaken without you giving me any more orders," he said, reaching down and rubbing the cat along its knobby back and picking it up.

He walked to the front door, unlatched it, opened it, set the cat out on the sandy ground and watched it loop away into the grainy darkness. Then he walked to his desk, sat down and took the time to clean his sawed-off shotgun while he waited for his coffee to boil.

In a narrow alley behind the adobe jail, Titus Boland slipped back down into his saddle. He had been standing atop his horse and looking in through a small, barred cell window above the cot where Luna had slept. He grinned at Fairday and whispered, "You can't know how satisfying this is going to be." He rubbed his sore chin in dark reflection. "Today I settle accounts with this lawdog for good."

Fairday handed him the reins to his horse, which he'd been holding for him. "Alls I ask is that you don't leave my pigsticker hanging in him when you're done," he whispered. The two eased their horses away from the window and along the building to the edge of the alley.

At his desk, Luna stood up and walked to the door when he heard the cat scratching to get back inside. "Already you want back in?" he said to the closed door, as if the cat could both hear and understand him. "You are getting to be more trouble than an old woman," he added, swinging the door open, looking down for the cat to come lopping in at his feet.

But instead of seeing the cat, he saw the wild-eyed face of Titus Boland staring grimly at him. Behind Boland's left shoulder he saw the same expression on the face of Leo Fairday. "Give it to him," Fairday hissed.

Before Luna could make a move to protect himself, Boland plunged Fairday's knife into his chest and watched the lawman stagger backward, both hands clutching the knife handle.

Boland stepped inside; Fairday followed, closing the door behind them. "Not that you asked, Lawdog," Boland said to the stunned peace officer, "but my chin is mending right along." He rubbed his chin. "I can't say much for my broken teeth though."

The two watched Luna stagger about and gasp for breath. "Pull it out and stick him again," Fairday said, his eyes lit with the excitement of watching a man die in front of him.

"Naw, this is good enough, for now," Boland said. He looked over at the freshly cleaned and loaded shotgun lying on Luna's desk. "Well, now, here's the very gun he busted my teeth with," he said, stepping over and picking it up. Luna backed against the bars of a cell and held on for support.

"You—you killed me," he gasped.

"That's right," said Boland, "and I ain't finished yet." He turned the shotgun back and forth in his hands, looking it over. He checked it, cocked it and pointed it at Luna from twelve feet away. "Say goodbye to your *little angel,*" he said mockingly.

"One moment is . . . all I ask," Luna managed to say, blood welling up and foaming around the knife hilt at his chest. "Let me make peace . . . with God."

"Naw, not today," Boland said in a flip and callous manner. "Maybe some other time." The eight gauge bucked and exploded in his hands.

"*Whoa, pal!*" Fairday remarked, watching Luna's head disappear into a spray of blood and gore all over the bars and the cell wall behind him. "You are a hard-nosed sumbitch, Boland," he said with a dark chuckle. He rounded a finger in his ear to lessen the ringing left from the deafening shotgun blast. Seeing the look Boland gave him as he opened the shotgun and reloaded it, Fairday added in a hasty voice, "Of course I say *sumbitch* with nothing but respect and admiration."

"Go get your knife out of him," said Boland, his chin and broken teeth feeling better already. "Let's get the hell out of here." He turned and began walking toward the open door as voices shouted back and forth along the dusty street.

Dawson and Caldwell had not only followed the tracks of the Barrows Gang; they had also followed the distant flames throughout the night, every now and then hearing the report of a single gunshot echo through the black, empty silence. By sunup, when the flames had died, they followed two rising spirals of smoke the rest of the way to the stone wall surrounding the Bengreen yard.

Riding inside the open gates, they saw the well, and beyond it the doors of the hacienda standing wide-open in the early-morning light. A hundred yards to their left beyond the walls they saw a few standing remains of blackened timbers amid the burned rubble of the small house where Ernesto and his family had lived. Nearby the house they saw the remains of the barn lying in a smoldering heap beneath its own rise of smoke.

"This was bad," Dawson whispered sidelong to Caldwell. Having seen their tracks leading here, already he suspected that the Barrows Gang had something to do with it. The two carried their rifles propped up and ready.

"Should I ride on over and see if anybody's alive out there?" Caldwell asked, nodding toward the spot where Ernesto's house had stood.

"In a minute, Jedson," said Dawson. "First let's see what we've got here."

As the two lawmen eased their horses around the well, they spotted Shaw sitting in the dirt twenty yards away. Anna Reyes Bengreen lay dead in his lap. Shaw sat with his right arm out of the sling, his Colt cocked and hanging loosely in his hand.

"Shaw," Dawson called out as the two stopped at a cautious distance. When Shaw didn't answer, he called out again. "Shaw, it's Cray Dawson and Jedson Caldwell. Are you all right?"

Shaw looked up from the dead woman's face, but only stared blankly, still not answering. Dawson gestured Caldwell forward alongside him. The two stepped their horses closer and stopped a few feet from Shaw, close enough to see the empty sling hanging from his wounded right shoulder. In his right hand Shaw loosely held his big Colt, cocked and ready to fire. Dawson saw a pile of spent brass shells lying strewn in the dirt beside him. A few feet away the ground had been chewed up, from where Shaw had fired bullet after bullet into the upturned dirt.

"We best walk easy, Jedson," Dawson said under his breath.

"You bet," Caldwell replied in the same manner. He lowered his rifle across his lap.

At a respectable distance, the two stopped and stepped down from their saddles. Caldwell lifted a leather canteen strap from around his saddle horn and brought along a canteen of water as they walked forward. He carried his rifle at his side.

"Shaw, I know you can hear me," Dawson said quietly but firmly. "We're coming over. Don't raise that gun toward us. We're your friends, remember?" He kept his rifle lowered also, just in case.

"Friends . . . ?" Shaw stared, but he slowly lowered the Colt to the ground beside him and cradled the dead woman in his arms. "I don't have friends," he said, lowering his face, gazing down at Anna's closed eyes. "Get back on your horses and ride away."

Dawson and Caldwell gave one another a cautionary glance and proceeded closer. "I'm afraid we can't do that, Shaw," said Dawson. "We're still your friends whether you like it or not."

"I don't like it," Shaw growled without lifting his eyes from the dead woman's face.

"Here, have some water, Shaw?" Caldwell urged cautiously, uncapping the canteen and holding it out to him.

Shaw looked at the canteen, considering it. But upon seeing that he would have to loosen his hold on the woman in order to take a drink, he turned his face away from Caldwell and said, "Why don't both of you leave. I've got things under control here."

"No, you don't, Shaw," Dawson said bluntly. "There's dead needing to be buried."

"I know how to bury the dead," Shaw said in a bitter tone of voice. "I've had plenty of practice everywhere I've been. I don't need your help."

"Yes you do," Dawson insisted, "so we best get to it. Caldwell and I are dogging some of the Barrows Gang. Their tracks led us here. They're the ones who did this. We'll help you do the burying, but then we need to get after them before they manage to strike again." He stared down at Shaw. "Do you understand me?"

"I understood you the first time," Shaw said, looking up at him, hollow-eyed. "Now get out of here. I don't *want* your help—I don't *need* your help. I'm taking care of *her*. . . . It's what she hired me to do."

"She's dead, Shaw," Dawson said, still blunt and straight to the point. "If you want to do something to help her, let's get her into the ground."

After a silent pause, Shaw said, "Dawson, Caldwell, you two are awfully hard to get rid of. What are you doing down here anyway? I heard somewhere that you became a U.S. federal marshal."

"I did," said Dawson. "Stand up. Help us get something done here."

Shaw looked at Caldwell. "What about you, Jedson? Are you working for the law too?"

"Yes, I am," said Caldwell. "I'm a federal deputy marshal. Now come on, Shaw. Help us out here."

"Help you out?" Shaw said. "I just want to be alone with her for a little while longer. Get away, go find some shade and sit in it."

Again, Dawson ignored his comment. "Go with us after the ones who killed her if you want to do something more for her. But let's get the dead into the ground. There's no time for grieving. There's no time for you to feel sorry for yourself."

Caldwell gave Dawson a harsh stare. "Take it easy, Cray," he said. "We've got time to give him a few minutes alone—"

"No, we don't," Dawson said with a snap, cutting him off. "Give him enough time alone, he'll end up with that gun barrel between his teeth." He looked back at Shaw. "That's what all the bullet holes in the ground is about, right, Shaw? All night you've been practicing killing yourself. You just haven't managed to keep the barrel pointed in the right direction yet."

"Shut up, Dawson, and stay out of my business," Shaw said, loosening his hold on the dead woman only a little as he stared up. "Whether I shoot myself or not is no concern of yours."

"Suit yourself," Dawson said. "We're after the ones who killed this poor woman. You can stay here and figure out how to die, if that best suits you." He glanced at Caldwell and said, "Let's go, Jedson. Save your water for the desert trail." He turned and started to walk away. Jedson stood up from where he'd kneeled beside Shaw, dusted off his trouser leg and started to follow Dawson back to the horses.

"I know who did this," Shaw called out. "It was a murdering snake named Titus Boland. Him and I had trouble in Matamoros. He shot me in the shoulder."

Dawson and Caldwell stopped and turned, facing

him without walking back. "I heard all about the shooting from Luna," Dawson said. "He told me you passed out in a gunfight." He gave Shaw a look of disgust.

"Luna has a mouth bigger than his face." Shaw reached out a hand and motioned it toward Caldwell's canteen. Caldwell looked to Dawson. Getting a nod of approval he walked back and held the canteen down to Shaw.

"*Gracias*, Undertaker," Shaw said. He adjusted the dead woman in his lap and took a swig from the uncapped canteen. He swished the water around in his mouth, spit a stream and wiped his hand across his lips. Looking back at Dawson he said, "It may be that Titus Boland has thrown in with the Barrows . . . but he's the one who did this. I know it down deep in my guts." As he spoke, he eased the woman off his lap and stood up.

"Are you going after him?" Dawson asked, seeing Shaw start to snap out of his dark suicidal state.

Shaw held the canteen up and poured water down over his head and face and swung his hair back and forth before answering. He looked all around, at the rising smoke, the carnage and ruin. Then he looked at Dawson and said flatly, "What do you think?"

Chapter 12

With the woman and Ernesto's son buried and wooden markers stuck into the ground to mark their graves, Dawson, Caldwell and Shaw rode in silence from the Bengreen spread onto the trail leading to Matamoros. Caldwell led three of the Bengreen horses on a rope—stragglers that the Barrows men had overlooked in their haste. He'd found the horses grazing on sparse clumps of wild grass beyond the burned barn.

When they had reached a distance of a thousand yards from the Bengreen spread, Caldwell brought Dawson's attention to Shaw who had stopped his horse for a moment and sat gazing back at the walled hacienda.

"Want me to lag back and stay close to him?" Caldwell asked.

"No, leave him be, Jedson," Dawson said quietly, the two of them staring back at Shaw. "He'll have to work it out for himself. We've done all we can do."

"Yeah, I suppose so," Caldwell said. "He'll be all right," he added as if to convince himself. "Shaw's as tough as they come."

"Right," said Dawson. He turned and nudged his horse forward with no more to say on the matter.

Caldwell caught up to him and asked, "Is there a problem between you and Shaw that I don't know about?"

"A problem?" Dawson said, tossing him a sidelong glance.

"Yes," said Caldwell, "ever since we rode up to him you've acted half cross and put out about something. Is it something I ought to know about?"

"Naw," said Dawson, staring ahead, "I've got no problem with him, at least no more than any man would have when he finds his friend working up the courage to kill himself."

"I can understand that," Caldwell agreed. "I expect that a man like Shaw has the courage. If he really wanted to die there would be no stopping him."

"Then what stopped him back there?" Dawson asked.

"It's complicated," said Caldwell, considering it for a second. "A man who *thinks* about pulling the trigger is still thinking there might be hope for something better. A man who goes ahead and pulls the trigger is a man who's saying he doesn't care enough about living to even stick around and see if his circumstances might change for the better."

"I can see what you mean by *complicated,*" said

Dawson with a thin smile. "A man has to be alive to see if life got better for him. I expect that means if he's dead he didn't really want it to?"

"That's interesting," said Caldwell, contemplating the matter.

"Yeah," said Dawson. "But to keep it simple, I happen to think that Shaw still has too much *wolf* in his belly to pull that trigger. He might think about doing it, but when it comes down to getting it done, his instincts won't turn him loose and let him do it."

"The *wolf* in his belly . . . ?" Caldwell worked on Dawson's explanation in his mind. "You're saying the same animal nature that brought him through every gunfight is the same nature that won't allow him to destroy himself?"

"Something like that," Dawson replied. "There's enough of the wild left in us to make us want to keep living. Someday maybe the wild will be gone . . . but for now we've still got it."

"You're saying we came from animals?" Caldwell asked pointedly.

"I'm not smart enough to speculate where we came from," said Dawson, "but wherever we come from, it was no gentle place. We slashed and ripped and hacked our way here from somewhere. It was no easy road and it's still not. We didn't learn to give up easy. I expect that nature or spirit or whatever you want to call it is still in us . . . so far anyway."

They both looked back at Shaw in time to see him turn his horse and ride to catch up to them. "You said Luna told you he passed out in the gunfight? You figure he got himself drunk enough to turn loose, get himself killed and get it over with?"

"Yeah," said Dawson, "but since that didn't work, maybe nothing else we just said amounts to a hill of beans." He allowed a thin, wry smile. "Maybe it's just luck and nothing else."

"What about God's will?" Caldwell asked, seeing Shaw draw nearer.

" 'God's will is what a sinner calls luck,' " said Dawson. "That's something I once heard a preacher say."

The two stopped talking as Shaw rode up close and drew his horse down to a walk. As they rode forward abreast, Caldwell leading the Cedros Altos horses, Shaw said in a steadier voice, "I should have said this earlier. Much obliged to both of you, coming along when you did. You're both friends—good friends—no matter what I said back there."

Without a word, Dawson and Caldwell touched their hat brims in reply. "Are you up to talking about a few things before we get to Matamoros?" Dawson asked, gazing ahead along wagon and buggy ruts on the widening, more traveled trail.

"That depends. What sort of things do you want to talk about?" Shaw asked in reply.

Dawson smiled to himself; he could tell Shaw was coming around. "I've been wanting more help out here, chasing the Barrows Gang. After what happened at Cedros Altos, I'm going back to the American consulate, ask one more time. I think I might get it now."

"Good luck," Shaw said with resolve.

Dawson looked at him. "This is a big gang, Shaw. It'll get bigger as soon as Redlow and Eddie hook up with Sepreano and his Army of Liberation. You'd be a fool trying to take them all on by yourself."

"I only want the Barrows," said Shaw. "I have no fight with Luis Sepreano. If Sepreano keeps his soldiers out of my way, I won't kill them."

"Are you drinking?" Dawson looked him up and down and sniffed the air between them.

"Not a drop," said Shaw, "but I will be when we get to town."

Seeing he was serious, Dawson said, "I wish you'd stay sober. I need a good gunman. I believe I can get the consulate to grant you a marshal's commission."

"Oh, wear a badge?" Shaw said. "Obliged, but no thanks."

"What's wrong with wearing a marshal's badge?" Dawson asked.

"You tell me," Shaw replied bluntly. "Neither one of you is wearing one."

Dawson's face reddened a little. "You know why we're not wearing ours," he said. "We've got no jurisdiction down here."

"Oh," said Shaw, looking back and forth between the two lawmen, "then what are you doing *down* here?"

"We're on a manhunt that's been agreed to between our government and the Mexicans. Neither side acknowledges us being here. We've got a free hand to deal with the Barrows, to keep them and Sepreano from getting too powerful."

"Let me see if I understand," said Shaw. "You think you might be able to get me a *badge* that I *can't wear* because I'll be doing a job that *nobody* on either side of the border wants to admit I'll be doing?"

Dawson frowned and stared straight ahead. "Wearing badges might make some folks think the U.S. government is taking sides in a people's rebellion."

"Oh? Isn't that the case?" Shaw said.

"It would be," said Dawson, "except we both know that Sepreano is a thief, not a leader of the people. He has to be stopped."

"Since when did being a *thief* keep anybody from leading the people?" Shaw asked.

Dawson let it go and shook his head. "I didn't know you had something against lawmen."

"I don't," said Shaw. "I just never pictured being one."

"Try picturing it," said Dawson, "at least until we bring down the Barrows.

"You're saying *bring down* the Barrows Gang," said Shaw, "not take them in for trial?"

"You heard me right," said Dawson. "We're taking them down. . . . It's one more good reason not to be wearing a badge."

Shaw nodded, in contemplation. Maybe I will stay sober when we get to town. This is sounding more interesting all the time." The three nudged their horses up into a trot and rode on in silence.

In Matamoros, a crowd had gathered along both sides of the street in front of the jail. Upon seeing the three Americans ride in off the trail that Boland

and Fairday had taken out of town, townsmen pressed in around them in a close circle. "Show them your badge, Cray," Shaw said in a teasing manner to Dawson, who rode beside him. "I bet that'll settle them down."

But before Dawson could respond, six uniformed *federales* and two Americans in business suits stepped forward from the direction of the American consulate office a block away. The soldiers shoved their way through the townsmen and cleared a path for the two Americans. One of the Americans, a tall, lean man with a gray goatee and matching hair showing beneath the brim of his bowler hat, raised a hand and called out in Spanish to the crowd.

"Listen to me! I'm Samuel Messenger, with the American Delegation." He pointed a raised finger toward the American flag waving above the consulate building. "I vouch for these two men," he said in their native tongue, motioning toward Dawson and Caldwell. "These two men are not with Sepreano and the Barrows Gang. You have my word."

"Who are they, then?" a townsman shouted back in English. "What are they doing with three of Judge Bengreen's horses?"

The American replied in English as he pointed out Dawson, "He bought the horse he's riding here the other day. Gerardo Luna introduced him to the horse dealer. He was Luna's friend." He looked up at Dawson and asked the same question under his breath, "What *are* you doing with these other three Bengreen horses?"

But Dawson didn't answer right away. Instead he

asked, "What do you mean I *was* Luna's friend?" He looked back and forth above the heads of the crowd. "Where is Luna? What's going on here, Messenger?" Looking all around he dreaded the answer before it came.

"Luna is dead. He was killed this morning before dawn by two of the Barrows Gang," said Messenger. He intentionally spoke loud enough for the crowd to hear him answer Dawson.

Shaw slumped in his saddle and shook his head slowly.

Sam Messenger continued speaking in a raised voice for the crowd's benefit. "I want all the good people of Matamoros to know that Gerardo Luna's killers will not go unpunished! Speaking on behalf of the United States government, I want everyone to know that my government will cooperate in every way in tracking these killers down and bringing them to justice. I will be staying at the American consulate building and personally overseeing the capture of the Barrows, and everybody associated with them."

Shaw, Dawson and Caldwell gave one another a look of disgust. "Messenger, let's go somewhere where we can talk in private," Dawson said, before the American could say any more to the crowd on the matter. "This is no time to step on a soapbox."

Messenger held a hand up to the crowd and smiled, but said sideways to Dawson, "You're wrong, Marshal Dawson. It's always the *right time* to try and get a better foot up in the game." Yet he lowered his hand and gestured toward Luna's office across the street.

The crowd parted enough to allow Dawson, Shaw and Caldwell to follow Messenger on horseback to an iron hitch rail where they stepped down and hitched their horses. Caldwell tied the lead rope to the three Bengreen horses next to his own and hurried to the open door where Shaw stood waiting for him, keeping an eye on the confused and angry townsfolk.

Once inside the office, Dawson wasted no time. He turned to Messenger and said, "The Barrows Gang struck the Bengreen spread last night. They killed Bengreen's widow and a family of Mexicans who still lived there. They rode away with the remaining horses she was waiting to sell."

"Oh my," said Messenger, contemplating things as Dawson spoke. "This is one more reason for the people to realize how important it is to stop Sepreano and his Army of Liberation. If he's riding with outlaws like the Barrows, he's no better than they are."

Dawson gave Shaw and Caldwell a glance, then let out a breath and said to Messenger, "Save all that for the crowd. We need to get after the Barrows."

"Don't take what I do so lightly, Marshal Dawson," said Messenger. "It's terrible what happened to Luna and to Bengreen's widow. But my job is to convince these people that Sepreano is no good for their country. I can best do that by showing the kind of men he allies himself with. So, before you judge me a fool and—"

"I'm not judging you, Messenger," Dawson said, cutting him off. "You do your job, I'll do mine." He gestured a gloved hand toward Shaw. "This is Lawrence Shaw. I'm sure you've heard of him."

"Yes, of course I've heard of Fast Larry Shaw, *the fastest gun alive,*" said Messenger, a look of distaste coming to his face. "In fact I've stepped over him a few times lying drunk on the street during my subsequent visits to Matamoros." He stared at Shaw as he added, "Luna befriended him, much like one would befriend a stray cur. He allowed him to sleep here in the jail on occasion. That was about the extent of the friendship as I saw it."

Shaw just stared flatly at him.

"Well, he's not drunk now," said Dawson, not wanting to discuss Shaw, "and I need help with the Barrows. I want you to swear him as a deputy."

"You've been in the sun too long, Dawson," said Messenger with a slight chuckle. He looked Shaw up and down critically, noting the sling on his right arm. "Look at him. Can he even pull a trigger, providing his hand isn't shaking too much to draw a gun—?" His words stopped short.

Shaw's left hand had streaked over to his Colt, which stood butt forward in a cross-hand draw, its slim-jim holster having been rigged to suit his needs. "That's the *draw* part, Mister," Shaw said, the Colt's hammer cocked, the tip of the barrel no more than an inch from Messenger's nose. "Want to see how I *pull a trigger*?"

Messenger's face turned pale, staring down the gun barrel.

"Easy, Shaw," said Dawson. Seeing in Shaw's eyes that this was strictly for show and that he had no intention of shooting the ambassador, Dawson played along. "Ambassador Messenger, this is the kind of man Caldwell and I need out there. We could use a dozen like Shaw. He has no qualms about killing men like the Barrows, especially since they killed his friend Luna. Unless you know of somebody better you can get on short notice, I want him with us."

Messenger looked up from the gun barrel and into Shaw's eyes as he said to Dawson, "There is help coming from Mexico City, or so the *federales* tell me. But they didn't say when or how many." He considered things and added, "Of course they say they will concentrate only on bringing down Sepreano. We must take care of the Barrows Gang on our own."

"That figures," Dawson replied in disgust. "Meanwhile I need any help I can get, *right here right now*. So what do you say?"

After a moment of consideration, Messenger sighed and said, "Perhaps I'm the one who has been too long in the sun." He looked Shaw up and down. "I'll get you a deputy badge, but you are forbidden to wear it on this assignment." Messenger raised a finger and added, "And if you get into trouble with any of the *rurales*—the *local* Mexican authorities—both the Mexican and U.S. government will deny any knowledge of you. Do you understand me, *Mr.* Shaw?"

"Sure," Shaw said cynically. "This sounds like the kind of job I've always wanted." He lowered his Colt, uncocked it and slipped it over into his holster.

"Now, if you gentlemen will excuse me, I'll be waiting for you at the cantina."

"I shouldn't be surprised," Messenger said sarcastically.

Looking at Dawson, Shaw said, "I'm not going there to drink. I told you I'll stay sober for now."

"I know what you said," said Dawson. "You don't have to explain yourself to me. Just be ready to ride when we come for you."

When Shaw had turned and walked out the door, Dawson gave Caldwell a nod. Without a word Caldwell turned and walked out the door himself.

Out front he looked all around the street for Shaw, but when he didn't see him he heard his voice say behind him, "Looking for me, Undertaker?"

Caldwell looked around at where Shaw stood leaning against the front of the building. With a slight shrug, he said, "Come on, Shaw, he just wants me to look out for you."

"Come on then." Shaw nodded toward the cantina two blocks away. "In case you're wondering, I'm going there to ask Max Manko who I need to see around here to join up with the Barrows brothers."

Caldwell gave him a strange look, but then he understood and said, "That's a good idea."

"Yes, I thought so too," said Shaw. "I'd like to think that all those weeks of drinking were worth *something*." He offered a wry grin. "At least we'll see if it's kept me in touch with all the wrong element."

Chapter 13

When Shaw and Caldwell walked into the Gato Perdido Cantina, they stepped around a couple dancing slowly to the music of an accordion and a guitar. The American wore a dusty black sombrero hanging down behind his shoulders by a thin hat cord. Metal studs ran the length of his buckskin trouser legs from his gun belt to his tall Spanish boots. He wore a single-action Colt like the one in Shaw's holster.

Without having to say a word to Caldwell, Shaw saw him take a step away and position himself sidelong at the bar in a manner that kept an eye not only on the American dancing, but also on the other two Americans in black sombreros at the end of the bar. The only other customer was a long-bearded elderly Mexican who sat sipping mescal from a clay cup at a table in the corner.

Shaw took note of the three Americans as he and Caldwell walked to the tiled bar. The American on the dance floor stared at Shaw until his raven-haired dance partner lowered the top of her white peasant dress and drew his attention to her naked breasts.

Upon seeing Shaw walk in, a gray-haired Mexican behind the bar immediately laid down a paring knife and a lime he'd been slicing and hurriedly wiped his hands on a ragged white apron. "Welcome, Senor Reed," he said, knowing that was a name Shaw had been going by when any strangers were within hearing distance. It was also a way of letting Shaw know that the men at the bar had been asking about him.

Shaw caught the warning. *"Hola, Max, mi amigo,"* he said without looking any closer at the three Americans.

"How is my favorite *abogado* today?" Max asked as he reached down and pulled up a fresh bottle of mescal from under the bar top. From the wall behind him he also took down a full bottle of whiskey and stood it beside the mescal. Then he reached down the bar and snagged two clean clay cups and stood them side by side. He started to uncork the whiskey, but Shaw stopped him.

"Your favorite attorney is fine, Max, but I'm not drinking today."

"Oh?" Max gave him a concerned look. "I hope you have been well. I have not seen you for a few days." He looked at Shaw's right arm in the sling and said in a secretive voice, "The last time I see you is when you were shot. I watch Sheriff Luna drag you out of the street." Upon mentioning Luna's name he quickly crossed himself. "I hope you have come to reap vengeance on his killers."

"That's why I'm here. As long as they're alive, they'll be in my gun sights, Max," said Shaw in the same lowered voice. "You can count on that." Without looking along the bar, he asked, "Now, what about these men?"

"*Si*, they rode in yesterday morning," said Max, even more secretively. "Always they are asking, 'Where is this Fast Larry? When will he be here?' " He slid the two men at the end of the bar a glance from beneath his lowered brow. "I told them Fast Larry is dead, but they say they know better. They say they heard in Brownsville that you were shot down in the street here. You must watch out for these men, eh?"

"*Gracias*, Max, I will," Shaw said. "Forewarned is forearmed."

Beside him, Caldwell let his jacket lapel lie open, putting his Colt in easy reach. He looked along the bar, seeing the two Americans staring back at him, drinking, talking quietly between themselves. As the musicians ended their song, the third American and the cantina girl left the dance floor, his left arm around her waist. They joined the other two, one of them handing him a clay cup of whiskey.

As Caldwell kept an eye on the three men, Shaw said to Max, "I'll try to take it outside if they force a gunfight on me."

"You must do what you must do," Max replied. He shrugged. "I will not have you risk your life to keep my walls from getting shot up."

Shaw nodded his thanks, then said, "I'm looking

for Charlie Pepper or his cousin Rady LaVease. Have you seen either of them around in the past couple of days?"

Giving Caldwell a look, the bartender hesitated before answering.

"Don't worry, this is my friend, Jed. Anything you can say to me, you can say to him."

"*Si,* I understand," said Max. He slid a glance back and forth along the bar, then said, "Pepper, his cousin Rady and some of their friends are hiding out at the old French fort settlement along the river. I am not supposed to tell anyone where they are, but I know you are not the law looking for them, eh? So it is all right."

Shaw only nodded, not mentioning his new appointment as U.S. federal deputy marshal. "I'm only looking for them for an introduction," Shaw said.

"An *introducción*?" Max asked, picking up the bottle of whiskey and putting it back on the shelf.

"That's right," said Shaw. "I once heard Pepper and LaVease say that if I ever wanted to ride for the Barrows brothers, they could tell me where to find them."

"Oh, *mi amigo,*" said Max, with a sour expression. "You do not want to ride for the Barrows. Think about this long and hard before you align yourselves with those outlaws."

"I'm not interested in riding with the Barrows, Max," Shaw explained. "I think the man who killed Luna is riding with them."

"I see," said the barkeeper. Before he could say

another word on the matter, a voice from the end of the bar called out, "Shaw! Fast Larry Shaw!"

Shaw had learned not to turn right away at the sound of someone calling his name unless he felt the next thing he would hear would be a gunshot. He continued looking at Max, and said in confirmation, "The old French fort settlement along the Río Grande?"

"*Si,*" Max whispered. He cut a nervous glance toward the end of the bar, then whispered as if Shaw might not have heard, "I think this one is talking to you."

"I know," Shaw said.

"*Hey usted, hombre!*" the man with the studded buckskins called out in bad Spanish. "Answer to your name! *Míreme, hombre!*" he demanded.

"Speak English before you hurt yourself," Shaw intervened. With no regard to the strategic position the three men had taken around them at the bar, he pointed at a slice of the lime Max had just sliced and asked, "*Puede I, por favor?*"

"*Si,* of course, have some," Max replied.

Shaw picked up the slice of lime, twisted it and held it to his lips. "*Gracias,*" he said.

"Here we go," Caldwell whispered, seeing the three Americans move along the bar toward them, the cantina girl slipping quickly away. At the corner table the elderly Mexican drained his mescal with one tall bob of his Adam's apple and managed to disappear like smoke. The two musicians did the same.

"I said, 'Hey you, look at me,' " the American in the studded buckskins said, stopping a few feet away and spreading his feet a shoulder-width apart.

"I heard you the first time," Shaw said. He pulled the juicy meat of the lime away from the rind with his teeth and chewed it as he looked the American up and down.

One of the others had spread out and now stood almost behind Caldwell. The third moved all the way around the bar, encircling them. The one facing Shaw gave up his bad Spanish and said in English, "I heard him call you *abogado.* An attorney, right?"

"His *favorite* attorney," Shaw said, correcting him.

"I heard this barkeeper call you Reed," the gunman said, "like you're Chever Reed, the attorney from Brownsville?"

"That is what you heard him call me," Shaw said, already realizing this man wasn't having any of it.

"Right, I did," the man said, shoving it aside, "only I know for a fact that you're not Reed, that you're Fast Larry Shaw. Reed is dead and in the ground." He poised, ready to do battle. "So, what have you got to say about that?"

Shaw picked up another slice of lime, pulled the meat off the rind with his teeth and chewed it slowly. Half turning his back on the man, he said bluntly, "Who am I talking to, and why?"

"Who? I'll tell you who," the man said, stiffening at the offhanded way Shaw treated him, as if he were no one Shaw should show respect to, let alone fear. "Down here I might be nobody." He nodded toward the east. "In Texas you've heard of me—I'm *Killer*

Pete Roland." He stopped long enough to let the name sink in, watching Shaw search his memory as he chewed the slice of lime and swallowed it.

"Killer Pete Roland . . . ," Shaw said, gazing off at the ceiling in an effort to remember. "No," he lied with finality, "I can't say that the name *Killer Pete* easily comes to mind."

Seeing that Shaw was taunting him, making him look bad in front of his friends, Roland said, "That don't matter, Mister. I know you're Fast Larry, and you know why I'm here?" He paused. Then he added grimly, "Let's get it done."

"One minute . . ." Shaw finished chewing the slice of lime, swallowed it and rubbed his fingertips on his shirt, his right hand lying limp in the sling. "What about these two monkeys?" he asked, without looking away from Roland.

"What about them?" Roland replied.

"While I kill you, are they going to be shooting holes in my friend here?" Shaw asked matter-of-factly.

"They go their own way," said Roland. He managed a tight shrug. "If they kill him while *I'm killing you*," he corrected Shaw, "I expect it's just his bad luck for backing the wrong man."

"Hear that, Undertaker?" Shaw asked Caldwell. "Killer Pete says you're backing the wrong man."

"I heard him," said Caldwell. He had taken a slow step back and half turned, giving himself the benefit of seeing the other two men, both of whom had bristled at Shaw calling them monkeys.

"What do you think?" Shaw asked him. Maybe

there's time for you to change sides. You could back Killer Pete here, my arm being injured and all?"

"I'll stay with what I'm dealt," Caldwell said, his dark eyes moving from one of the gunmen to the next.

"Stop wasting time, Shaw," said Roland.

But Shaw ignored him and asked the other two, "What about you hombres? You've got no qualms about your amigo here coming to gun down a man whose shooting arm is in a sling?"

"So much the better, far as I'm concerned," said one of the men. "Your wounded shoulder is his big gain, the way I look at it."

"Who are you, Mister?" Shaw asked the other gunman, not looking around at him.

"I'm Clifford Noonan," the gunman said flatly, staring hard at Caldwell.

"Undertaker," Shaw said to Caldwell, "don't you kill Clifford. I want him, soon as I finish Killer Pete. Do you hear me?"

"I hear you," said Caldwell, in the same flat, calm voice. He turned his cold stare away from Clifford Noonan and toward the other gunman.

"I said stop wasting my time and let's get this done, Fast Larry!" Roland shouted, his nerves starting to become frayed from Shaw's slow, stalling manner. "I come here to kill you! I didn't come here to be put off, listening to a whole bunch of—"

Two shots exploded from Shaw's Colt. The first bullet ripped through Killer Pete's chest and sent a spray of blood and heart fragments streaking along the tile bar top. Even as Shaw fired the first shot, he'd spun toward Noonan. The second shot slammed Noonan backward before his hand closed around his gun butt to draw.

Caldwell froze, seeing the third man throw his empty hands in the air. "Don't shoot! Please don't shoot!"

Shaw stood calmly, his Colt smoking in his hand. "Go for your gun," he said quietly. "You came here for a fight—a fight is what you get. Now fill your hand."

Caldwell stood watching, stunned, aware that although he himself was considered to be a top gun hand, his barrel had made it only halfway up from his holster before Shaw's second shot killed Noonan.

"This was a mistake. I didn't want to come here, Mister, I swear I didn't!" the man pleaded. "I told Pete to stay home. But no! He swore he could take the Fastest Gun Alive!"

"Draw your gun, you coward." Shaw insisted. "I'm not leaving you alive to come throwing down on me some dark night. You're leaving here on a plank."

Seeing the look in Shaw's eyes, Caldwell said, "Easy, Shaw. He doesn't want to fight. Don't kill him. Don't let him turn you into a murderer."

"Turn me into a murderer?" Shaw gave him a dark, strange look. "If I'm not a murderer now, what the hell do you think I am?" He turned the smoking Colt toward the young gunman and cocked the trigger. "Die with that smoker in your hand or in your holster. It's the only choices you get today."

"I'm not drawing! Everybody look!" the young

man shouted. "I'm not making a reach for my gun! All I want to do is get out the door and across the Río! I swear that's all!"

"Don't kill him, Shaw," said Caldwell. "Call it a personal favor to me. I'll be obliged if you let him live."

"It's a mistake, Undertaker," Shaw said, reluctantly lowering his Colt and easing the hammer down. "I know it's a mistake." He shook his head and held the Colt loosely in his hand. "What's your name, Mister?" he asked the gunman, who let out a tense breath.

"Bob Jones," the man said quickly, waiting, watching to see the gun slip into the holster.

"Yeah, I bet," said Shaw. He eyed the man. "Bob Jones, if you ever come at me again, don't have plans made for the next day."

"I—I understand," the man said, backing away toward the door as he spoke, seeing Shaw drop the Colt to his side.

As the man disappeared out the door, Shaw looked at Caldwell and said, "There, are you satisfied?"

But before Caldwell could answer, a series of shots rang out from the open doorway where the young man stood fanning his Colt toward the bar. Shaw raised his Colt deftly, before Caldwell could reach for his. One shot hammered the gunman in his chest and sent him flying backward, dead in the street.

Outside on the street, horses nickered loudly. A woman screamed at the sight of the dead man flying out of the cantina doorway in a spray of blood. "I told you it was a mistake," Shaw said with a bitter snap in his voice. He dropped three empty cartridges out of his Colt, replaced them and slipped the gun into its holster. "Next time listen to me."

The two had turned to the bar when Dawson walked into the cantina, his Colt out, prepared for anything. Seeing Shaw and Caldwell both eating a slice of lime, he let out a breath and slipped his Colt into its holster. "All right, what happened?" he asked, stepping over to them. He looked to see if any bottles or shot glasses stood in front of Shaw.

"Don't worry, I'm sober," Shaw said. On the other side of the bar, Max nodded in agreement when Dawson gave him a questioning look.

Caldwell cut in, "We came looking for a couple of fellows who can tell us where the Barrows hole up." He nodded at the bodies on the floor. "This one called Shaw down for a fight." He shook his head. "I suppose you can see the rest of it."

"Yes," said Dawson, "I can see." He turned to Shaw and said, "It never stops with you, does it?"

"It hasn't yet," Shaw said.

"Messenger won't like this," said Dawson. "He's a government man. He won't understand that there's always men trying to kill you."

"Oh?" said Shaw. "Then tell him something a government man *will* understand." He worked his left hand open and closed. "Tell him I killed them because I needed the practice."

Dawson let the remark go. "Who are the men you came looking for?"

"A murderer and horse thief named Charlie Pepper, and his cousin, Rady laVease," said Shaw. "Max told me where to find them. I say we go pay them a visit. It could save us searching all over the desert if we lose the Barrows' trail."

"All right," Dawson nodded. He looked all around at the bodies on the floor and outside at the onlookers gathering in the street. "Let's drag these two out of here and get moving."

"Go," said Max with a wave of his hand. "Don't worry about these two. I can have them moved for a shot of tequila."

"*Gracias,* for all your help," said Dawson, reaching out and placing a gold coin on the bar. "Please let it be heard that this was self-defense."

Max grinned and nodded toward Shaw. "The people of Matamoros know that with this one, it is always self-defense."

Chapter 14

The three lawmen left Matamoros and traveled north toward Reynosa, to a long-abandoned and crumbling stone fortress the French had built for settlers along the banks of the Río Grande. Caldwell led the string of three of Bengreen's Cedros Altos horses with them for spares in case a horse were to bruise a tendon in the rocky terrain. One of the spare horses carried a small load of trail supplies.

When they'd stepped down from their saddles to water the horses at the river's edge, Shaw had walked his horse a few yards away to a stretch of bracken, cane grass and cottonwood saplings. There he stared out across the swirling river current while his horse lowered its muzzle and drank its fill.

While Shaw was out of hearing distance, Caldwell turned to Dawson and said in a guarded yet eager voice, "I have never seen anything like it in my life! It looked impossible, what he did."

"He's fast," said Dawson. "You get no argument from me in that regard."

"Fast?" Caldwell shook his head. "No, I'm fast. You're fast. But this . . . this was eerie," said Caldwell, "almost unnatural."

"He was in the right, though," Dawson said, also gazing off across the river. "That's the thing about Lawrence Shaw—I've never seen him come out wrong."

"Yes, he was most certainly in the right," said Caldwell. "But he was so fast it appeared that those two never stood a chance against him—and it seemed like he knew they didn't have a chance from the start."

"I know," said Dawson. "Afterward you almost wonder if it really was fair, even though they came forcing the fight on him."

"Yeah," said Caldwell, considering it, picturing it over again in his mind. "Then what he said afterward, about killing them because *he needed the practice*?"

"I know he's hard to take sometimes," Dawson said. "But I always remind myself that he's stood in front of an awful lot of gun barrels. He knows that no matter how fast he is, there's a great reckoning coming, a time when somebody faster will be standing in front of him. Whatever he says about his life, or the men he's killed, I figure he's earned the right to say it."

Caldwell grimly contemplated Shaw's predicament, then said, "Fast or not, right or not, I wouldn't want to be in his boots. Half the time he's wanting to end his own life. The other half, he's shooting down anybody who comes along to face him." He shook his head. "It makes no sense to me."

"It probably makes even less sense to him when he thinks about it," Dawson replied. He looked off to where Shaw came walking back, leading his horse behind him. "I'm glad he's riding with us, not against us."

When the rest of the horses had finished taking water, the three mounted and rode north along the river until the evening shadows spread long across the rugged terrain. At dark they saw torch fires burning and followed the flickering light until they came to what were once the main gates of the French settlement. At a length in the wall where the stone had fallen and lay strewn about on the ground, they stepped the horses along carefully.

At a shorter wall inside the old fortress, a voice called out in Texan English from among a pile of fallen stones, "Stop right there. That's close enough, you hombres. Who the blazing hell are you? What the blazing hell are you doing here?"

Shaw spoke up. "It's Lawrence Shaw, Rady," he said. "You told me if I ever wanted to join the Barrows Gang, come look you up."

"Yeah, so?" the voice said.

"So, I'm looking for them. I want to join the gang," Shaw said.

"Keep looking," the gunman said. His rifle lever clicked back and forth. "You can go join the Mexican navy for all I care. You're not welcome here, and that goes for the two jakes riding with you. We're declaring this place Robber's Roost from now on."

"Hold on, Rady," said Shaw. "This old fort has always been a place where anybody on the run could come cool their heels. You can't just ride in and take it over."

"Can, have and will," said Rady, feeling more confident as he talked. "Anybody comes here unwelcome, dies here, unless we say otherwise. Now get going! I'm starting to get cross just talking to you."

Shaw lowered his head and said to Dawson and Caldwell, "He wouldn't be talking this bold if he didn't have rifles covering us."

"Yep, I hear you," said Dawson, neither he or Caldwell looking around at the shadowy rocks and trees surrounding them. "Think we ought to back away?"

"Not without an argument," said Shaw. "If we back off too easily, they'll figure we're coming back on them later."

"You know these men. Play it your way," Dawson said.

"What the blazing hell are you two talking about down there, Shaw?" Rady asked gruffly. "Don't think you're going to shoot your way through us. This is our world you've stepped into. We run it. We call all the shots."

"We're talking about how I brought my friends all the way out here, thinking you'd make us welcome," said Shaw. "Now we're this far out without a place to stay. What's gotten down your shirt anyway?"

"I'm done talking, Shaw," said Rady. "Back out of here right now. Unless the Fastest Gun Alive is fast enough to duck a bullet, this is one fight you're going to lose—"

"Whoa now, Rady!" said another voice. "Take it easy. That's no way to treat pals."

Shaw cut a guarded glance at Dawson and said quietly, "That's his cousin. He must've decided he likes the horses."

"Shaw, it's me, Charlie Pepper," the voice called out. "Pay no mind to Rady. He's been chewing cactus all day."

"Charlie," said Shaw, "I rode out here to talk to you. Can we ride in there without Rady shooting at us?"

"Hell yes, you can," said Charlie Pepper. "Ride right on. We'll drink ourselves some good rye whiskey . . . if you've got any, that is."

Shaw called out, "*Gracias*, Charlie. Of course I do." But as he nudged his horse forward he said under his breath to Caldwell and Dawson, "Watch yourselves. It looks like this could turn bloody before the night's over."

"I thought you know these two," Dawson said, nudging his horse forward.

"Knowing them doesn't make them my friends, Cray," Shaw replied.

"Great," Dawson said under his breath. "Are they going to tell us anything?"

"You can count on that," Shaw said, nudging his horse along beside him. Caldwell followed, the Bengreen horses in tow, his right hand resting near his gun butt.

Once inside the shelter of the old fort walls, Rady LaVease, Charlie Pepper and three other men stepped out of the shadows, rifles in hand. The three other men drew in close around Caldwell and the three spare horses. Seeing the Cedros Altos brand on the animals, one of the men, a half Cheyenne outlaw known as Red Panther, ran a hand along a horse's side across the brand.

"It is a dangerous thing, to lead such fine horseflesh through such wild country," he said, with little effort to conceal the threat in his voice.

"I wouldn't have it any other way," Caldwell said, not backing an inch. He jerked the lead rope slightly, causing the horses to step away from the Indian, and the other two men gathered around him.

Shaw gave Dawson a look, letting him know to keep an eye on Caldwell as he turned in his saddle and asked Panther, "Tell me something, Indian. Are you still carrying that big bowie knife you took off the dead teamster over at Hyde City?"

Panther stared at him with a stiff, mirthless grin and patted the knife's bone handle beneath his shirt. "The knife follows me everywhere."

"Careful it don't get itself stuck in my friend's ribs, else it'll be following you to hell," Shaw said bluntly, making no attempt at offering any more courtesy than he felt they'd been shown.

Hearing Shaw, Caldwell heeded his warning and stepped his horse another foot away, leading the string, and stared down at Red Panther.

"Hot damn, Red," a lean Montana outlaw named Tyler Wilson chuckled. "It sounds like Fast Larry knows you pretty well."

"I know him better than I care to," said Shaw as

he reached around and took a tall bottle of whiskey from his saddlebags. Pitching the bottle down to Charlie Pepper, he said, "Cut the dust, Charlie. I need you to tell me where the Barrows hole up this side of the border."

Pepper grinned, looking at the bottle of rye in his hands. "I'll say one thing, Fast Larry. You sure as hell know how to come calling." He pulled the cork with his teeth and blew it away, as if it was no longer needed. "Tell me, how do you manage to stay alive with that right arm out of business?"

"I do the best I can," Shaw said, he and Dawson watching Pepper take a long swig and rub his shirt-sleeve across his lips.

Passing the bottle on to LaVease, Pepper grinned slyly and said to Shaw, "But I doubt there's enough whiskey in the world to make me tell where the Barrows hide out." He looked around with his sly grin. "What would these fellows think of me?"

Shaw looked disappointed. "All this time I thought we were friends."

Rady pointed a finger and said, "I know you're a hard case and a killer, no different from us. But I look at these two and I see badges in their eyes, clear as day." Reaching around, he gestured a hand for the bottle as Rady lowered it from his mouth. Grinning, he hurriedly took another long swig. "Looks like you wasted good whiskey on us gringo desperados for nothing, Fast Larry."

Feeling emboldened by Rady's attitude, one of the riflemen, a cattle rustler and burglar named Arch

Deavers, said to Caldwell, "Why don't you step down from there and hand us that lead rope? Three horses is too many for any one man."

"These two are lawmen," Shaw said bluntly to Pepper, paying no attention to the men surrounding Caldwell and the spare horses. "The fact is, so am I."

A silence fell over the men. Shaw looked all around slowly, then said, "I want to know where to find the Barrows, and you're going to tell me, else I'm going to start dropping your pals."

"Like hell you are!" shouted Red Panther. He started to swing his rifle around at Shaw. But Shaw's left hand streaked over, drew his Colt and fired before the Indian could get a shot off. Panther flew backward on the rocky ground with a bullet hole in the center of his chest.

The other men tensed, ready to fire. But upon seeing guns in the hands of Dawson and Caldwell as well as Shaw, they froze for a second, and that second was all it took. Shaw said in a calm tone, "Who's next?" His gaze and his smoking Colt centered on Tyler Wilson. "How about you, Wilson?"

"Me? Why me?" Wilson said, looking frightened.

"Because I never liked you anyway," Shaw said in a cool tone.

Wilson's nerve ran out quickly. "Tell him, Charlie! To hell with the Barrows! Tell him what he wants to know!"

"Like hell," said Charlie, still holding the bottle of whiskey. "They can't kill us all!"

"Of course we can," said Shaw.

Chapter 15

The fight had commenced. Dawson had seen it coming but had hoped somehow to avoid it. Coming here was a mistake. He should have realized what would happen. This was how Shaw did things, fast and reckless. But it didn't matter now, he thought, his Colt bucking in his hand.

Tyler Wilson had seen Shaw turn his eyes to Charlie Pepper as he spoke to him. He took it as his chance to make a move, not realizing Shaw had only looked away in order to bait him. But Dawson knew it. As Wilson tried to swing his rifle up for a shot, Dawson's shot nailed him, lifted him backward and flung him to the dirt. Caldwell, seeing the fight erupt, shot Arch Deavers as the gunman swung his rifle away and drew his big Remington from its holster. Deavers got off two quick shots, both streaking wildly past Dawson and Caldwell, before Caldwell's shot killed him.

As the bullet flew, Shaw had calmly shot the rifle

from Charlie Pepper's hand and left him standing, hugging the bottle of whiskey while he tipped his gun barrel just enough to put a bullet through Rady LaVease's chest. LaVease staggered backward, rifle still in hand, and sank to his knees. He stared at Shaw in disbelief as blood pumped hard and steadily from his chest. "You two-hand-shooting . . . sonsa-bitch," he managed to say to Shaw. Then he pitched face forward in the dirt, a pool of blood spreading beneath him.

Charlie stood with his eyes squeezed shut, as if that would be all it took to keep bullets from slicing through him. In the ringing silence, Shaw said, "Well, Charlie, it looks like nobody will ever know you told us anything."

Pepper opened his eyes slowly and looked all around, his rifle on the ground, his hand bleeding from Shaw's bullet creasing it, his gun still holstered on his hip. But the bottle of whiskey was still intact. "Damn it," he said, seeing his cousin lying dead in the dirt. "I just had to get my hands on them horses." He looked at the three spare horses, shook his head, then threw back a long swig of whiskey. "All right, go ahead, chop me down," he said to Shaw.

"Huh-uh," said Shaw, "you're still going to tell me where the Barrows hole up." He gestured with his gun barrel. "Have another drink."

Pepper took another long drink and said, "What if I don't? What are you going to do about it, kill me? Hell, let her buck. I ain't scared of anything you do to me."

"I can see you're not," said Shaw, "and I respect

you for it." He tipped his gun barrel in another drinking gesture. "Go on, toss it back."

Pepper nodded thanks and took another long swig, the whiskey starting to have an effect on him. "You are sure loose and easy with your drinking stock, Fast Larry. I have to say I admire that."

"My pleasure, Charlie," said Shaw. "Drink up now. It'll be years before you taste any more whiskey, if you *ever do*."

"Oh," Pepper said in a slurred voice, "what's that supposed to mean?"

"It means, now that I'm a lawman, I'm taking you across the border and turning you over to the law in Brownsville."

"You wouldn't do that, would you, Fast Larry?" Pepper asked, his tongue sounding thicker. "I never know you to jackpot a man."

Shaw shrugged. "I'm a lawman now, Charlie. This is what us lawmen do." He gave a thin smile and added, "Now drink up. Let's get going."

"Damn . . ." Pepper stood considering things for a moment. "Well, hell, I expect I don't owe the Barrows anything, come to think of it."

The three sat waiting, watching in silence as he took another drink and said, "All right. You want to know where you can always count on finding the Barrows." He nodded west. "Head for Durango. Redlow and Eddie like the high country. The gang has a whole valley all to themselves up near Canto Alto, a place called Puerta del Infierno."

"Hell's Gate," Shaw translated.

"Yep." Pepper gave his sly grin. "Sounds inviting,

don't it?" He took another drink and wiped a hand across his mouth. "I hope you find them. I hope they kill all three of you sonsabitches."

"Much obliged for your help, Charlie," Shaw said calmly, without looking around at the dead strewn on the ground. "Now, lift your shooting iron easy like and let it fall."

"Ha!" Pepper said, sounding even drunker as the whiskey he'd drunk so quickly caught up to him. "Are you afraid I'll grab it up and get the drop on you, Fast Larry?"

"No," Shaw said, "I just know you to be a back-shooting son of a bitch. I'm hoping we can leave here without having to kill you, now that you've told us what we wanted to know."

Rage flashed in Pepper's eyes. "How do you know I didn't make it up? What makes you think I was telling you the truth? Maybe you ain't as damned smart as you think you are—"

Charlie Pepper's words stopped short as Red Panther's knife spun whistling through the air and stuck deep in his heart. The three lawmen turned as one, seeing Red Panther on his feet, letting out a war cry, his arms spread high, his shattered chest covered with dark blood. Shaw's shot hit him first, knocking him back a step. Dawson's and Caldwell's shots staggered him farther backward until he flipped over a fallen wall stone. His boot heels landed upright atop the stone.

Shaw stepped down from his horse and hurried over to where Pepper had sunk to his knees, his right hand jerking the knife from his chest, leaving a fountain of blood spilling forward. "I didn't mean for this to happen, Charlie," Shaw said. "I would've kept my word."

"You . . . always did," Pepper managed to say, his life draining quickly. He managed to keep from dropping the whiskey bottle until Shaw took it from him and pitched it away.

"Were you lying about the Barrows?" Shaw asked, stooping down in front of him, holding him upright at arm's length, barely missing the spewing blood.

"I . . . should have," said Pepper. "I just didn't . . . think to." He collapsed, dead.

Shaw laid him back onto the rocky ground, stood up and looked up at Dawson and Caldwell.

"Do you suppose we can trust what he told us?" Dawson asked. As he spoke he looked around the carnage.

"I believe him," said Shaw.

"Then I hope you're right," Dawson said in a tight voice. Caldwell sat quietly, his Colt still smoking in his hand.

Seeing the hard expression on Dawson's face, Shaw said, "All right, spit it out. What's eating at you?"

"We shouldn't have come here," said Dawson. "We're tracking Barrows' men. That was good enough. I said so to begin with."

"Yeah," said Shaw, "good enough until tonight or tomorrow when a wind moves across this desert floor and clears every hoofprint."

"I'm saying these men wouldn't have had to die if we hadn't come here," said Dawson.

"These men are killers and thieves, not different

than the ones we're chasing. I wanted information. I got it. If this gets me closer to Titus Boland, that's all that matters to me. If it gets you Fairday, the Barrows brothers and their whole gang, it shouldn't matter to you either."

Dawson said, "Maybe it shouldn't, but it does."

"What are you saying, Cray?" Shaw asked. "If my ways are too hard and bloody to suit you, say so. We'll split trails right here with no hard feelings."

When Dawson didn't answer right away, Shaw turned to Caldwell and said, "What about you, Undertaker? Have you got any problems with the way I go about getting something done?"

Caldwell had broken open his gun and begun reloading. He gave Shaw a look, then said to Dawson, "I've got to be honest, Cray. We could play cat and mouse with the Barrows across this desert until we all die of old age. All of these border outlaws are in cahoots. So what if they're dead. They meant to kill us, take these horses. To hell with all of them."

Shaw looked only mildly surprised by Caldwell's words, but Dawson appeared taken aback. Yet, after a moment of thought on the matter, Dawson let out a tense breath, knowing he needed Shaw, knowing that Shaw and Caldwell were both right about the men lying dead on the ground. These men had every intention of killing them, taking the horses, the supplies and leaving their bones to bleach in the desert sun.

"We're riding together until we've done what we set out to do," Dawson said finally. He looked at Shaw. "But from now on, we follow the Barrows' trail. I know there's more killers and rogues than there are sand lizards out here. Let's stick to the ones we're after." He backed up his horse a step, turned it and nudged it back toward the trail.

"He didn't mean anything, Shaw," said Caldwell, finishing his reload and shoving his Colt down into its holster. "You know how he gets after a shooting."

"Yeah, I know," said Shaw. "He always has to question what he does and why he does it." He stepped up into his saddle and looked over at the whiskey bottle lying on its side on the rocky ground, some of the amber rye still puddled inside it.

"We all handle things our own way," Caldwell commented, "depending how the world looks to us."

Shaw backed up his horse, turned it and followed Dawson toward the trail, taking one last look toward the whiskey bottle, then looking off toward Dawson. "There's times I envy how the world looks to him."

Caldwell turned his horse and followed, leading the three-horse string behind him.

The three lawmen stopped long enough to fill their canteens along the banks of the Rio Grande. They filled four extra canteens they'd taken from the dead men's saddle horns before dropping the saddles from the horses' backs and setting them loose in a flatlands rich with tobosa and grama grass. When they'd finished preparing the canteens and allowing their horses to drink their fill, they rode purposefully, picked up the tracks they had been following before they'd turned off to the old French settlement.

For the rest of the afternoon they followed the

tracks farther out onto the desert floor, the terrain changing gradually from stretches of sparse grasslands to even sparser scatterings of desert scrub. Blades of yucca stood plump and spiky around them among rolling hills of yellow-white sand. At length the yucca gave way to sotol, patches of saltbush, javelinabush and mesquite until even those slowly disappeared behind them on the dry, scorching land.

For more than two hours a hot northwest wind had grown from a warning purr to a deep, sinister whistle. With his Stetson tightened low onto his brow, Dawson stepped down from his saddle, picked up a discarded mescal bottle by its woven grass handles and looked at it for a moment as if it might reveal something of its former recipient.

Also stepping down, lead rope in hand, Caldwell looked at where the tracks they followed veered off to their left and headed southwest. He raised his coat collar and tugged his hat down tight against the sting of wind-driven sand. Turning the horses sidelong out of the stinging sand, he shouted above a roaring wind gust, "They must've seen this coming and headed for shelter! Maybe we should too."

Dawson nodded in acknowledgement; yet he looked to Shaw who stepped down and stood huddled in a riding duster he'd unrolled from behind his saddle. "What's over that way?" he shouted above the wind.

"More sand and wind the next twenty miles," Shaw shouted in reply. "Then there's Rock Station."

Dawson pitched the mescal bottle away and shook

his head. Knowing that by morning the tracks they were following would be gone, he sidled over nearer to Shaw and asked in a more normal voice, "Did you see this thing coming?"

"This time of year, you have to figure on it," Shaw said, also lowering his raised voice as the wind slacked off for a moment. "How long since you've ridden across this desert?"

Dawson didn't answer, but now he realized that Shaw had been right, going to the outlaws for information. Hell, he admitted to himself, he'd realized it all along. Shaw had wandered the Chihuahuan Desert like some restless ghost since his wife's death—he knew what he was talking about. "What's beyond Rock Station?" Dawson asked in a raised voice, the wind slamming back after its lull.

"Nothing," Shaw answered in the same manner, his duster collar flapping on his cheek, "leastwise nothing these jakes will be interested in. They're going to want to get those stolen horses housed somewhere. Being in good standing with Sepreano won't buy them a thing if the *federales* catch them pushing a string of Bongreen's horses with the Cedros Altos brand still on their rumps."

"Which way will they be headed when this wind dies down?" Dawson asked.

Shaw considered it for a moment, his hat brim blown down against the side of his face by another stinging wind gust. "Nobody is loco enough to take a string of horses out onto this desert unless they intend to cross it." He nodded northwest into the strong hot wind. "Come morning I'd say they'll be headed back in the same direction, taking those horses to Sepreano."

Dawson and Caldwell both nodded, considering what he'd said.

Shaw continued, saying loudly, "I can't picture Sepreano being anywhere southwest of here. He's a big man now. He's through hiding. He wants the people to see his face. Wherever he goes, he's going to want to start drawing a crowd."

"Durango?" Dawson asked in a shout as another hard gust slammed them.

"Until we find new tracks leading us another direction, Durango's a safe bet," Shaw shouted back.

"Then we best find ourselves a place to lay these animals down, try to keep this sand from skinning us all alive," Dawson said. Squinting, looking all around, he saw nothing more than a swirling wall of yellow-gray sand in the wind-whipped evening light.

Chapter 16

Outside of Rock Station, the sandstorm had not yet hit as Titus Boland, Leo Fairday, Tomes and McClinton met up with the rest of the Barrows' horse-stealing party. Fairday had been beside himself with excitement. He told Redlow and Eddie Barrows about Boland killing Lawrence Shaw in the doorway of the Bengreen hacienda and stabbing Gerardo Luna and shooting him with his own shotgun. The gun now hung by a strip of rawhide around Boland's shoulder. When Fairday had finished, Redlow looked Boland over appraisingly, as if seeing him in a whole new light.

"Well, well," he'd said, "it looks like we've got the man who killed the Fastest Gun Alive riding with us, Brother Eddie. Not to mention that worrisome Mexican lawman. What do you think of that?"

"Killing Luna wasn't nothing," said Eddie, unimpressed. Without looking at Boland, he continued, saying, "As for Fast Larry, it's about damned time somebody put that drunken dog out of his misery." He nudged his horse over for a better look at the six Bengreen horses strung out on a lead rope behind Fairday. "It took four of you men to rustle six horses out of there?" he asked, sounding annoyed.

"Ease up a little, Eddie," said Redlow. He nodded toward the rest of the Bengreen horses the gang had gathered in the raid. "This gives us a tally of twenty even fine horses now. Sepreano is going to be as pleased as a pig sucking honey."

"Yeah, you think so?" said Eddie, not giving in without an argument. "What about all the men we've lost? Two at the horse raid . . . six more at the old ruins. That doesn't please me a damned bit."

Seeing the questioning look on Boland's and the other three's faces, Redlow explained, "Shaw killed Brady Lawton and Phil Gaddis at the horse barn."

"Maybe it wouldn't have happened if we hadn't split up and you four had cut out on your own," Eddie said.

But Redlow looked all around at the men and said, "Or maybe if somebody hadn't set the barn blazing, Shaw wouldn't have had a target."

Fairday cut in, asking, "Did you say *six men* dead at the old ruins?"

"That's right," said Redlow. "Paco, Blue Joe, Delby, Wally, Pockets Dan and Indian Jack, all of them killed." He nodded toward Giles Sweeney who had joined them along the trail. "Giles told us he'd heard shooting. We went and checked on our way here and found their bodies."

"Killed by the same two lawmen who were tracking you, Leo," Sweeney called out, "is what I figure."

"You better keep all your damned figuring to yourself then," Fairday warned, his hand instinct-ively clasping his gun butt. "Don't go accusing me of anything. I didn't ask to be dogged by the law!"

"That's enough, Leo," Redlow said. "We've all lost some pards to those sonsabitches . . . who have no right even being down here poking around in the first place."

Fairday took a breath and calmed himself down and said as if contemplating everything, "So Fast Larry killed Lawton and Gaddis before my pal Bo-land here stopped his clock. . . ."

"Yeah, and he sent a bullet whizzing right past my nose," said Lying Earl Sunday. "I raised my rifle and took aim at him. I would have shot him dead too, had it not been for somebody bumping into me."

Fairday looked at Redlow and saw him shake his head slowly, discounting everything Lying Earl had said. Ignoring Lying Earl, Redlow said to Titus Bo-land, "I don't mind telling you, Boland, a bold man like yourself is going to go far with this bunch." He gestured him forward. "Come over here and ride be-side me into Rock Station. Let's talk some." He ges-tured at the short ornate shotgun that had been Luna's little angel. "I always wanted to take myself a look at that scattergun."

"Careful, if you cock it," Boland cautioned him as he rode forward, took the strap from his shoulder and handed the gun over to him. "It's got a hair trigger."

"Mr. Careful is who I am," Redlow grinned, taking the gun in his hand and examining it closely. "I just want to carry it awhile. There's satisfaction in holding a dead lawman's gun."

Turning the six-horse string over to Drop the Dog Jones, Fairday said, "Careful with these hosses, Dog. I've grown attached to them."

Dog took the string without comment and led them behind him. Fairday, Tomes and McClinton settled in with the rest of the riders while Boland rode in front between the Barrows brothers. Eddie Barrows kept his horse a few feet ahead of Boland and Redlow and rode in sullen silence, while around them the wind had begun to whir and swirl with sand.

By the time they'd ridden past a weathered, hand-carved signpost that read ROCOSA ESTACIÓN, the wind had increased. Sand obscured the men's view of much of the small village until they stopped in the middle of the dirt street and looked at a half-dozen horses standing huddled at an iron hitch rail out front of a dingy cantina.

"I'll be damned," said Redlow, in disgust, staring at the animals with their worn-down Mexican- and Californian-style saddles and tack. "These lousy bummers have stuck their horses where we wanted to hitch ours." He looked at Boland. "That's rude, wouldn't you say?"

"Damned rude," Boland replied, getting into the same frame of mind as Redlow.

The owners of the horses had posted a guard out

front of the cantina. Seeing the riders gather in the dirt street, the guard pushed up the lowered brim of his sombrero and stared with interest. He started to turn and step inside to warn his comrades of the new arrivals. But before he could, Redlow raised the scattergun he still held in his hand and asked Boland, "Do you mind?"

"Be my guest," Boland replied, swinging down from his saddle, the others doing the same. Wind-whipped sand whistled around them.

Inside a dimly lit cantina, four Mexican bandits, who had traveled down from the high country, sat at a battered table playing cards with a German mine operator from Monterey. Two more of the bandit party stood at a bar drinking, one with his arm wrapped around the fleshy waist of Rock Station's only prostitute.

With an aura of fire, blood and gore surrounding and trailing him, the guard burst through the front door, launched forward by a blast from the shotgun. Behind the slain guard, Redlow Barrows leaped inside with the smoking shotgun hanging from its strip around his neck. In his right hand a big horse pistol bucked up and down steadily with each blazing shot.

On Redlow's right, Boland stood with his feet shoulder-width apart, firing into the men at the table as they scrambled to save themselves. Behind Boland the rest of the gang quickly crowded inside, each of them firing at the bar, the table and at the cantina owner as he ran screaming toward a rear door. On the ground outside the rear door a disheveled man wearing a ragged serape watched what was on, but only for a moment before scurrying away on all fours beneath the screaming wind.

As bullets riddled the German's chest and sent him flying backward from the table, one of the bandits snatched up a long French pistol from his waist sash and fired at the gunmen as he leaped from his chair. Landing on the tile and dirt floor, he scrambled behind the end of the bar, bullets biting and slicing into him.

The two men at the bar had managed to return fire, one of them holding the fleshy woman in front of him as a shield. She screamed in pain and terror as bullets hit her. Behind her the bandit felt her blood splatter on his face as he emptied a big German pistol toward the gunmen inside the doorway. Beside him, his drinking comrade fired four shots before bullets from Drop the Dog Jones and Giles Sweeney felled him.

Only seconds from the time it had started, the gun battle had ended. The bandits lay dead or dying on the blood-strewn floor; powder smoke hung in a dark cloud. Outside, the wind whistled and roared.

"Hot damn! What a row!" Redlow shouted as the firing slacked off. On the floor in front of the bar, the fleshy whore lay sprawled faceup atop one of the bandits, her bloody mouth and eyes open wide toward the low thatched ceiling. "Finish them off, men," he said. Looking over at the dead guard who lay almost in two pieces on the floor, he said to Boland, "I see why Luna called this his little angel." He patted the smoking shotgun hanging from around his neck. "What say I hang on to her for just a little while longer?" He grinned widely. "I'm enjoying the hell out of it." He reached a gloved hand out to Boland for a reload.

Boland handed him the thick shotgun load without answering. Redlow reloaded the eight gauge as they stepped forward. Boland lowered his gun barrel toward the bloody, grimacing face of one of the men from the table. The dying man said in a strained and halting voice, "You make . . . a bad mistake . . . gringo. Do you know who . . . I am?"

Redlow gave him a curious look and said, "No, I suppose we don't. Who *were* you?"

"I am . . . Carlos Sepreano. . . . My brother is . . . Luis Sepreano."

"Ooops!" Redlow gave a little laugh and glanced at Boland.

"We are going to . . . join him," the dying man gasped.

"Not anymore, you're not." Redlow shrugged, appearing unconcerned with whom they'd shot. "I'll tell him you should have hitched your horse somewhere else."

"Hitched my horse . . . ?" The man looked disturbed and confused.

"Yep, you heard me," Redlow said. He lowered the shotgun inches from the man's puzzled, trembling face and pulled the trigger.

Boland stepped back, spitting the dead man's blood from his lips and wiping flecks of meat and bone from his face.

"Damn, Redlow!" said Eddie Barrows. "Let somebody know when you're going to do something like that!" From six feet away he'd caught some of the blood spatter. "Look at me, damn it!" He spread his arms to show the mess on his riding duster.

"Look at *you*?" Redlow laughed. "Hell, look at me! Look at Titus here. We'll be wearing this man's face for the next month if we don't find some bathing water."

"You heard who he was," said Eddie. "How are you going to square that with Sepreano when we meet up with him?"

"Simple." Redlow's grin widened. "It's just more of them damned lawmen's handiwork—the rotten, murdering sonsabitches!" He looked over at the dead cantina owner lying near the rear door. Then he waved the smoking shotgun around over his head. "Looks like drinks are on the house, amigos."

The men rushed to the bar, over it and around it. They hastily grabbed down bottles of tequila, rye and mescal from shelves on the wall. Boland looked over at Giles Sweeney who, bowed at the waist, stood against the front wall. "Redlow, take a look at this," he said in a quiet tone.

Redlow turned, looked at Sweeney and said, "Giles, what's ailing you? You look like you caught a bullet in your guts."

Sweeney tried to give a smile, but it looked stiff and pained. "Hell, that's because *I did* catch a bullet in the guts," he replied in a rasping voice. Beads of sweat stood on his dusty forehead. "But I'll be all right," he added, holding a hand out as if to stop them from going to any bother on his account. "I just need to catch my breath and get a swig or two down my gullet."

"Come on now," Redlow said, "we all know better than that. A gut shot ain't something you push aside and go on with."

"Maybe—maybe there's a doctor here," Sweeney said, his knees clamped together like a man badly needing to relieve himself. His right hand gripped his belly tightly.

"You know better than that, Giles," said Redlow. "If there was a doctor in this pig rut, I doubt you'd want his fingers poking around in your guts."

"I'm . . . just saying that I ain't done for, Redlow," Sweeney said.

"Oh yeah, you're done for," said Eddie Barrows. He and the rest of the men had seen what was going on. They stopped what they were doing and stepped forward from the bar, liquor in hand, watching with interest as they twisted corks from bottles and drank. "You know how the thing works. Same for you, same for any of us." He stepped forward, raising his Colt from its holster.

"Damn it, Red! After all we've been through," said Sweeney, turning an appeal to Redlow. "Can't I at least get a drink or two? Tell everybody adios?"

"Somebody give him a bottle," said Redlow. "This is our old pal Sweeney."

Drop the Dog Jones stepped over quickly and put a bottle of rye in Sweeney's bloody trembling hand. "So long, Giles, ole pard," he said. Then he stepped back out of the way.

Sweeney turned the bottle up, took a long swig

and swallowed it. The fiery whiskey came back up in a bloody spray. "Oh my sweet aching hell!" Sweeney wailed in pain, dropping the bottle, both hands going to his belly, squeezing his burning intestines.

Redlow watched the bottle roll on the tile-and-dirt floor, whiskey splashing from it. "See what I mean?" he said to Sweeney. He turned and nodded at Eddie. "Close him down, Brother."

Eddie fanned three shots, each hitting Sweeney in the center of the chest in a tight three-inch pattern.

"Damn it all," said Drop the Dog as Sweeney slammed back against the wall, then sank to the floor. "There just ain't nothing fair in life. Not one damned thing."

"All right, everybody," said Redlow, seeing the grim look on Drop the Dog's face, "we'll liquor up till this wind dies down some, but we're waiting for it to stop altogether. We're circling back around to the main trail." He grinned again and gave his brother a wink. "I need to hurry and tell Sepreano what happened to his poor brother, Carlos."

Eddie shook his head as he dropped his Colt back into his holster. "And I'm the one they call crazy." But he knew his brother was right. After they had killed Luis Sepreano's brother, Rock Station was no place to be, storm or no storm. Leaving before the wind died would get them out of town and get their tracks covered. Seeing the knowing look in his eyes, he called out, "You heard my brother. Get to drinking. We ain't got all night."

Chapter 17

Before daylight, while the last vestiges of wind whirred in the distance, Shaw stood up from beneath a layer of sand like a man rising from a grave. He pulled his bandanna down from across the bridge of his nose. He shook himself off, drew his Colt from its holster, shook it, blew on it and checked the action. He looked toward the sound of his horse as it also rose up, shaking itself. The animal stood spread-legged in an indention left from where it had lain huddled down on all fours, sheltered beneath a low cut-bank edged with rock and brush.

Along the low cut-bank the other horses stood and shook and snorted until once again the air thickened with billowing dust. Shaw coughed and spit and lifted his canteen strap from around his neck. He uncapped the dusty canteen, took a small sip, swished it and spit it out. Then he took another sip and swallowed it. He coughed again.

Nearby, Dawson and Caldwell stood up, dusted

themselves off and pulled down their bandannas. "I heard shooting," Dawson said, gazing off in the direction of Rock Station as he uncapped his canteen, rinsed his mouth and spit. "It sounded like Luna's little angel a couple of times."

"I heard it too," said Caldwell, following suit. With the dusty lead rope coiled over his shoulder and canteen in hand, he walked toward the horses. "It sounded like hell broke loose for about two or three seconds. Then it got quiet. . . . Then some more shots followed." He looked back and forth between Dawson and Shaw as if welcoming their take on the matter.

"I heard it too." Shaw fished his fingers beneath a mound of sand and found his saddle horn. "Maybe everybody got drunk and killed one another," he offered sourly. He hefted the saddle, sand pouring from it, and walked it over to his horse. "But I doubt it," he added. "Most likely they tipped horns with some of the local desperados. There's plenty of them around here."

"Whatever it was, I plan on being up trail from them when they come back from Rock Station," Dawson offered in a hoarse, dust-stricken voice. "Maybe we can surprise them and get this over with." He picked up his saddle, shook it out and carried it to his horse while Caldwell strung the lead rope on the Bengreen horses and prepared them for the trail.

When they had watered the horses with a few precious drops poured into their hats, they saddled, mounted and rode on until the sun stood fiery and bright in the eastern sky. The fresh sand lay loose beneath the horses' hooves. Any signs of hoofprints from the day before had been swept away, so when they came upon fresh tracks coming from the direction of Rock Station, the three slowed their horses to a halt and stared after the tracks lying ahead of them.

"Missed them," Dawson said bitterly. "They rode on through the night."

"After cutting all the way over to Rock Station they didn't even wait out the storm?" Caldwell asked with a curious look.

"So it appears," said Shaw, looking back through the swirling heat along the trail from Rock Station. "Makes a fellow wonder just what happened in Rock Station, the shooting and all."

Dawson stared along the trail with him. Finally he said, "Think one of us ought to ride back and see?"

Shaw considered it. "Somebody must've died in Rock Station. Whoever it was, it scared the Barrows enough to send them off into the storm. . . ."

"So, it might be good to know what happened," Dawson said as if finishing a thought for him.

"That's what I'm thinking," said Shaw. He nodded toward Rock Station. "Figure three hours there, three back. I can take one of the spare horses, cut straight across land to you two if you stick to the trail." Shaw looked at him, then nodded toward the fresh tracks leading away from them. "There's water three hours ahead at Agua Cubo. I'll try to catch up to you there. If I don't, you won't be too hard to follow. Lag back if you can. Try not to get into a gunfight with them until I get back."

"We'll try," said Dawson. He nodded at the spare

horses. "Pick one and get going. We'll look for you back by dark tonight."

As Dawson spoke, Caldwell freed one of the spare horses from the string and had it ready for Shaw when he nudged his horse over to it. Shaw turned the spare horse by its mane, pointed it back along the fresh tracks leading from Rock Station and gave it a slap on the rump with his gloved hand. The horse took off at a trot. "Don't step on any rattlesnakes," Shaw said to Dawson. Then he booted his horse out behind the spare horse, following it at an easy pace.

Before Shaw and the spare horse had turned into two streams of swirling dust, Caldwell asked Dawson, "He seems to be doing all right, doesn't he?"

"Yes, I believe he does," Dawson said staring after the streams of dust. "There's something about having men wanting to kill him that always seems to make him want to stay alive."

Caldwell shook his head and turned his horse back to the trail. "It does appear that way," he said, looking back over his shoulder as the two rode on.

Shaw followed the hoofprints back to Rock Station in less time than he thought it would take. An hour along the trail he spotted the tin thatched roofs of the town rising up amid the wavering heat. Stopping only for a few seconds, he stepped down and brushed his palm back and forth beneath a thin strip of shade under a stand of saltbush. There he found a small, smooth pebble, which he ran under his hat brim through his damp hair to cool; then he stuck it in his mouth. He switched saddles to the spare horse, mounted it and rode on.

At noon, in the blazing sun, he felt relieved to see the weathered hand-carved sign reading ROCOSA ESTACIÓN. Atop the sign a black buzzard leaped upward and flew away in a great batting of wings. "Thank God," Shaw murmured. He spit out the pebble and rode on. But as he approached an abandoned donkey cart that sat half buried over months of shifting sands and desert winds, a rifle shot rang out.

Feeling the bullet slice past his head, Shaw dived from the saddle, his Colt out and cocked toward the weathered cart. Another shot came from around the edge of the buried cart. The sound of the shots brought a group of seven men up from the cover of sand and running forward toward him, some with guns, others with poles, hand-sized stones and pitchforks.

Seeing what had likely happened, Shaw fired two quick shots. One shot hit a shovel blade with a loud *twang* and sent it flying out of a man's hands. The other shot thumped into the donkey cart dangerously close to the edge where the two shots had come from. The seven men dropped to the ground for cover.

Shaw quickly called out to them in part Spanish, part English: "Hombres. Don't shoot, *por favor*! I am not one of the men who was here last night! I am an American lawman. I'm here tracking these same men!"

"Oh?" a voice called out. "Yet you come from the direction they rode away. How is that so?"

Shaw shook his head, and said in English, "That requires some explaining, I know. But I am tracking them. I just happened to stay on the trail toward Durango. They cut over to Rock Station to lay out the storm."

A pause, then the same voice called out, "If you are a lawman *americano*, why are you here doing what is *our government's* job?"

"That's a good question," Shaw said, having no short or reasonable answer at hand. "But that's how it is. Your government and mine have me and a couple of others looking for the Barrows Brothers Gang—the ones who were doing all the shooting we heard last night, is my guess?"

There was another pause while the men discussed what he'd said. Then the same voice said, "If you are a lawman, where is your badge? We saw no badge when you came riding up to our town."

Shaw let out a breath and shook his head again, realizing how weak his story sounded. "All right, that's something else that requires explaining. I have a badge in my saddlebags, but I'm not allowed to show it. Neither your government nor mine will admit that I'm here with their approval."

He knew it should take more than that, yet Shaw waited for a moment, and was surprised when the voice said, "*Si*, we understand. Stand up and keep you hands raised. We will talk more about this out of the noonday sun."

"Good idea," Shaw said to himself, holstering his Colt and standing slowly, his hands clearly in sight. Twenty-five yards away the seven townsmen stood up slowly, watching with wary eyes, weapons in hand. Around the corner of the donkey cart, a young man stepped into sight, holding an ancient-looking French rifle at port arms.

"Wait!" said another of the seven men as Shaw walked closer, "I know of this hombre! He is a drunkard and a killer the people of Matamoros call Fast Larry!"

"Whoa," said Shaw, seeing the man's words cause a tenseness to set in. "I am Lawrence Shaw. But that's nothing to get spooked over." He raised his hands higher. Both horses tagged along behind him. "If any of you know Gerardo Luna, you'll know that was his shotgun blast that I heard last night. The man carrying that gun killed Gerardo Luna. That's partly why I'm out here, *sober*," he emphasized, to the man who called him a drunkard and a killer.

"You come to avenge your friend Luna?" the first man asked.

"Yes, that's part of it," Shaw said, not wanting to get into what had happened to Anna Reyes Bengreen. "Luna was a friend of mine. If I wasn't a killer I would have to be a damned fool, trailing these kind of men, now wouldn't I?" He looked back and forth across the somber, distrusting faces. Less than a hundred yards behind them Rock Station stood behind a veil of wavering heat.

After a silence, the man who had first spoken nodded and motioned for the others to lower their weapons. As they did so, he said to Shaw, "These men made a bad mistake last night. They killed Carlos Sepreano."

"Carlos Sepreano . . ." Shaw stopped and let the name sink in. Now he realized why the Barrows had to get out of town during a sandstorm. "Some kin to Luis Sepreano, I take it?" he asked.

"*Si*, his brother," the man said. "They think no one saw them kill Carlos and his friends, but this man saw it." He pointed to a thin, ragged man standing nearby.

Shaw looked the man up and down, starting to realize that if Dawson and Caldwell were on the Barrows' trail, there was no doubt the gang would blame the killing on the two *americano* lawmen to get themselves off the hook. "What is your name?" Shaw asked the vagrant, the man who had seen the massacre through the rear door of the cantina before crawling away.

"I am—I am Simon," the thin man said hesitantly, looking first to the others before answering. As soon as he'd answered, he stepped back as if wanting to disappear from sight.

"You have to come with me, Simon," Shaw said bluntly, as if there was no room for any further discussion of the matter.

The thin, ragged man gave the other man a worried look and said, "I cannot go with him, Pedro! I am not able to travel! I must stay here in Rocosa Estación! Tell him I cannot go!"

But Pedro seemed to consider the matter as he asked Shaw, "The Barrows Gang will cause the death of more innocent men? Men like Gerardo Luna unless our new friend Simon tells Luis Sepreano what happened to his brother, Carlos?"

"If Redlow and Eddie Barrows can get to Luis Sepreano and make him believe that it was us three lawmen who killed his brother, Carlos, here last night, you can bet Sepreano will have our heads on a stick for it."

Pedro thought about it for a few more seconds, then said, "Yes, it is so. Luis Sepreano will kill whoever killed his brother, Carlos." He turned to Simon. "That is why it is important that you ride with this man. You must seek out Luis Sepreano and tell him what happened to his brother. Sepreano will kill the men who killed not only his brother but also the men who killed Gerardo Luna. This is how things must work themselves out."

"But what am I to do?" Simon pleaded. "I have no horse, no food, no supplies."

"No mescal," a voice from among the men said, causing a ripple of laughter.

"I know how it feels to need a drink," Shaw said. He gave the other men a stern look that caused them to stop laughing under their breath. "My horses need water—so do I." He nodded toward Rock Station behind the men and said, "I'll buy you some mescal if that's what it takes to get you leveled out."

"You will?" said Simon. He took on a different, more positive appearance. His voice even strengthened. "A whole bottle, senor?"

"*Two* whole bottles," Shaw said. "More than that if you still want it after we get to where we're going."

"And just where are we going?" Simon asked, uncertain of what he was letting himself in for.

"All the way to Puerta del Infierno, if we have to," said Shaw.

"To the gates of hell?" Simon looked apprehensive. But it appeared that Shaw's promise of two bottles of mescal outweighed his apprehension as he rubbed his dirty hand on his trouser leg.

"Yes, to Hell's Gate," Shaw said in all earnestness, "or until we reach Sepreano and tell him what happened here last night."

Simon summoned up his courage. "If it is to the gates of hell that I must take myself, then it is to the gates of hell I will go." He nodded as he looked all around at the others.

While Simon and the others turned and walked back toward the Main Street of Rock Station, Pedro stepped forward, took the spare horse by its lead rope and walked alongside Shaw. "You will be doing this man a favor if you do not let him drink any more than it takes to keep his hand from shaking and his forehead from sweating cold sweat. For the week he has been here, he is always with a bottle in his hands. I think he is greatly troubled, this pitiful vagrant."

"I understand," Shaw replied, feeling his face redden a bit in reflection. "I've been through all that myself."

PART 3

Chapter 18

Dawson and Caldwell approached the small village of Agua Cubo with caution, knowing the Barrows Gang had to have stopped there to water their horses less than five hours before. On a sandy ridge a thousand yards away, Caldwell lay prone on the hot ground and scanned back and forth along the narrow dusty street with a long, brass-clad telescope.

"Any sign of them?" Dawson asked. He sat stooped on his boot heels behind Caldwell, the reins and lead rope to the horses in hand.

"Only the tracks they left riding in," Caldwell said without taking his eye from the lens. Out front of the village cantina, a hefty man sat with a bloody bandanna pressed to his forehead. The door of the cantina lay broken in the street. Discarded food, empty bottles and remnants of broken furniture lay strewn everywhere. "It looks like they helped themselves and moved on."

Dawson looked back impatiently along the trail

and said, "Shaw should be catching up to us by now. We need to make a move on this bunch before they align with Sepreano's men."

Caldwell scanned his lens past the village and along the trail headed west. The fresh tracks wound out of sight across the sand, upward into an endless stretch of hills. "They're gone. I see no need for us roasting out here waiting for Shaw when we could be cooling ourselves and resting these horses in some shade."

"Yeah," Dawson said, standing, squinting down at the wavering heat surrounding Agua Cubo, "let's ride down. I'm giving Shaw a little longer, and then we're getting back onto their trail. I don't want to risk another windstorm wiping out their tracks. We were lucky yesterday. But sooner or later luck can turn on you."

"I hope it hasn't turned on Shaw," Caldwell said. He collapsed the telescope between his gloved palms, stood up and dusted himself off with his hat.

Dawson handed Caldwell his reins, but kept the lead rope to the two spare horses. Caldwell slipped the telescope into a long leather case and shoved the case down onto his saddlebags. Stepping up into his saddle, he followed Dawson and the spare horses down a long, steep hillside of loosely spilling sand.

Across a stretch of flatlands dotted with cactus, tarbush and mesquite, they followed the Barrows' tracks onto the narrow street and headed toward a stone well out front of the ransacked cantina. When the owner of the cantina had stopped the two riders and the spare horses coming into Agua Cubo, he'd put away his blood-spotted bandanna, run inside and returned with a long club in hand.

"I have had all I can stand of you *gringos ladrones y criminales*! By thunder, this time I will pound you into the dirt!"

"Hold it right there," Dawson said in a strong tone, holding up a hand to stop the man before he stepped toward them. "We're not thieves and criminals, Mister. We're tracking the men who did all this." He swept a hand along the littered street. A skinny dog lifted its muzzle, licked cornmeal from its nose and stared curiously at the two lawmen.

"All of you gringos are the same!" the man raged, waving the club above his head. Yet he made no move forward. "You take whatever suits you. You pay nothing to the man who works to earn his keep!"

As the cantina owner spoke, townsfolk ventured into sight as if from out of nowhere. They gathered close, yet at a safe distance from the armed Americans. One of the men stepped out from the others and said to the cantina owner, "Be quiet, Phillipi. These men are not the ones who treated you badly."

"They are gringos. They are all the same," the man repeated insistently, dismissing the matter.

"No," said the townsman shaking his head, "if they were *those* kind of men, they would have shot you down and already taken what they want from you." He looked up at Dawson and Caldwell and said, "Pay no attention to him. He has suffered much abuse at the hands of those men." He gestured a hand out along the tracks leading across the sand flats to the distant hills.

"I understand," said Dawson, he and Caldwell keeping an eye on the angry cantina owner. "We came here only for water, for us and our animals." As he spoke he reached into his vest and pulled up two gold coins. "We pay for our food and drink." He gazed toward the cantina owner and rubbed the coins together. "We don't take anything without paying for it, *comprende*?"

The cantina owner hesitated, running a hand back over his bruised and cut forehead and through his thinning hair. Finally he nodded stiffly. *"Si, comprendo,"* he said. "I must ask you to overlook my lack of hospitality. It has been a trying day—"

"We understand," Dawson said cutting his apology short. "The quicker we can water our horses and get some food and water in our bellies, the quicker we can get after the men who did this to you."

"Step down, and welcome to you, *mi amigos*," said the cantina owner, his eyes going back to the gold coins in Dawson's hand. "If I were a younger man, I would ride with you myself. I would take my revenge on these sons of pigs for what they did to my beautiful Cantina de Flores."

Dawson and Caldwell stepped down from their saddles and led all four horses to the town well. Dawson looked his cream-colored Barb over well while the big horse snorted, shook sand from its black mane and stuck its muzzle into a horse trough beside the well's surrounding stone wall.

While the horses took water, Dawson and Caldwell drank from a gourd lying atop the stone wall and filled their canteens for the trail ahead. When the animals had drunk their fill, the two lawmen fed each one with a handful of grain from a small bag among the supplies. Then the two walked into the cantina and stood at the bar, where the owner had set a bottle of rye whiskey and two glasses.

"To cut the desert dust from your throats, eh?" the cantina owner said with a grin.

"*Gracias,*" said Dawson. He lifted the glass to his lips and tossed back the shot.

Caldwell raised his glass and did the same. But as he swallowed, he noted a slight bitterness and caught a faint, unpleasant scent arising from the shot glass. "Oh no," he said, turning to Dawson who stood with the same stunned look on his face. "We've been poisoned!"

They both turned in time to see the cantina owner disappear out the back door, leaving it batting back and forth on its hinges. Caldwell drew his Colt and tried running toward the door. But Dawson only stood clutching the bar edge, watching him as if the whole thing had begun turning into a dream.

Caldwell's legs fell limply out from under him as each step crumpled him toward the floor. "Wait up, Jed," Dawson tried to call out to him. Yet his own voice sounded strange and distant to him. He swung his head back and forth, hoping to clear it. He turned backward to the bar, bracing himself with both hands along the edge, his feet spread to try to balance himself in the swaying cantina.

Looking toward the front door as he felt his consciousness being drawn farther and farther down a swirling black hole, Dawson saw the cantina owner, who had run out the back door, suddenly step inside, followed by Leo Fairday, Drop the Dog Jones, Billy Elkins and a famed Texas assassin named Deacon Kay.

"Well, well," Fairday said with a cruel grin, the four men spreading out, their guns still in their holsters, "you did a damned fine job for us, Phillipi. I expect we won't have to kill your *esposa* after all."

"*Por favor*, let her go now," the cantina owner pleaded, casting a remorseful look at Dawson and at Caldwell. "May God forgive me for what I have done."

"God don't forgive nobody for nothing, you horse's ass," Leo said bitterly. "You're wife is in the stone building out back. Better take a knife—we had to hog tie her. She wasn't a lot of fun."

Phillipi hurried across the floor again, and once again out the back door. On the dirt floor, Caldwell, his eyes out of focus, tried to raise himself up onto his knees. His gun wobbled back and forth until it fell from his hand. At the bar Dawson sank to his knees, one hand still clinging to the bar edge, his right hand reaching limply for his gun butt.

"Come on, Dawson boy! Draw that smoker! I know you can do it!" Fairday teased.

Drop the Dog Jones drew his big LeMat pistol and pointed it at Dawson just in case. "Don't go goading him into shooting us," he said to Fairday.

"Put that gun away, Dog," Fairday laughed. "He's done for." He stepped over to where Dawson, clinging to the bar with one hand, kneeled. "Hear that, Dawson? You're done for," said Fairday. He reached a boot out and kicked Dawson's hand away from his Colt. "Just so's you know, it was me who killed you both. I had Phillipi put enough poison in that rye to kill a full-grown bull elk. How's dying treating you?" he asked in a devilish voice, wearing the same cruel grin.

Dawson struggled, feeling himself sink farther and farther away. "Leo Fairday . . . You son—you son of—son of a—"

"So long, Dawson. I sure loved watching you die," said Fairday.

Drop the Dog, who had slipped his gun back in its holster, grinned at Leo as Dawson fell the rest of the way to the floor. "You sure don't let up on a fellow, do you, Leo?" he said.

"Hell no," said Leo, "not this one especially. He's caused me more trouble than any one man ought to go through. This son of a bitch!" He gave Dawson a kick and spit down on him. "Throw them both over their saddles. Let's go show Redlow and Eddie how smooth this went." He looked back down at Dawson again with a grin and said, "Big tough lawmen, Cray Dawson and his deputy. I took them both to the ground without so much as a whimper."

With the two horses watered and the canteens refilled, Shaw and Simon Campeon left Rock Station and cut across a line of low rocky hills to Agua Cubo. By the time they had arrived, the afternoon sun had begun to simmer low and red on the western horizon. Looking the town over well from a distance, they rode onto the street of the small, dusty village.

As Shaw thought about the bottle of rye in his saddlebags, he turned to the thin, pale man riding beside him and asked, "How are you holding up, Simon?"

"I could drink a river of whiskey," Simon replied, rubbing a dirty hand on the belly of his faded, ragged serape. "But I know that it is most important to you for me to stay sober enough to tell what I saw when the time comes. So I will," he said with marked determination.

Shaw nodded and said, "Good man," as they rode well past the town and stopped out front of the cantina.

A few of the townsmen had seen them riding in and had quickly disappeared from sight. Shaw eased down from his saddle and looked all around warily, as if expecting an ambush.

"What's wrong?" Simon, having ridden bareback, asked as he slid down from the spare horse's back.

"I don't know, but something doesn't feel right," said Shaw in a lowered voice. "These folks act like they're apt to spook at any minute."

"Yes," said Simon in stiff but good English, "I see it too. It is not good, no?"

"We'll just have to see," said Shaw. "Stick close beside me. Do you have a gun?"

"Do I look like a man who can afford a gun?" Simon asked in reply.

"No, I suppose not," said Shaw. The two men stepped inside the cantina's vacant doorway. The door that had been torn from its hinges stood against the inside wall. The broken furniture and other strewn items had been gathered from the street. But the cantina owner's forehead still bore the cut and the bruised knot from his earlier encounter with the Barrows. He stared nervously at Shaw from behind the bar.

"Welcome to my cantina, senor," he said to Shaw in an unsteady voice. He gave one quick look and ignored Simon, owing to the condition of the man's ragged clothes and his deadbeat demeanor. "What can I get you to drink?"

Ignoring the offer, Shaw said, "I'm supposed to meet two men here."

The cantina owner shrugged. "As you see, there is no one here this evening. But it is still early."

Shaw turned and looked at the broken door standing against the front wall. "These men are *Americanos* like myself." He looked back and forth along the narrow, dusty street.

"Perhaps these men will show up later," the owner said as Shaw turned and walked over closer to the bar, still looking all around the small cantina. "There have been no strangers ride into Agua Cubo for the past four—"

His words stopped short, Shaw's left hand came up quick, his Colt in it, cocked and ready. The tip of the gun barrel lifted the man's chin. His eyes opened wide.

"Don't even try lying to me," Shaw hissed, his right arm coming out of the sling, his right hand gripping the man by his shirt. "I saw the hoofprints coming in and going out. Now answer me like your life depends on it. Where are those *Americanos*?"

Simon stared as if in disbelief.

"*Por favor*, senor! Don't shoot! I had to do what I was told! The gringos were going to kill my *esposa* if I did not do as they said!"

"What *did* you do?" Shaw persisted. "Where are my friends? If you don't want to die, you'd better start talking."

The cantina owner broke down and quickly told him everything. Simon stood by listening in silence. When the owner had finished, Shaw turned loose of his shirt and gave him a shove backward. "I should kill you anyway," Shaw growled. But he lowered his gun grudgingly. "What was it you slipped into their drinks?"

"It is called Shanghai tonic," said the owner. "It is what animal doctors use on large animals. It is also what the shipping companies in your country used to knock out sailors and shanghai them."

Shaw paced back and forth. Simon watched his eyes go to shelves filled with bottles of rye and mescal along the wall behind the bar. "Anything you like, it is free," said the owner. "You only have to name it."

But Shaw didn't name it. He rubbed his left hand idly on his trousers and said, "If my friends are dead, there won't be enough desert for you to hide in."

Shaw stomped out onto the street where the horses stood. Simon followed. "If you no longer need me, Senor Shaw," he said meekly, "I will stay here in Agua Cubo." He gestured a hand toward the open doorway. He started to turn back to the doorway.

"No," Shaw said, grabbing him by his ragged serape and stopping him. "You're not going back in there and drinking yourself into a stupor. I need you now worse than before. If my friends are alive, it's only so the Barrows Gang can blame them for killing Sepreano's brother. Do you understand me?"

Simon considered it and said, "*Si*, I think so. But if they join Sepreano, how will the two of us get Sepreano's ear, in order to tell him what really happened?"

"Let me worry about that when the time comes," Shaw said, realizing he had no idea how to pull it off. "Get your horse watered. I'm not letting up. We're staying hot on their trail."

Chapter 19

When Dawson had lost consciousness, the cantina had been swaying before his eyes. Now, as he awakened slowly in the waning evening light, he saw nothing but sand and small rocks swaying and drifting past his face with each step of the cream-colored Barb. When he tried reaching up and rubbing his throbbing head, he found that his hands wouldn't do as he'd wanted. It took him a second to realize that he was lying tied down over his saddle. Looking back, he saw Caldwell lying in the same manner, his bare head bobbing lifelessly with each step of his horse. Was Caldwell dead . . . ? Slowly Dawson recalled what had happened to the two of them.

The last thing he remembered hearing had been Fairday laughing close to his face, telling him that he and Caldwell were dying. Dawson took a deep, thankful breath and let it out. Well, that much wasn't true, he told himself. Now that he knew he was still alive, he wanted to find out why. It certainly wasn't because Fairday didn't want him dead—

"Well well, pards," Fairday said to the other three men, cutting off Dawson's train of thought, "look who's back among the living." He sidled his horse in closer, reached his right foot out of his stirrup and raised Dawson's head with the toe of his rough, dusty boot. "I bet you figured the next face you'd see would be ole Satan himself."

"How's—how's Caldwell?" Dawson asked in a thick voice.

"Stop right here, Dog," Fairday said to Drop the Dog Jones, who had led Dawson's horse all the way from Agua Cubo.

As Drop the Dog stopped and the cream-colored Barb stopped behind him, Dawson looked back and saw the other two outlaws ride up closer. Caldwell's horse was being led by Billy Elkins. Deacon Kay rode along beside him. "Why are we stopping?" Kay asked. "We've got a long way to go to catch up to the others."

Fairday said in a mocking tone, "Mr. Federal Marshal Crayton Dawson here has a few questions he'd like to ask us, Deak. I felt it only polite that we stop here and answer them for him, don't you?"

Kay looked down at Dawson with daggers in his eyes. "For my money, I'd as soon split both their heads and leave them lying out here to bake up good and plump for the buzzards." He nodded at the still-unconscious Caldwell.

Fairday, with Dawson's face still lifted on his boot

toe, grinned. "There now, Marshal Dawson, does that quiet any questions you have going round in your lawdog head?" He jerked his boot away roughly. "If he keeps talking, I'll clip off his ears first, then his tongue if he keeps it up," he said to Drop the Dog. "That's an old Apache way of shutting up a prisoner."

Recalling the gruesome condition of the young woman Fairday had staked down on the desert floor when this manhunt had begun, Dawson decided it wise to keep his mouth shut unless he was spoken to.

"How come you know so danged much about Apache ways, Leo?" Drop the Dog asked, riding on, Dawson on the Barb in tow behind him.

Fairday said sharply, "Never you mind how I know. I just know is all."

They rode on.

At dark, they stopped only long enough to water their horses at a shallow puddle of water at the base of a hill line and relieve themselves, and allow Dawson and Caldwell to do the same. Then they rode upward, climbing onto a meandering hill trail under the thin light of a half-moon. In the middle of the night, they stopped again, this time on a high precipice overlooking the sand flats they left behind them.

"Untie them," Fairday said to Drop the Dog. "I'm throwing one of them off this edge. I want to hear how loud they can scream."

Dawson heard him, but he knew it was only Fairday taunting them again. He looked back toward Caldwell but he couldn't make out his face in the purple darkness. Caldwell had been conscious the past couple of hours, but they hadn't been able to talk.

"I'll let our good marshal here decide which one goes off the edge," Fairday said. "What say you, Marshal Dawson? Who should I throw off, you or your loyal deputy here?"

"Throw yourself off, Leo," Deacon Kay cut in, speaking in a somber voice, "if you want to get rid of some of the stink in this world."

Elkins and Drop the Dog both laughed under their breath. But Fairday saw no humor in it. "You have no cause to talk to me in that manner, Deak," he said in an angry but even tone of voice.

"I get sick of hearing somebody take overbearing advantage just because they're holding all the cards," said Kay. "Either kill these two wretches or else shut the hell up about it."

Fairday, aware of Deacon Kay's reputation for viciousness and murder, decided to step back from any further argument on the matter. "Hell, I can't kill them, Deak. You know that—else I already would have, and not in a pretty manner. Eddie and Redlow want them alive to take to Sepreano for killing his brother, Carlos, back in Rock Station. Marshal Dawson here is going to feel the wrath of Sepreano sure enough."

"Then quit picking at him till then," Kay said bluntly. "It's starting to raise my bark every time you do it."

Dawson listened intently, realizing why he and Caldwell were alive. Now he understood what must've taken place in Rock Station, and why the Barrows Gang had left there in the midst of a raging sandstorm.

Fairday had to make some sort of comeback to Kay, or face looking timid in front of the other two men. "Well, excuse the hell out of me, Deak," he said with a chuckle, hoping to lighten the air a little. "I'm not being overbearing. The fact is I was going to cut them loose after I scared them both good and proper. I figured it'd be easier on all of us if they rode sitting up."

"Dawson is a U.S. federal marshal, Leo," Kay said quietly. "Do you really think you're scaring him with your schoolboy teasing? If you do, you haven't been walking streets near as mean as the ones I've been on."

He called over to Dawson. "Marshal, how scared are you of getting thrown off a cliff?"

"About as much as I am of dying in my sleep," Dawson answered in a level tone.

"There, Leo," said Kay, "that's what he thinks of dying." Kay shook his head, walked over, took out a knife from his belt and sliced through the rope that ran from Dawson's tied hands, under the Barb's belly and wrapped around Dawson's feet.

"Try anything funny and we'll kill you!" Fairday warned Dawson.

"Jesus, Leo!" said Kay in a tried tone of voice. "He already knows that." He pitched his knife to Drop the Dog and said, "Dog, cut the deputy loose." Then he said to Fairday, "Think you ought to warn the deputy too?"

Humiliated by the muffled laugh that rose from Elkins and Drop the Dog, Fairday changed the subject, saying, "I don't know about the rest of yas, but I'll be glad when we get to Hell's Gate and hook up with Sepreano. I'm ready for a few days of lying back and taking it easy."

"I'm all for that myself," said Drop the Dog, watching Dawson and Caldwell slide to the ground and stretch their aching bones before stepping into their saddles, their hands still tied, but this time sitting upright. Dawson had listened to every word, getting an idea where they were going. He hoped Shaw had made it back to Agua Cubo, knowing that if he had, there was no doubt he'd found out what had happened. That meant he was back there somewhere on the sand flats right now, headed this way.

As the four men mounted their horses, Dawson and Caldwell managed to get close enough for Dawson to ask under his breath, "Jed, are you all right?"

"Yeah, I believe so," said Caldwell. "How about you?"

Dawson only nodded.

"I thought for sure we were both done for back in Agua Cubo," said Caldwell.

"Yeah, that was Fairday's idea of having a little fun," Dawson whispered.

"You heard what they said," Caldwell whispered, "about blaming us for killing Sepreano's brother? What do you suppose that's all about?"

Dawson had to let his question go unanswered when Drop the Dog said harshly right behind them, "Shut up, or we'll tie a gag around your mouths."

Throughout the purple moonlit night they rode, across high trails that neither Dawson nor Caldwell had ever ridden. Dawson did not risk asking and possibly bringing trouble for himself or Caldwell. Instead, he rode on in silence, feeling the night air grow chilled around them on the mountain trails. Besides, he thought to himself, he didn't need to ask. He was already certain they were headed for Hell's Gate.

At daylight, Lucky Dennis Caddy, a gunman from Utah Territory, rode back from the edge of a high overhang and over to Eddie and Redlow, who sat at a licking campfire, sipping coffee from tin cups. "Fairday and the others are coming up the trail."

"Good," said Redlow.

"Are they bringing anybody with them?" Eddie asked impatiently.

"Yeah, two men. Both with their hands tied, it looks like," said Caddy.

"It's about damned time," Eddie commented, letting out a breath.

Redlow motioned for Caddy to pour himself some coffee. When the outlaw had done so, he stepped carefully into his saddle and rode back toward his guard position. Redlow grinned and said to Eddie, "See? Fairday *is* good for something."

"Yeah, right," said Eddie, "he's good for trickery and deceit. The sonsabitch has gotten to where he lies more than Lying Earl."

Redlow chuckled. "Now that would be some *serious* lying, Brother. Lying Earl even lied once about his boot size. He went limping around for a year complaining about his sore toes."

"Yep, that's Lying Earl all right," said Eddie. "But I believe Leo has gotten worse."

Hearing the two talking from across the fire, Titus Boland laughed stiffly along with them. His mouth was much better now, his lips getting used to the sharp edges of his broken teeth. Redlow nodded toward Boland and said to Eddie, "I'm not saying Leo is anywhere near as good a man as Titus there. But he tries. Damn, how he tries."

Staring hard at Boland, Eddie said, "I guess I just don't see what you do in this man. He still hasn't showed me much."

"Oh really?" said Redlow. "You act like killing the Fastest Gun Alive is just an everyday occurrence." He sipped his coffee after tipping his steaming cup toward Titus across the fire. "Here's to you, Titus. Whether Brother Eddie here sees it or not, you've damned sure shown your worth to me."

Eddie ignored his brother's praise of Titus Boland. He stood up, slung the last few drops of coffee from his mug and looked over to where Fairday and the others rode up into sight, Dawson and Caldwell riding closed in between them. "Let's go over and hear about how Leo captured these two lawdogs for us."

Standing, Redlow slung the grinds from his cup and set it beside the fire. "Come join us, Titus. I want you to get familiar with how things are done around here. Once we meet up with Sepreano, I'm going to be putting you in charge of certain situations." He winked. "Provided you've got no qualms about killing anybody I want killed."

"None at all," said Titus. He stood and dusted off the seat of his trousers, then followed the Barrows brothers and some of the other men over to where Leo had stepped down from his saddle.

"Both of yas down from there right now!" Leo barked at the two hand-tied lawmen. He grabbed Caldwell and pulled him down roughly to the ground. Before he could turn and get his hands on Dawson, Redlow and Eddie watched Dawson slide easily from his saddle and stand facing them.

"So you are the marshal who never learned where that border runs, eh, Crayton Dawson?" said Redlow.

"They offered me the job. I took it," Dawson said, offering no more than he had to on the matter.

Redlow, Eddie and the rest of the men looked at Caldwell on the ground as Dawson ventured his hands down and helped him to his feet. "Just the two of you," Eddie remarked. "Now that was damned bold thinking on somebody's part." He stepped closer to Dawson and said with a menacing stare, "I'm betting they'll change their minds when Sepreano sends both your heads home on a stick."

Dawson said calmly, "We're not the only ones. There'll be others after us."

"They can die too," Eddie said. He grinned. "But I have to admit you two jakes came along at the right time. We saw what you did to Carlos Sepreano in Rock Station, how you killed him with Gerardo Luna's little angel."

Dawson glanced at Luna's shotgun hanging around

Redlow's neck by its strip of rawhide and understood what had happened. "I suppose it doesn't matter that we weren't even in Rock Station?"

"Naw, not at all." Eddie chuckled. The rest of the men laughed along with him. "Sepreano will be so happy to get his hands on the two of you, he won't take time to listen to what you've got to say. Hell, who wouldn't deny killing Carlos Sepreano, knowing what Luis is going to do to you." He grimaced and added in a pained tone of voice, "Whoo-eee! I hurt just thinking about it."

Dawson stood firm, even when Eddie leaned in almost nose to nose with him. "But we know you did it. We all saw it. Unless you are calling all of us liars."

Dawson didn't reply. He saw Eddie Barrows' clenched white knuckles and knew the outlaw would jump at any opportunity to beat a defenseless man.

Caldwell saw it too. Trying to draw Eddie away from Dawson he said, "*I'm* calling you a liar, Barrows." He stood braced, ready for whatever Eddie Barrows might do.

But Eddie saw what Caldwell was up to and he laughed as he stepped over in front of him. "Do you hear this one, hombres?" he said to his men. "He's standing up for his boss!" Without warning he shot a knee up into Caldwell's groin. Caldwell doubled over and fell gagging to the ground. Two men grabbed Dawson to keep him from throwing himself onto the outlaw in spite of his tied hands.

Eddie Barrows turned away, as if dismissing the matter altogether. To Redlow and the others he said,

"From here on, we leave two riflemen guarding our back trail all the way to where we're going." He looked at Andy Mack and Teddy Barksdale who stood nearby. "You two, go first," he said. "Drop back a mile and keep us covered."

"How many warning shots if we see somebody trailing you?" Mack asked.

"Just one," said Eddie. "If we don't hear any more than one we'll figure you was shooting at a lizard. We hear more shots, we'll get the idea somebody was coming up on us. We're not idiots, Andy," he added with a hard stare.

"Sorry, Eddie," said Andy. He and Barksdale hurriedly walked away toward the horses, mounted and rode away. Dawson watched them leave as he reached down and helped Caldwell rise stiffly to his feet.

Chapter 20

Shaw and his new companion, Simon Guerra, had also ridden long and hard throughout the night. From a ledge overlooking the wide, steep hillside, Shaw had caught a glimpse of Dawson and Caldwell earlier as Fairday and the others led them out of sight around a turn in the high trail. The two lawmen were alive, sitting up and looking around. That's good, Shaw told himself.

An hour later, from a similar ledge higher up and cut deeper into the hillside, Shaw watched the two riflemen ride down quietly and take a thin, narrow path leading up toward the trail he and Simon were on. "Two riders are coming," he said, turning to the ragged Mexican sitting in the dirt, his arms clasped around his knees. "Are you all right?" Shaw asked, already knowing what had the man looking haggard and sick.

"*Si,* I am all right," Simon said bravely. He stood up and turned to Shaw. "I am not giving in to wanting a drink, no matter how I feel . . . not until I know I can stand it no longer."

"That's the way to beat it," Shaw said. The rye was still in his saddlebags, but so far Simon had resisted asking for it.

"What about the two riders?" Simon asked, changing the subject.

"They're headed up this way," said Shaw. "The Barrows sent them out as rear guards, I figure." As he spoke he raised his Colt, checked it and dropped it back into his holster.

"You are going to shoot them?" Simon asked timidly, looking at the Colt on Shaw's hip.

"No," Shaw said, "gunshots would be a dead giveaway we're following them. I'll have to slip in close, use a knife on them."

"A *knife*?" Simon gasped, his hand almost clasped over his mouth.

"That's right, a *knife*," Shaw snapped at him. "Have you got any better ideas?" He had to keep himself from becoming impatient with this timid drunkard. Simon had a lot to deal with all at one time, Shaw reminded himself. He noted the stunned look on Simon's face and let out a breath. "Pay me no mind, Simon," he said. "The fact is I must still be sweating out some months of heavy drinking. I still catch myself a little edgy. It still takes me a minute to think straight."

Simon seemed less tense. "I understand. I know that you must do as you must to save your amigos. Forgive my fear and my ignorance of such things."

Shaw nodded. As the two walked to the horses, he stooped enough to draw a big bone-handled knife from his boot well. Seeing it, Simon stepped a bit wide of him, an apprehensive look on his face. "Forgive me again for asking," he said, "but after you kill these two men, will the Barrows not send others?"

"Yep, I'd count on it," Shaw said. "Once these two don't come back, I'll have to be prepared to kill the next two, maybe more after that."

Simon looked troubled. "But if you kill these men, however quietly, will the Barrows not realize something is wrong when they do not return? Will they not be alerted that someone is back here following them?"

Shaw didn't answer. Of course they would, but what else could he do about it? It wasn't as if he had any choice in the matter. *Wait a minute. . . .*

"You're right, Simon," Shaw said, as an idea came to him.

"I'm right?" Simon shrugged his thin shoulders, looking even more confused.

"I'm not going to kill these men, gun, knife or otherwise," said Shaw. He slid the knife back into his boot well. "The best way for them not to know we're back here is to not *be* back here."

"Oh . . ." Simon looked even more confused.

"Yes," said Shaw, "in this kind of terrain, we can get in front of them and still stick with them wherever they're going."

"I see," Simon said, but he still didn't look too clear on what Shaw had said. As he sorted through

Shaw's words, he used his fingertips, as if counting. "We will get around in front of them, and we will anticipate where they are going—"

"Never mind. Just stick with me," Shaw said. He could see that the man's thinking was still veiled by a fog of alcohol. He swung up into his saddle; Simon did the same.

"I must apologize again for being too stupid to understand," Simon said as they turned their horses toward a thinner, more concealed trail. "I have not always been this way."

"Think no more about it," Shaw said. "Truth is, you gave me the idea."

"I did?" Simon sat upright.

"You stopped me long enough to make me think things over," said Shaw. "That was a great help."

"Then I am honored," said Simon. He cut a glance toward Shaw's saddlebags. Shaw saw the look and realized how badly the man must be wanting a drink right then. He wasn't going to make the offer; yet, if Simon asked, he certainly wasn't going to refuse him. But Simon seemed to force himself to look away from the saddlebags and heel his horse forward. "Onward then," he said. "I am grateful that you have allowed me to do my part. It makes me feel the way a real man is supposed to feel. I am sick of feeling like a drunkard and a derelict."

Shaw just looked at him. He understood.

They rode on, gaining ground by following one thin, treacherous path after another. The two pushed the horses as much as they dared, but it paid off. By late afternoon they had swung around the Barrows, and stood a mile ahead of them in the shelter of afternoon shadows. Looking back and down, they could see the gang's glowing campfire on the hillside.

"Now we simply stay ahead of them and move as they do?" Simon asked, not seeming quite as puzzled now.

"Something like that," Shaw replied. He wasn't sure just yet how he would pull it off, but ever since they had circled and gotten in front of the Barrows, he'd been thinking about making a move on the Barrows and taking Dawson and Caldwell back before the gang met up with Sepreano. He had no doubt that Sepreano would kill them once the Barrows told him they killed his brother.

"Now we are going to spend the night up here, above them, *si*?" Simon asked.

"No," Shaw said. "We're going to put some distance between them and us tonight. They're going to have to come down and cross some lower hills tomorrow. If I catch them off guard, I can take down enough of them to allow my friends to make a run for it."

Simon blinked and swallowed hard. "A gun battle? Against such odds as this? I—I am afraid I can be of no help to you. I have no experience with firearms."

"Don't worry, I do," Shaw said. "I can catch them in a tight place with no cover. I can do a lot of damage in very little time."

"But how will your friends know it is time for them to make a run for it?" he asked.

"They'll know," said Shaw. "That's the only part of this that I feel certain about. When they see men falling, they'll know it's me making my move. They'll hightail it while I keep the gang busy ducking for cover."

Simon shook his head. "May God be with you, senor," he said. "I only wish I could help."

"When the shooting starts, you stay down out of the way. That *will* be helpful." Shaw didn't want to mention it yet, but as far as he was concerned, once he saw that he'd gotten Dawson and Caldwell away from the Barrows, Simon would be free to ride away.

"Oh, Senor Shaw," Simon said. "You will not see me once the first shot is fired. I will be hiding under a rock."

"Good," said Shaw, "I'm glad we understand each other."

The two rode on through the encroaching darkness.

At daylight, Shaw had found a spot on a hillside facing the trail the Barrows Gang would have to ride down. They would have to cross a low valley and a rolling stretch of flatlands. This was the spot, he told himself. He checked his rifle, taking all of his ammunition out of his saddlebags and counting it.

He could do it from here, he decided, gazing down. He saw where the high trail spilled down onto the wide-open flatlands. From here he could fight an army, he told himself. Unrolling a canvas bandoleer and shoving his ammunition into each slot until it was full, he slipped the bandoleer over his shoulder and walked over to where Simon lay sleeping in his ragged serape.

"Simon," he said quietly, "time to wake up."

The thin Mexican rolled quickly to his feet and whispered in a near panic, "What is it? What is happening?"

"Nothing yet," said Shaw. "But the Barrows will be coming down that trail any time. I think it best if you cut out now."

"Cut out?" Simon shrugged, looking uncertain of Shaw's meaning.

"It's time for you to leave. Get on the horse and go home," said Shaw.

"But your friends," said Simon. "What will become of them? Who will tell Sepreano what really happened to his brother, Carlos?"

"If what I'm getting ready to do here works, my friends will be all right. I'll wipe out the biggest part of the Barrows Gang right here. The rest of them will scatter. It'll be over, as far as I'm concerned." He'd thought it out. The Barrows Gang would be finished if his plan went his way. Once the Barrows and Titus Boland were dead, and Dawson and Caldwell were freed, it was over. Sepreano wouldn't even know about his brother's death until news reached him from other sources.

"*Si*, I understand," said Simon, "but what if it does not go as you plan? What happens to you and your friends then?"

"I expect we'll be dead and it won't matter," Shaw said. Then he gave Simon a pointed look and said, "What's wrong with you, Simon? Don't you want to leave? This hillside is going to become a hard killing ground any minute now."

"Oh, senor," Simon said, hurrying, grabbing his horse's reins, "believe me I am ready to leave, provided this is what you want me to do. But if you wish for me to stay, you only have to say—"

"Go, Simon," Shaw said. But as he looked at the thin Mexican, past him he saw a long column of armed men ride into sight on the lower rolling flatlands. "Hold it!" he said. "Get down. Riders coming."

Looking closer at the riders from his crouched position beside Simon, Shaw saw the assortment of both Mexican cavalry caps, as well as sombreros and tied-back bandannas. Men in mixed uniforms rode side by side with men in peasant trousers and range clothes. "The Army of Liberación!" Simon whispered. "It is too late. Sepreano's army is here!"

Shaw considered quickly, deciding how far away the riders were. Looking in the other direction, still high up on the hill trail, he saw Barrows' men riding down, taking their time, in no hurry, expecting nothing. "No, you can make it, Simon," Shaw said. "Leave now and stay high up on the hillside. They won't see you for the chimney rocks and trees."

"But you, your plan?" said Simon.

"Get going," Shaw said. "You've done all I can ask of you. I'm obliged."

Shaw watched him slip up onto the horse bareback and ride out of sight along the edge of the long hillside. He turned facing the other direction and watched the trail for a moment, estimating that the Barrows would be moving into sight within a half hour.

"Good," he said aloud, looking the other way and seeing Sepreano's men riding across the flatlands from the other direction, still a long distance away. He could do it. It would be cutting things close, but he could get it done. He visualized it. When the Barrows rode into sight he would start dropping them. Dawson and Caldwell would make their getaway. He would join them. All this before Sepreano's soldiers could get here? *All right, it's risky. . . .* But this was what the situation called for.

Suddenly he heard a loud, fearful cry from the trail Simon had taken around the hillside. Looking out along the hill, he saw Simon, the spare horse and all, sliding and tumbling down the long, sandy hillside. Twenty yards down, the horse found footing, stopped, stood up and shook itself off. But Simon continued rolling and sliding, screaming at the top of his voice.

"Oh no, please shut up!" Shaw growled under his breath. He watched the Mexican flail his arms as he slid, kicked, tumbled and screamed, raising a cloud of dust that could be seen all across the hills and flatlands.

When Simon finally did come to a stop, he stood no more than thirty yards up the long hillside, loose sand pouring down around his ankles. From three hundred yards away, four of the soldiers raced forward toward him. The rest of the column swung in his direction like some long, curious serpent.

"Don't try to run," Shaw advised under his breath, as if Simon could somehow hear him. "That's it, stand still, keep your hands in sight. Take it easy. . . ." He watched the soldiers arrive at the bottom of the hill, the one in front raising a pistol toward Simon.

Even at such a distance, Shaw thought he could see the look of anguish and fear on the ragged Mexican's face as Simon turned a glance in his direction, then slowly started walking down to the soldiers. Behind him, the horse had begun a careful descent, picking its footing and half walking, half sliding until it and Simon reached the bottom at about the same time.

Shaw glanced toward the hill trail the Barrows would ride down. Then he looked back down at Simon and let out a breath. He couldn't leave him in Sepreano's hands, especially not after he killed the Barrows. Rifle in hand, he turned and walked toward his horse, knowing his plan had been ruined. Now it was his turn to cut a glance toward his saddlebags. He could use a drink, he thought. But he quickly put the thought aside. Dawson's and Caldwell's lives depended on him. He shoved his rifle into its boot and stepped into his saddle. *When a plan goes bad, it's time to get another plan. . . .* He turned his horse and booted it out along the same path Simon had taken around the hillside.

Chapter 21

On the flatlands, Simon stood in a cloud of dust that he and his horse had created. His horse had trotted over and stopped beside him. Three of the riders had gathered around him. The fourth, a large barrel-chested man, wearing a thick, tangled beard with panther teeth and the skull of a small bird, a reptile and a rodent braided into it, looked down at Simon from atop his horse. As he curled his lip in a sneer, his front tooth revealed a gold cap with a half-moon carved in it. When he spoke, his voice sounded as if it came from deep within a dark cave.

"What are you doing in my desert?" he demanded of Simon, speaking in low-border Spanish.

Simon replied, his Spanish more polished and properly refined. "Your desert?" he said meekly, exhibiting an ignorance of this kind of man and what his words were meant to convey.

The big man gave the three soldiers a nod. One of them reached out with his pistol and cracked Simon on the side of his head. As Simon crumbled to the ground the other two caught him, stood him up and shook him like a rag doll. Less then two hundred yards away the rest of the column proceeded toward them at an unhurried pace.

"What are you doing in my desert?" the big man repeated, this time in a little stronger tone.

"I—That is, we—" Simon stammered, clearing his head. "My friend and I are traveling to Durango."

"What friend?" the man asked, looking all around until at the top of the long hillside, he saw Shaw stepping his horse down carefully toward them. Shaw carried his rifle left-handed, sticking up from his thigh, his right arm still in the sling.

Seeing the look on the big man's face, Simon said quickly, "There is my friend now." He looked up at Shaw and shrugged his thin shoulders. Shaw only stared flatly. Singling out the soldier who'd hit Simon with his gun barrel, he focused on him coldly until the soldier actually took a step back.

Damn it, Simon. . . . The long hillside wasn't presenting any problem. Shaw kept his weight back on his saddle and held his reins up and back firmly, helping the horse negotiate the loose sandy soil without incident. Nearing the bottom he stopped his horse fifteen feet up and said down to the big Mexican, "Why is *your* soldier hitting *my* friend?" The way he asked indicated that he held the big Mexican personally responsible.

As Shaw spoke he took note of the approaching column, the distance between them growing shorter and shorter as they hurried up their pace. He saw there was no way for him and Simon to get away, not across this loose, sandy flatlands.

The big Mexican heard the tone in Shaw's voice and saw his thumb lying over the hammer on his rifle. He gave his men a quick look, preparing them for the coming gunplay. Then he said to Shaw, "I asked him what I now ask you, gringo," he said in stiff English. "What are you doing in *my* desert?"

Shaw's thumb slid down the small of the rifle stock, cocking the hammer easily. "Funny," he said, "I'm under the impression this is *my* desert."

The big Mexican gave a dark chuckle. The three soldiers stepped sidelong, putting some room between themselves. All they needed now was to see the big Mexican make his move and get the killing started. "You gringos make me laugh," the man said, his hand easing up toward the handle of a big Remington holstered on the center of his chest where two bandoleers of ammunition draped on his shoulders crossed in an X. "You think every piece of ground you step on is yours, eh?"

"It *is* a shortcoming we all share," Shaw replied calmly. "Now touch that pistol, I'll save you ever having to take another bath." Beneath Shaw his horse seemed to freeze in place.

"Hold it, Manko!" a voice shouted from the head of the column, seeing what was about to happen from twenty yards away. Shaw sat like a statue, his left hand poised, his eyes fixed straight into the big Mexican's, as if the other men were not even there.

The big Mexican relented. He eased his hand down from the gun butt and let out a breath. The three men eased down too. Shaw remained as still as stone.

"It is lucky for you, gringo," the big Mexican growled, "lucky for both of you, that my *capitán* does not want me to kill you just yet." On the ground Simon stood with his hands clasped tightly together in front of him, his eyes squeezed shut.

Shaw still didn't respond. He continued staring coldly until at length the column stopped a few feet from the big Mexican and a man wearing a dusty military tunic said in a New Zealand accent, "As you were, Sergeant Manko." He looked at Simon and the three men on the ground. Then he looked at Shaw curiously and said, "What are you doing out here? Don't you know there is a war going on?" He finished speaking and gave Shaw a bemused look.

"Yes, I know there's a war going on," Shaw said, speaking for the first time since he'd taken his stand. He paused long enough to nudge his horse the rest of the way down off the hillside. "I came out here looking for Luis Sepreano and his army." He paused, uncocked the rifle and lowered it across his lap. "It looks like I must've found him."

"No, you haven't found General Sepreano, only the Army of Liberation," the New Zealander corrected.

"That's close enough to suit me," Shaw replied, pushing up his hat brim.

"He lies," the big Mexican cut in. He gestured toward Simon. "This one already told me they were headed for Durango."

"Yes," said Simon, wanting to help, "in our search

for Sepreano. I heard we would find him in Durango."

The big Mexican said, staring harshly, "I would have gotten the truth out of them if you had not come when you did."

Shaw returned the harsh stare, but he kept silent.

"Who are you, Mister?" the captain asked, giving Shaw a curious, scrutinizing once-over. "You look very familiar to me."

"My name is Shaw . . . Lawrence Shaw." As he spoke, Shaw gave the big Mexican the same harsh stare. "My friends call me Fast Larry." He dreaded even saying the name. But if this was the kind of tight spot being the Fastest Gun Alive would get him out of, then so be it, he told himself.

"Lawrence Shaw!" The captain looked taken aback for a moment. "My God, man, it *is* you!"

Shaw turned his eyes away from the big Mexican and gazed at the New Zealander. Simon watched in silence, seeing a change come over the captain.

"I saw you in a shoot-out in Hyde City." He paused, then said, "But wait, I heard you were dead, killed up in the Montana mining country."

"A false report," Shaw said flatly. "You know how easily rumors get started."

"Yes, I do," the New Zealander said. He stepped his horse closer. "I may have also heard that you were *alive,* drunk and on *the boards* in Matamoros."

"I was down and out in Matamoros," Shaw said. "But I got off the boardwalks, sobered up and now I'm looking for work—gun work, the thing I do best."

The big Mexican cut in again, saying to Shaw, "How much gun work are you capable of, with your gun hand in a sling? We're going to need to see some proof of what you have to offer."

"You had your chance to see some proof," Shaw said. "You turned it down." As he spoke, his left hand moved idly to the small of his rifle stock and rested there.

"That'll be enough, Sergeant Manko," said the New Zealander. You and your men get back into formation."

When the big Mexican and the other three men had ridden over and into the column, the captain said to Shaw as if in private, "It appears you and Manko have gotten off on the wrong foot. He's not the sort of man you want to anger."

"If I had a dollar for every man like him I've killed, I wouldn't be looking for a job killing more," Shaw replied.

"I see," the New Zealander said, offering a trace of a smile. "I'm Captain Rhineholt. I'll ask you to ride back with us and meet General Sepreano himself. It's not everyday a man with a reputation such as yours comes to join our cause."

"Your cause . . . ?" Shaw questioned. "I figured you to be a mercenary, like me."

"That's true," said Rhineholt, lowering his voice a little more. "But I am an officer of the ranks. If I don't support the cause of *liberación,* what business do I have here?" His eyes went to Simon as he spoke. "What about you there?" he asked, taking in Simon's ragged, derelict condition. "Are you also a gunman looking for work?"

Simon looked stunned that the captain would even ask such a question.

"He's my guide," Shaw said. "I'm not familiar with this part of the country," he lied. "I hired him to help me find Sepreano's army." He offered a thin smile. "I didn't think he'd find it by falling into your laps."

"I think you hired him because you felt sorry for him," the captain said in an even quieter voice. "I've heard it said that sympathy is a virtue a man in our position can't afford to have."

"Maybe." Shaw shook his head and added, "At any rate, I hired him. But now that I'm here, I won't be needing his services any longer." He raised his voice toward the ragged Mexican and said, "Hear that, Simon? You can turn around, ride on back the way we came."

Rhineholt called out to Simon in a much stronger tone, letting Shaw know he was not to be manipulated. "No, you're riding on in with us." He turned to Shaw. "If the general wants him to ride away, so be it."

Simon, looking shaken by everything that had happened, asked Shaw in a nervous voice, "Now that we have found the Army of Liberación, perhaps I may ask you for some of my pay?"

Shaw understood what Simon wanted. "Sure, why not, if you think you really need it now." He paused as if to give Simon a chance to change his mind.

"Oh, yes, please, I need it very badly," Simon said, almost in desperation.

Shaw gave the captain a look as he reached back, pulled one of the bottles of rye from his saddlebags and pitched it down to Simon.

"I understand what sort of guide you hired for yourself," Rhineholt said between the two of them. "But what I fail to understand is *why*?"

"He said he knew this country," Shaw lied again. "That was good enough for me." He nodded at the bottle of rye in Simon's dirty hand. "He was sure willing to work cheap enough."

"Yes," said Rhineholt, "sort of a mercenary of a lower caliber, wouldn't you say?"

Shaw didn't answer. He and Simon had both done enough to keep themselves out of trouble. He needed to get to Sepreano now and convince him that Dawson and Caldwell had nothing to do with his brother's death.

Simon nervously stepped farther away as he pulled the cork from the bottle of rye and took a long swig. To Shaw's relief, instead of taking another drink, he corked the bottle. But then, like any other drunkard would do, he shoved the bottle up under his serape without offering the captain a drink.

Shaw gave the captain a look that showed sympathy for the ragged Mexican and at the same time disapproval for his rudeness. "I hope you'll forgive Simon's lack of manners, Captain Rhineholt," he said quietly. "It's been a long, dry ride for him." He spoke low enough for the captain to hear, but not Simon.

"Think nothing of it, Mr. Shaw. I make it a practice

never to drink when I'm on duty," the captain said matter-of-factly.

They both watched Simon turn and climb up atop his horse. Suddenly, from the column, Sergeant Manko came riding up quickly and slid his horse to a halt in a rise of sandy dust. "*Capitán*, to our west," he said, handing the captain an American-made telescope. "There are many *federales* coming! We must be gone from here before they see us."

Rhineholt took the telescope and scanned the distant hilly horizon until he came upon the long column of soldiers. He took on a concerned look and said as he stared through the telescope, "They have a Gatling gun, and a small field cannon. What nice presents those would make for the general."

"There are many of them," Manko said in a warning tone of voice.

"Yes, Sergeant, too many, for a scouting group our size," Rhineholt said, lowering the lens and collapsing it between his palms. "I'm afraid we'll have to avoid them, if we're lucky enough to do so. We came searching for the Barrows, but we're not going any farther north. Turn the column around, Sergeant. We're heading back. The Barrows know where we will be."

Shaw wasn't about to mention that the Barrows were a half hour or less on the other side of the hill. Until he could see a way to get Dawson and Caldwell safely out of their hands, he was going to have to play things by ear. He looked at Simon to see if he understood. But he couldn't read anything in the blank look that had come upon the ragged Mexican's face.

Chapter 22

Leo Fairday and Lying Earl Sunday had been scouting the trail thirty yards ahead of the others when they spotted the column of *federales* riding toward the steep hills. "Uh-oh, I think they saw us!" said Leo, jerking his horse to a halt and spinning it around on the trail. Beside him Lying Earl did the same. As soon as they had ducked back behind the cover of overhanging brush and scrub-tree limbs, Leo asked, "Do you think they saw us, Earl?"

"One of them looked me right in the eye," Lying Earl said. "I saw him pull a gun from his holster. Another second, I believe he would have started shooting."

"You saw all that, from more than three hundred yards away?" Fairday gave him a bemused look, realizing that Lying Earl would always live up to his nickname no matter what the situation.

"Damned right, I saw all that," said Lying Earl. "I'll tell you something else I saw—"

"Never mind," Fairday interrupted, shaking his head. He peeped out and down on the distant flatlands through the brush for a second, getting a better look. "Maybe you'd best let me do all the talking when we get back to Redlow and Eddie," he said, stepping his horse back and nudging his boots to its sides.

"Suits the hell out of me," Lying Earl said indignantly, hurrying his horse along behind him as Fairday rode away.

But moments later when they'd ridden up to Eddie and Redlow on the trail, Earl hurried his horse forward ahead of Fairday and started speaking rapidly to the Barrows brothers. "There's *federales* coming—must be near a thousand of them!"

Redlow and Eddie looked past Lying Earl and watched Fairday shake his head, discounting Earl's words.

"How many are there, Leo?" Eddie asked.

"I wasn't lying," Earl grumbled under his breath. Then he backed his horse away and fell into a sullen silence.

"It's a large column, Eddie," said Leo, "maybe a hundred, give or take. We saw them only for a couple seconds. But I saw they're pulling a small cannon and a Gatling gun on a flatbed."

"All right," said Redlow, already making plans to avoid the soldiers, "let's get pulled back and into some cover until they pass below."

"Whoa, Brother!" said Eddie. "Didn't you hear Leo? They've got a cannon and a Gatling gun."

"That's right, and we don't," said Redlow. He

started to back his horse up a step in order to turn and tell the men to take cover.

Eddie grabbed his horse by its bridle. "But we *will have,*" he said, "as soon as we ambush them and take theirs away from them."

Redlow jerked his reins, pulling the bridle from his brother's hand. "Don't talk crazy, Eddie! We've got all these stolen horses to deliver, and two prisoners to worry about keeping quiet if we plan on pulling an ambush. Which *we don't,*" he added with stern emphasis.

"Listen to me, Brother," said Eddie, keeping his horse alongside him. "We're on a winning streak here. Can't you see it?"

"Yes indeed, I see it," said Redlow. "We've got the horses for Sepreano. We've got the two law dogs to feed to him for his brother's death. That's our winning streak. Let's not go doing something to mess it up."

"Think about this, Red," Eddie said in a dead-serious tone, reaching out and once again grabbing his horse's bridle. This time he saw that Redlow had already started to bring the horse to a halt as he considered Eddie's words. "Sure, we bring him the two men who killed his brother. That's a good thing, but it doesn't carry much weight." He waved a gloved hand toward the strings of horses some of the men were leading. "These are damned fine horses. Sepreano is going to be most happy with them. But what kind of men bring horses?" He stared intently at Redlow for an answer.

"Horse thieves," Redlow said, starting to get his brother's point.

"Right you are, horse thieves," said Eddie, leaning in closer from his saddle. "But what kind of men attack a well-armed column of soldiers and bring in cannons and Gatling guns?"

With a trace of a smile, Redlow made and said in a tone mimicking Luis Sepreano, *"Hombres duros en negrilla, eh?"*

"That's right, 'Bold hard men,' " Eddie repeated in English, returning Redlow's thin smile.

Redlow called out to Lucky Dennis Caddy, "Lucky, you and Drop the Dog take the horses and the lawdogs off the trail into the brush. Tie those two good and tight and stuff their bandannas into their mouths. Then you catch up to us, Dog. Caddy, you stay here with the horses and the prisoners. Keep them quiet."

"Want me to stab them both in the heart?" Caddy asked, looking Dawson and Caldwell up and down. "That'd keep them quiet."

"Did I say stab them in the hearts?" Redlow asked, his voice turning testy and sharp.

Caddy looked disappointed. "No, you didn't. Sorry, Red."

"Only if they try giving you any trouble, Caddy," Eddie cut in, giving the two lawmen a look, letting them know what to expect if they tried anything. "In that case you can stab them in the heart as many times as you feel like it. Only don't use any guns or make any loud noise. Got it?"

"Got it," said Caddy. He and Drop the Dog both nodded. Taking the lead ropes from the hands of the other men, they gestured for Dawson and Caldwell to follow the horses off the trail and onto the brushy, rock-strewn hillside. Without saying a word, Dawson gave Caldwell a look that said, *Here's our chance,* as the two stepped their horses along, their tied hands holding their reins and their saddle horns.

Along the base of the steep hillside, Redlow, Eddie and their men split up. Seven of them hurried across a thirty-yard stretch of sandy soil and took cover in a bed of half-sunken boulders overlooking the trail. The remaining six spread out a few feet up the hillside and waited behind cover as the column of Mexican regulars approached their position unexpectedly. "If a dozen of us can take their fieldpiece and Gatling gun, they deserve to lose it," Redlow whispered, getting into the spirit of battle.

Eddie grinned beside him and whispered in reply, "Hope you don't go getting superstitious on us, but there's thirteen of us, not a dozen."

A grim look of apprehension started to come over Redlow's face, but he shook it off. "Superstitious or not, once they ride into this cross fire and Elkins and Boland close around behind them with their rifles, it's going to look like a hog killing in there." He nodded at the narrow trail. "We catch them off guard, keep firing, they won't have time to ready their fieldpiece or man their big gun."

"Now you're talking, Brother Redlow," Eddie said.

He gave his brother a slap on the back of his sweat-darkened shirt.

High above them, in the brush on the hillside, Lucky Dennis Caddy crouched down, staring through a tangle of brush toward the approaching column of soldiers. Twenty feet behind him the two lawmen stood with their backs to the scrub juniper he'd tied them to. A knife stood stuck in the ground a few feet from the juniper. Caddy had stuck it there in case Dawson or Caldwell managed to remove their mouth gags and tried to warn the soldiers.

What Caddy didn't realize was that as soon as he'd finished his job tying the lawmen and walked away to watch the coming battle on the flatlands below, Dawson and Caldwell had strained and pushed upward with their legs until the shallow roots of the juniper had begun to rip loose from the dry, loose soil. Staring intently at the knife standing in front of them was all the incentive they needed.

In a determined pull, the two felt the short juniper give up its hold on the ground and send them both tumbling forward. Caddy heard the thrashing of dry branches as the two landed with a thud. He turned in time to see them scurry the last few inches and flip the tree in a way that allowed Caldwell to get his tied hands on the knife. "Oh hell! Get away from there!" Caddy shouted, keeping his voice down as much as he could. He ran toward them, his gun out, but his mind warning him not to fire it.

Caldwell had begun hacking on the rope behind his back. "Hurry, Jed!" said Dawson, twisting himself around, scrub tree and all, putting himself between Caddy and Caldwell in order to give Caldwell the precious seconds he needed to finish cutting himself free.

Caddy leaped around Dawson, his gun raised for a swipe at Caldwell's head. But as he swung, Caldwell's freed hands came from behind his back. He'd braced himself, ducked the swinging gun barrel and stabbed the knife blade deep into Caddy's chest. Caddy staggered backward, the impact of the knife causing him to fire a shot wildly from his Colt before Caldwell grabbed it from his hand.

Caldwell fired two more shots into Caddy's already mortally wounded chest, sending him backward to the ground.

"Keep firing!" Dawson yelled, trying to see through the brush and determine how close the soldiers were to the ambush awaiting them. "Get his rifle! Fire at the soldiers! Warn them!"

Caldwell ran to Caddy's horse and jerked a repeating rifle from its boot. He levered a round into the chamber as he raced forward to where Caddy had stood watching the trail below. . . .

At the head of the column of soldiers, a lean young corporal's horse jumped and bolted sideways as a rifle bullet stuck the sandy, rocky ground near its hooves. Even as he settled the spooked animal, his arm went into the air, warning the troops behind him. Beside him a seasoned captain and his sergeant, who had been looking upward toward the sound of the gunfire, also settled their horses as they both raised an arm toward the following column.

Along the hillside, Redlow and Eddie had heard the shooting from above them. "Damn Caddy! They're not riding in!" said Eddie, seeing the soldiers stop short of riding into their cross-fire ambush.

"Then fire, *damn it*!" Redlow shouted, already aiming his rifle and firing, knowing full well their element of surprise was gone, and their targets were not going to fall for their trap.

On the hillside high above the melee, Dawson and Caldwell hurriedly gathered the lead ropes to the Bengreen horses. Climbing into their saddles, they led the string of horses up onto the trail, Caddy's horse tagging along behind.

"We need to find ourselves a place higher up above the trail," Dawson said as they rode. "I think I saw one on our way here."

"Lead the way," said Caldwell, quickly reloading Caddy's pistol as he spoke. He carried Caddy's gun belt, full of bullets, thrown over his shoulder.

Dawson, with Caddy's rifle in hand, rode upward, leading some of the horses behind him. Caldwell followed, leading the rest. Below them the powerful sound of the Gatling gun began exploding back and forth along the base of the hillside, eclipsing the sound of rifle and pistol fire from the Barrows Gang. "Give them hell, *federales*!" Caldwell yelled back over his shoulder, knowing that Dawson was unable to hear him above the fray.

They rode almost a half mile upward along the winding trail, leading the horses until they spotted a long, high ledge above them. "This is it," Dawson said, not stopping, but veering off the trail and onto a steeper, narrower path. "We'll have to take the horses out of sight, down here. We'll make our way up there on foot."

While the two climbed the rocky footpath and took a good firing position along the jagged edge, the battle continued to rage along the base of the hillside. Redlow and Eddie had fallen back to their horses under heavy fire from the Gatling gun. As their men scattered, grabbed their horses and made a run for it, the Barrows brothers climbed into their saddles and took their chances riding away along the base of the hillside.

Along the other side of the trail, the bodies of Teddy Barksdale and Fred Townsend lay at the bottom of a long smear of blood leading down from the boulder standing above them. "That damned Caddy!" Eddie shouted. "I'll kill him when I get my hands on him!"

"Don't you know he's dead already, you fool?" Redlow said harshly. "The lawdogs killed him! Can't you figure that out for yourself? You and your 'lucky streak we're on'! Where is that lucky streak now?"

Eddie didn't answer. He clenched his teeth and rode on.

The Mexican soldiers, seeing the gang break up and race away, sent riders in pursuit of them in every direction. The captain and sergeant stayed back with the main column, making sure not to weaken their ranks so much that the cannon and Gatling gun sat underprotected on the flatlands floor.

Dawson and Caldwell remained ready. Hearing the battle lessen and spread out as the soldiers chased the fleeing men, they watched the trail until at length they saw a rise of sandy dust start drifting upward along the trail toward them. "We best kill them quick and get back down," said Dawson. "The soldiers behind them won't know which side we're on until we get a chance to explain it to them."

When Andy Mack and Deacon Kay raced into sight below them, the two lawmen stood as one and fired. Dawson's rifle shot picked Elkins up from his saddle and launched him backward. Elkins hit the trail dead, and rolled another twenty feet before coming to a halt as four soldiers came charging upward into sight.

Caldwell fired three pistol shots, each one hitting Deacon Kay and knocking him out of his saddle.

Dawson and Caldwell stood tensed, waiting, expecting more men. Then when they saw the soldiers, they ducked down quickly and Dawson shouted, "Don't shoot! We're on your side. We're *americano lawmen*!"

"*Americano* lawmen?" The four soldiers looked back and forth at one another. After a moment's pause, a voice called out, "Stand up with your hands in the air, and walk down here! If you try to run we will shoot you dead!"

"Sounds fair to me," Dawson said to Caldwell, letting out a breath of relief. "This must be the *help* the Mexican government said they would send."

Chapter 23

Walking slowly with their hands raised, Dawson and Caldwell looked down the edge above the trail. On the ground they watched a soldier walk over and nudge Elkins with the toe of his boot, making sure he was dead. A few feet away another soldier, his pistol cocked and pointed forward, had stepped down beside Deacon Kay. But the soldier jumped back with a start as the wounded gunman struggled up onto one knee, one hand raised, the other hand clutching his bloody chest.

"We're not with them," said Dawson, stepping around the rock from the steep footpath onto the edge of the trail. "We were their prisoners. We fired the shots to warn you there was an ambush waiting for you."

"Oh, I see," said the lean young corporal whose horse had reared at the rifle shot. He held a cocked pistol toward Dawson's chest. "You are the ones who almost shot me from my saddle?"

"No," said Caldwell, "we weren't trying to shoot

you, or you wouldn't be standing here. That was a warning shot to get your attention. You saw who was waiting for you between those two stretches of rock, didn't you?"

The corporal didn't answer, but he did seem to ease down a little, enough for Dawson to say, "We're both lawmen. We're tracking the Barrows."

"On my side of the border?" the young corporal said with a harsh stare.

"But with your country's permission," Dawson countered quickly. "We're supposed to get some help from your government. In fact, we thought that you—"

On the ground, Deacon Kay cut in a coughing, rasping voice, "He's telling you the truth, Corporal. They were our prisoners. We were taking them . . . to Sepreano. He would have . . . killed them."

"Obliged, Kay," said Dawson. He and Caldwell both gave the mortally wounded man a surprised look, not expecting any help from any of the Barrows Gang.

"Ah, what the hell . . ." Kay coughed and clutched his chest even tighter. "When a man is dying he can . . . afford to be generous, I reckon." He took a breath and struggled to continue. "We're the Barrows Gang. We've thrown in with Sepreano's army. We were going to . . . meet him. These lawdogs were hounding us. We took them prisoner . . . and were going to tell the general that they . . . killed his brother, Carlos."

"Take it easy, Kay," said Dawson. "Try to save your strength."

"Yeah . . . for what?" Kay rasped. He nodded up at the soldier holding the gun on him. "This peckerwood . . . is going to finish me off. Ain't you?" As he asked, his bloody hand left his chest, reached inside his shirt and pulled out a small hideaway gun.

Seeing the gun swing up toward him, the young Mexican pulled the trigger. Kay's head snapped back with the impact of the bullet. He pitched backward in the dirt, a puddle of blood spreading beneath his skull.

Dawson started to say something, but before he could, the corporal rushed him and Caldwell toward the spot where they'd tied the horses. "Are there any more of you up here?" the corporal asked.

"One more," Dawson said, still thinking that Shaw must be somewhere on the trail behind them. "He should be coming along any time."

"I see," the corporal said, sounding skeptical.

Dawson once again started to say something, but again the corporal cut him off, this time telling him curtly, "Anything you say to me, you will only have to say again when we get to my *capitán*. Dawson took that as a polite way of telling him and Caldwell to shut up.

As they walked along through the brush around the large rock, one of the soldiers hurried to the top of the ledge and came back carrying the pistol, gun belt and rifle the two had left lying on the ground. Caldwell and Dawson looked at one another with a sigh of relief they hadn't breathed in days.

"You can believe us when we tell you, we are both

mighty pleased to see you," Dawson said over his shoulder, still holding his raised chest high.

"You can lower your hands," the corporal said, appearing to believe what the two had told him.

"*Gracias*, Corporal," Dawson replied. He and Caldwell lowered their hands as the soldiers unhitched the horses and motioned for them to get mounted.

Random gunshots still resounded on the sand flats below, but the Gatling gun had fallen silent as they turned the horses onto the trail and followed it down to the base of the steep hill. Once they were upon the flatlands, the other soldiers spotted them riding across the trail. By the time they stopped and sat atop their horses in front of the captain and the sergeant, the gunfire had ceased altogether. "Who have we here, Duego," the captain said, looking Dawson and Caldwell up and down with close scrutiny.

"*Capitán* Agosto," the young corporal said as he gave a salute, "these two men were waiting atop a ledge on the hill trail." He gestured toward Dawson. "This one says they are on our side, that they warned us of the ambush and in doing so, kept us from suffering casualties."

"Oh, so we have them to thank," the captain said, appearing cautiously grateful. "What do you make of all this, Sergeant?"

"If he is telling the truth," the big sergeant cut in gruffly, "then we are fortunate that they warned us." He glared at Dawson as if to decide whether or not to believe him.

"They had all of these fine horses, *Capitán*," said

the corporal. "If they wanted to get away, they could have. But they did not flee. Instead they stopped the two men we were chasing. One of the men said that the gang had been holding these two prisoners."

The captain fell silent for a moment, considering everything. During the pause, Dawson said, "Captain, I'm U.S Marshal Crayton Dawson. This is my deputy, Jedson Caldwell. We were told that Mexico would be sending us some help when the time came. I figured that was you and your men. Am I right?"

The captain only gave a thin, sly grin and said, "*Por favor*, allow me to ask all the questions, *U.S. Marshal Dawson*."

From the other side of the rocks along the trail, a rider came racing up to them at breakneck speed and slid his horse to a halt in a spray of sand and rock. With a hasty salute, he stared anxiously at the captain until the officer said, "Speak."

"*Si, Capitán*," the man said, "we have found a spot on the trail where the men we were chasing gathered back together and rode on across the desert."

"In which direction are they headed?" the captain asked, already rising in his stirrups and stretching for a look through the stirred dust and wavering heat.

"Toward the hills southwest," the man said, pointing as he spoke.

Dawson cut in. "They're headed for a valley up in the hills known to be the Barrows Gang's hideout, Captain. It's called Puerta del Infierno. It's my belief that Sepreano and his men will be gathering there too. The Barrows were bringing him these horses."

He gestured toward the Bengreen horses strung along behind them.

"Ah, a place known as Hell's Gate," the captain said, still weighing Dawson's words. "How fitting that we should all travel to such a place as Hell's Gate, each in search of our enemies." Then he asked as he watched Dawson's eyes closely, to see what his answer would be. "Tell me, Marshal Dawson, do you know the way to Puerta del Infierno?"

"No," Dawson was quick to point out. "But that's where they're headed. If you want them, they're leaving us plenty of tracks to follow."

"Ah, yes, and it is for the first time that we have tracks to follow!" Looking at his sergeant, the captain said, "Assemble the men, Sergeant. I think it will be I who will be known as the one to have followed Luis Sepreano to the gates of hell, and there killed him."

On their way toward the valley where Puerta del Infierno lay hidden between two towering hill lines, Shaw, Rhineholt and the others heard the distant sound of gunfire far behind them. They looked back only now and then in curiosity until the firing had stopped and the desert floor lay in silence.

"Anything we should be concerned about?" Shaw asked Rhineholt, in a way that included himself in with Sepreano's Army of Liberación.

"No," said Rhineholt. "The *federales* are always chasing their tails out here. They probably shot up some poor band of gypsies crossing the flats—mistook them for us most likely." He chuckled under his breath.

"All right . . ." Shaw smiled slightly. "It's going to feel good riding with a bunch that wields so much power and has so much confidence."

"That's Sepreano for sure," said Rhineholt. "If it wasn't I wouldn't be riding with him."

"It sounds like you and I ride *gun* with an outfit for the same reasons," Shaw said, wanting to know as much as he could about Sepreano and his men.

"Oh, and what's that?" Rhineholt asked.

"Money," Shaw said flatly. He gave Rhineholt a knowing grin.

"You hit it dead center, Fast Larry," Rhineholt replied. He gave a guarded look around to make certain they weren't being overheard. "They can stuff all the *liberación*, all the *common good*, all the *flags, politics and fireworks.* When the money runs out, *I* run out, usually one step ahead of it, if I'm lucky enough to make it happen that way."

"Here, here," Shaw said in agreement. The two chuckled quietly together.

They rode on.

As afternoon shadows fell long across the hillsides and flats, they rode up along a high ledge, following its path until the land leveled off and led down into a valley of broken rock and patches of wild grass. In the first purple shades of night, Rhineholt brought the men to a halt. He gestured Shaw's attention ahead where the valley narrowed and funneled in between two rocky hillsides.

"There it is, Hell's Gate," he said. "Could you ever imagine a better hiding place than this? There's room to hide an army here. Sometimes I believe the only reason Sepreano let the Barrows join his forces was to find out about their hideout."

"I can understand that," Shaw said, looking all around, taking in the desolate, endless land.

Noting the eeriness of the place, Simon made the sign of the cross on his chest as he looked up and saw a dark, winged predator glide silently past their heads. Then, seeing the two look at him, he said, "Forgive my superstitious peasant ways, senors. But all my worthless, drunken life I have lived in fear of reaching the gates of hell, and yet, here I am." He wobbled a bit in his saddle. "I have arrived at the gates of hell of my own accord."

Rhineholt replied, "Haven't we all?"

Simon fell silent.

Shaw eyed the half-full bottle in his hand. But he made no comment. Instead he said to Rhineholt, "I hope you'll allow him to get some food in his belly and get some sleep—sober up some before we meet Sepreano."

"Don't worry," said Rhineholt, nudging his horse forward, signaling the men to follow him, "you won't be seeing Sepreano tonight."

"Why is that?" Shaw asked.

"He conducts no business after dark," said Rhineholt. "The general believes in allowing his men to let off a little steam at night."

"I can live with that kind of attitude," Shaw said, looking all around at the dark, vast terrain. "Can't you?"

In the rocks to their left a coyote let out a long, sharp howl. "I can, if that's the way it is." Rhineholt shrugged. "He says it makes the men more eager to make it through another day. That's the Mexican way of looking at things, I suppose." He passed Shaw a look.

Shaw only nodded, not knowing Rhineholt's opinion on the matter, and not wanting to cross views with him.

"I don't mind telling you, Shaw," Rhineholt said, lowering his tone of voice a little, "it's good to talk to someone like myself for a change."

"Like yourself?" Shaw asked.

"Nothing against the Mexicans," said Rhineholt, "but I'm convinced I could raise a better grade of soldiers from among the *aborigines*, if you get my meaning."

Shaw got his meaning. He wasn't going to tell the man that he had lived much of his life among the people of Mexican hill country. He wouldn't mention his friend Gerardo Luna, his deceased wife, Rosa, the widow Anna Reyes Bengreen. . . . The list went on in his mind. But this was no time to discuss such matters. Instead he passed the subject aside, saying, "I expect it would be hard to have a Mexican revolution without *Mexicans.*"

"That's true," Rhineholt said wistfully, "but it would sure make things go a lot smoother."

They rode on.

By the time they rode through an ever-narrowing corridor through the rocks, Simon sat slumped and limp in his saddle, the bottle of rye dangling loosely and almost empty in his hand. Sidling close to him, Shaw eased the bottle out of his fingers without disturbing him. He looked at the amber liquid, swirled it and considered taking a drink. Yet, thinking about Dawson and Caldwell, knowing he needed to keep his wits sharp for their sakes, he reached back, slid the bottle into his saddlebag and rode on.

Chapter 24

The jagged hills surrounding the valley served as a natural wall against the outside world. Entering the valley through a narrow corridor of stone, Shaw could see nothing but darkness on either side of him. He heard only the clacking of their horses' hooves resounding off stone. Looking up into the darkness, he saw where the walls seemed to end against a purple moonlit sky.

Riding beside him, Rhineholt said, "A damned impressive place, eh, Mr. Shaw?"

"Yes, most impressive," Shaw replied. He wanted to ask if there was another way out, but he decided this was not the time to do so.

Rhineholt continued, saying, "This valley was once the lair of a Spanish warlord. His private army kept the peace among local tribes. They put down any rebellion and protected Spanish gold-mining interests from marauding Apache. Wait until you see the place."

"A *private* army," Shaw said. "It sounds like mercenaries have had a stake in the game here for a long time. Looks like your profession is secure."

"You mean *our* profession," Rhineholt said. "Yes, as long as there's money and power changing hands, there's going to be work for men like you and me protecting it. That should make you happy, knowing there's always a high price for a fast gun."

Shaw didn't answer.

A hundred yards farther into the valley, a series of torchlights rose up on the horizon as riders came forward to meet them. At the same time riders began to rise up as if from the darkness and flank them on either side as the corridor of stone grew wider and opened up onto a stretch of flatlands. "Sit tight, Shaw," Rhineholt said. "Everybody has to go through this. Our general is a most cautious man. He doesn't want to be caught off guard in the middle of the night with his face buried between some senorita's breasts."

"Heaven forbid," Shaw said wryly.

As the torch carriers rode in closer, their light fell across the riders already on either side of Rhineholt's column. Shaw saw the same mixed clothing of peasant trousers, French uniform tunics and range clothes that Rhineholt's men wore. He heard voices murmur back and forth in a mesh of bad English and border Spanish, all of it about his and Simon's new faces among the men.

Hearing the murmurs, Rhineholt held a hand up and said to the men, "It's all right. I'm bringing these two men in. They're going to be riding with us." He gestured toward Shaw as they continued riding. "This one you have heard most of. His name is Lawrence Shaw. He's also known as the Fastest Gun Alive."

Shaw touched his hat brim but stared ahead, used to the sort of mixed and edgy reaction his presence always conjured from a band of gunmen like these. Of course they'd heard of him; he knew it. Every saddle tramp, bummer, murderer, no-account on the frontier had heard of him, he reminded himself. Wasn't it his name and reputation alone that had gotten him and Simon here to Hell's Gate?

"He is going to ride with us?" a voice asked Rhineholt.

"That's right, as soon as we ride in and I get the general's approval," Rhineholt said. Looking at Shaw he added, "Which I see no problem doing, once General Sepreano hears who you are."

"Obliged," Shaw said, without looking at him. Instead he kept his eyes straight ahead, seeing a wide glow of light grow more clear on the turn of the horizon, beginning to reveal the outlining stone-walled ruins of an ancient Spanish castle.

"What about this one?" a voice asked, referring to Simon. "Who is he?"

"He's with me," Shaw said with finality on the subject.

Another twenty minutes passed before the column of men reached a pair of iron and timber gates. With a wave of Rhineholt's hand the gates began opening with a creaking and groaning of rope, winches and chain. Looking at Shaw in the torchlight, Rhineholt said with a short grin, "As if this land itself wasn't protection enough, the gentleman warlord decided he needed these monsters." He gestured toward the huge gates.

"Maybe they're meant to keep people in, as well as out," Shaw remarked, sizing everything up.

"Yes, maybe so," said Rhineholt. "Perhaps that's why this place is called Hell's Gate."

The opened gates came to a shuddering halt. Shaw nudged his horse forward, riding beside Rhineholt through a stone wall that he estimated to be eight-foot thick. They crossed a courtyard where soldiers, bottles of whiskey and tin cups of coffee in hand, stood around a large fire watching them.

At an iron hitch rail out front of a small room attached to the main structure, Rhineholt waved the rest of the column toward a long lean-to livery barn and stepped down from his saddle. As Shaw stepped down beside him, he had to take Simon's horse by its bridle in order to stop it. Rhineholt shook his head and gestured toward the small, dark room. "You can leave him in there for the night," Rhineholt said, pointing to an open doorway. "I have to go report to the general."

"Obliged," said Shaw.

As Rhineholt left to report to Sepreano and tell him whom he had brought back with him, Shaw looped Simon's arm over his shoulder and walked him inside the small, empty room facing the courtyard. "All right, my friend," Shaw said, realizing that Simon was too drunk to hear him, "you stay here and sleep it off while I take a look around."

"*Si*, I will . . . ," Simon murmured incoherently in a thick voice, his head bobbing loosely on his chest.

Shaw lowered him onto a cot covered with a faded Mayan blanket and turned and walked out onto the stone-paved street. He followed some of the men he'd ridden in with toward a dimly lit building where laughter and music spilled out of the open doorway and windows. Out front of the building, Sergeant Manko and a few men stood puffing on black cigars. They stared hard as Shaw walked past them and into the crowded storage building the soldiers had turned into a cantina.

In the darkness on a stone balcony overlooking the street, General Sepreano stood watching, his hands resting on the stone rail. A few feet behind, spread around him in a protective half circle, stood four personal bodyguards. Standing behind the bodyguards was Rhineholt, his holster empty, his Smith & Wesson revolver lying on a table where one of the guards had laid it before allowing him into the room.

"How good is Fast Larry Shaw? Or, should I ask how good *was* he?" Sepreano asked Rhineholt in stiff English.

"When I saw him shoot three men in Hyde City, he was *damned good*," said Rhineholt. "In fact, I have to say he was the best I'd ever seen, then or since."

"I see," said Sepreano. "And all of the drinking you said he did?" Sepreano asked without looking around at him. "What has that done to him?"

"That I can't say," Rhineholt replied. "But he's looking for work, like all the others we've hired. We find out pretty quick if they're good enough for the job." He shrugged. "They're either good enough, or they're soon dead."

"Yes, but that is so with all the others," said Sepreano. "But this is the Fastest Gun Alive, eh? We deserve to see him at work." He turned a tight grin back over his shoulder, then returned his gaze to the street below. "Tell Manko to push him, see what he does."

"With all respect, General," Rhineholt said cautiously, "Manko is one of my top men. I would hate to lose him."

"*Si*, and I would hate to lose you, New Zealander," Sepreano said in a threatening tone. "Would you prefer I have Jessa here go tell him?"

"No, sir, General," Rhineholt said quickly. "I will see it right away." He turned on his heel military style and walked away. The guard followed him to the door, picked up Rhineholt's gun by its barrel and handed it to him, butt first.

Inside the cantina, Shaw had ordered a cigar and two bottles of whiskey. He stood puffing the cigar as the bartender stood a shot glass in front of him. When the bartender started to pull the cork on one of the bottles, Shaw said, "Let it sit."

The bartender nodded, stepped back and walked away down the bar toward his other customers. Shaw heard the buzz among the drinkers as he puffed his cigar, but he didn't turn toward them until finally one of them ventured down the bar and stood beside him. "The men you rode in with say you are Lawrence Shaw, the Fastest Gun Alive? It is so, *si*?"

"Yes, it's so," Shaw replied flatly, having learned

long ago not to answer that any other way. He gave the man a cold stare, enough to cause the man to raise his hands slightly in a show of peace.

"No, Senor Shaw," the man said, "I do not come looking for trouble. My name is Raoul. We heard that you are joining us. I only wish to invite you to have a drink with us." He gestured a hand along the bar toward the other drinkers, who nodded with respect and tipped their clay cups and glasses toward him.

"*Gracias*, all of you," Shaw said, touching his hat brim toward the drinkers. Then to Raoul he said, "But I'm not drinking tonight. I'm not in a drinking mood."

Raoul looked at the two bottles of whiskey standing on the bar. "But these are for you, *si*?"

Shaw only looked at him, not feeling like explaining himself. Taking three gold coins from his vest pocket, he pitched them down on the bar and called out to the bartender, "This is for my whiskey and smoke . . . and another bottle, for Raoul and the bar."

The drinkers nodded again and thanked him with another tip of their cups and glasses. Raoul said, "*Gracias*, I hope you will soon be in a drinking mood."

"You and me both," Shaw said. He puffed the cigar up to a glowing red coil and tucked one bottle into the sling along his right forearm. Carrying the other bottle in his left hand, he turned and walked out the open doorway.

As he started along the stone tiles, he caught a

glimpse of Rhineholt ducking into the same doorway he'd gone into earlier to report to Sepreano. Glancing up at the dark balcony, he saw only the darker outline of men looking down toward him. All right, Shaw told himself, the general wanted to see what he was buying. . . .

Out of the darkness along the stone walkway, Manko and two other men stepped out facing him. "Stop right there, Fastest Gun Alive," Manko demanded, his big hand poised near his gun butt. The other two men stepped sidelong, spreading out, each with their gun hands poised in the same manner.

But Shaw didn't stop. He took a few more steps, his head down slightly as if he didn't see them. "You! I told you to stop!" Manko bellowed without backing an inch as Shaw drew closer.

Shaw stopped abruptly, as if seeing the three for the first time. "What do you want?" Shaw asked, looking back and forth across the three, standing only three feet from the big, powerfully built Mexican.

"What do we want?" asked one of the men in a Texas accent. "Son, how'd you manage to live this long? You can't tell when three men have come to kill you?"

Shaw said with a flat, blank stare, "What three men?"

On the balcony, Sepreano saw the two men step in closer to Manko. He saw Manko reach out to give Shaw a shove back, giving them both more fighting distance. He heard the big Mexican say, "Draw!"

But instead of seeing Shaw go for his gun, he saw

the whiskey bottle in his left hand swing upward in a long half circle and crash against Manko's thick chin in a spray of blood, broken glass and whiskey.

"Kill him, Chico!" the Texan shouted, as Manko staggered backward and rocked to a shaky halt. Sepreano watched Shaw pull a cross draw as the other two men made their play. But instead of reaching for his gun, Shaw's left hand grabbed the other bottle by its neck, jerked it from the sling and brought it crashing in a roundhouse swing against the Texan's jaw, a second before the man could get his gun up from its holster.

The third man managed to clear leather, but he dropped his gun and screamed when Shaw brought the jagged broken bottle neck back around across his face.

Shaw kicked the gun away, stepped in and buried his right-boot toe in the man's crotch. "I told you, he's good," Rhineholt said to Sepreano atop the balcony. He sounded a bit smug now that he'd seen Shaw in action again, this time without firing a shot.

Sepreano didn't seem to hear him. He stood watching with rapt attention as Shaw walked forward calmly, took the stunned and staggering Manko by his thick forearm, and started guiding him, quicker and quicker with each step until he launched him face-first into an upright iron post supporting a long overhang.

Along the balcony rail, the bodyguards looked at one another, bemused, as the overhang shuddered and Manko fell backward, full-length onto the stone tiles. Without looking up, Shaw turned and walked away in the darkness. Sepreano stood staring at the three men lying knocked out on the street below as men from inside the cantina ran out to see why the building had trembled. "Well, General, what do you think?" Rhineholt asked. "Does Fast Larry ride with us, or not?"

Without looking around at Rhineholt, the stoic general said over his shoulder, "I have not yet seen how fast he draws his gun."

Chapter 25

Throughout the night Shaw sat on a straight-backed chair and stared out across the darkness in anticipation of the Barrows Gang's arrival. In the center of a stone courtyard flames licked upward from a large fire where some of the men lay nearby on blankets, having drunk until they fell backward in an alcoholic stupor. But not him, Shaw reminded himself. He'd stayed awake, kept vigilant by strong, tepid coffee he'd boiled earlier at that same licking fire and poured into his canteen. While he'd waited for his coffee to boil, he'd watched some of the drinkers from the cantina haul the three men out of the street and out of sight. If there had been hard feelings over what he'd done, no one had made it known to him.

Simon lay motionless on the bare cot in the corner behind him, for all purposes a dead man, the sound of low, deep snoring his only proof of life. But Shaw managed to ignore the snoring and dozed lightly now and then until dawn peeped rosy and bright above the eastern edge of the earth.

With first light the sound of the large front gates creaking open piqued Shaw's attention. Standing, he walked to the open doorway for a better look as seven riders goaded their tired horses inside, onto the stone-tiled courtyard. They dropped from their saddles. Searching the haggard faces in the thin morning light, Shaw recognized Titus Boland among them, yet he saw no sign of Dawson or Caldwell as the gates began creaking shut.

Now what . . . ?

Standing, he took off his gun belt, turned the holster around for a right-handed draw and strapped the belt, slung low the way he always wore it, back around his waist. He tied the holster down to his thigh with the strip of dangling rawhide.

Now he would go ahead and do what he'd vowed to himself to do, he told himself, answering his own question. Had Dawson and Caldwell ridden in, prisoners of the Barrows, he would have freed them. But since that hadn't been the case, all he had to do was kill Titus Boland. Maybe his two friends had gotten away on their own. He hoped they had, as he clenched and unclenched his right hand.

But maybe they were dead, he also had to consider. Either way, it made no difference now. He looked down at his right hand as he continued clenching and unclenching his fist in the sling. This was what had to be done now. Nothing else mattered.

As the Barrows men gathered around a well and drank cool water from gourd dippers, Shaw stepped forward from the doorway and moved closer, staying in the shadows, out of sight, listening closely, his focus locked on Titus Boland.

On the stone balcony outside the general's room overlooking the courtyard, one of the bodyguards jumped to his feet and grabbed his rifle and big Remington revolver as he heard Shaw's voice call out in a rage, "Titus Boland, you woman-murdering son of a bitch."

No sooner had the bodyguard jumped up from his chair than the doors on the balcony burst open. Sepreano and two more guards hurried out onto the balcony. The two guards carried their repeating rifles at port arms. The general stood at the rail and looked down at the remaining Barrows Gang gathered at the well. Since he had been interrupted during his morning shave, a white linen bib hung from Sepreano's shirt collar. One cheek was still lathered with shaving soap. His personal attendant, razor in hand, had followed close behind him.

The bodyguard on Sepreano's right said, "I will go and stop this before it starts, General."

But Sepreano would have none of it. "No, leave them alone. Do nothing until they are finished." He stared down with rapt fascination. On the street below, Rhineholt stepped into view, a rifle in his hands. He looked at the general for orders. But Sepreano deftly waved him away without taking his eyes off Shaw. Rhineholt stepped back and lowered his rifle. He also watched with great interest as Shaw stepped forward, his right arm still in the sling.

Standing by the well, water gourds in hand, Redlow and Eddie Barrows had both turned toward the sound of Shaw's voice. In disbelief, Titus Boland murmured, "Shaw . . ."

"Shaw?" said Redlow, also staring in disbelief. "You said you *killed* Fast Larry Shaw!"

"I did kill him," Boland said, unable to work this out in his confused mind. "I shot him. I saw him fall."

"You lied," Redlow said flatly.

"No, I didn't lie," Boland insisted. "I swear, I did shoot him. I saw him fall!" he repeated.

"Yeah," Redlow said with a sneer, "you reached down and put two in his head. Ain't that what he told you, Leo?"

"He sure did, this no-account sonsabitch," said Fairday, pitching his water gourd aside in disgust. "I ought to kill you myself."

"No, you're all wrong. This man is not Shaw. I killed Shaw!" said Boland. "I killed him, damn it!"

"You killed a defenseless woman!" Shaw bellowed, not wanting to talk, not wanting anything but to kill, or to be killed. He'd prepared himself for either outcome.

"Brother, I told you not to trust this lousy saddle tramp!" said Eddie. As he spoke, he stepped away, taking Redlow by the side of his shirt and pulling him along until Redlow got the message and moved away on his own. "Let them shoot each other to pieces," Eddie said just between the two of them. "There's who we've got to worry about right there." He gestured a nod up toward Sepreano.

Redlow glanced quickly up at Sepreano. Then he looked at Boland and said, "Well, Titus, it looks like you'll just have to kill him again." He tapped his fingers on the barrel of Luna Gerardo's little angel still hanging around his neck by its strip of rawhide.

Boland looked at Shaw's right arm, still in the sling, but his gun holstered on his right hip, set up for a right-hand draw. "Yeah, I can do that easily enough," he said, taking a step forward.

All around the courtyard soldiers had armed themselves instinctively. In the morning light, Sepreano had jerked the white linen bib from his collar, wiped shaving soap from his face and thrown the cloth aside. He stood rigid, watching the scene unfold below him. To the guards on either side he said, "We are no longer common banditos. We are civilized *políticos*, eh?" He gave a stiff wink. "When it is over, kill the one still standing."

"*Si*, General." The two guards nodded. They both raised their rifles and levered them quickly in preparation for their task. Shaw heard the metal-on-metal sound, but didn't bother looking up. He knew what it was; he couldn't care less.

Boland cut a quick glance upward, then back to Shaw. He didn't care either. As soon as Shaw's body hit the ground, he would make a leap for cover behind the stone wall running the girth of the well. And Shaw's body *would* hit the ground, he told himself. He had faced him down once before and shot him—and that was when Shaw had two good arms. All right, Shaw was drunk, he had to admit. But that didn't matter. He could take him; he *would* take him.

As if reading his thoughts, Shaw called out, "I've been saving this for you, Boland." He reached down, pulled the sling from his right arm and tossed it back over his shoulder. "I haven't fired a shot with my right hand since you caught me drunk and shot me on the street in Matamoros."

"I shot you fair and square in Matamoros, Shaw!" Boland shouted. "And I never killed a woman in my life. I don't know what you're trying to pull, but it's not going to save you. You're dead!"

Boland tensed. He made a fast grab for his gun. But the tip of his gun barrel never cleared the top of his holster.

Shaw's bullet hit him, dead center of his chest. On the balcony, Sepreano blinked as if his eyes had just fooled him. He had heard the first shot and seen Boland stagger backward, but what he had not seen was Shaw's gun leave its holster. The other thing he did not *clearly* see was Shaw's left hand fan three more shots, each one slamming Boland in almost the same spot before the falling gunman hit the ground.

There it is, Shaw thought. *That much is done. . . .*

Staring straight ahead at Redlow and Eddie Barrows, he opened his Colt, flipped out the spent cartridges, replaced them quickly and held the gun loosely toward the two stunned outlaws. "Where's Cray Dawson and Jed Caldwell?" he asked flatly, as if any answer they gave him would be the answer that would get them killed.

On the balcony, the two bodyguards had raised their rifles and taken aim, ready to fire. But hearing Shaw's question, and seeing his lack of concern about the two rifles pointed down at him, was enough to raise Sepreano's curiosity. "Wait, don't shoot," Sepreano said, holding a hand toward the two riflemen.

On the ground, Rhineholt stepped back out into sight. Right behind him on the street, Simon stood staring, his hair disheveled, a frightened, shaky look on his face.

"What is this man talking about?" Sepreano called down to the Barrows. "Who are the two men he speaks of?"

Redlow seized this as the opportunity to tell him about his brother, Carlos. "He's talking about two murdering American lawdogs who were hounding our trail, General," he said. Stepping forward and looking up at Sepreano with his arms spread, he continued. "We were on our way here—"

"You were supposed to bring me horses," Sepreano said, cutting him off. "Where are they?" He looked at the six dusty, bedraggled men and the seven overridden horses. "Where are the rest of your men?"

Redlow said, "We had a whole herd of horses for you, General—fine horses from the Bengreen Cedros Altos spread over around Matamoros. But those two lawdogs took them. We were holding them both prisoners, bringing them here to you. We set an ambush for some *federales*. Things went bad, and while we fought to save our lives, the lawdogs escaped and took off with the horses."

"An ambush?" Sepreano glared down at him.

"You were told to lie low and avoid the *federales*. Is that not what I ordered everyone to do?"

"Yes, I know that, General," said Redlow. "But we saw they had a cannon and a Gatling gun. We couldn't resist bringing those to you as a present—call it a token of our respect and admiration."

"Oh? And yet, where are they?" Sepreano asked, spreading his hands.

"It was a terrible fight, General. Things didn't go the way we planned. We lost some good men."

The general recounted. "Let me see. You lost the horses you were bringing me. You lost the cannon and Gatling gun you were bringing me. You lost the two lawdogs you were bringing me." He paused as if in contemplation, then asked, "What is it I pay you to do?"

Redlow's face reddened as laughter rose from Sepreano's men. He started to say something in his and his brother's defense, but before he could, Sepreano settled his soldiers' laughter with a raised hand. "Why were you bringing these lawdogs to me? I have no use for these *lawdogs*." He gave a wicked grin. "Unless I wished to see them wiggle on a stick above a fire."

Shaw was glad he hadn't been wearing the badge Dawson gave him.

Eddie Barrows cut in, "Believe me, you'd want to see these two wiggling over a fire, General."

Redlow gave his brother a look, silencing him. "This is the part that grieves me to tell you, General," he said to Sepreano, shaking his head slowly, "but these two lawdogs killed your brother, Carlos."

Shaw waited, not wanting to respond at that moment. He had Simon, a witness if he needed one. But if what Redlow said was true, that Dawson and Caldwell had stolen the Bengreen horses and made a getaway, he wasn't about to mention Simon seeing the gunfight that had gotten Carlos Sepreano killed. To hell with the Barrows. Now that Titus Boland was dead and Dawson and Caldwell were safe, he was ready to clear out of there.

"Carlos, Carlos . . ." Sepreano gripped the stone-balcony railing as if needing it for support. He shook his bowed head in silent grief for a moment. Then he collected himself, raised his head and wiped his fingertips to his eyes. Pointing down first at Shaw, then at each of the Barrows brothers he said, "You, you and you, get up here. I must be able to look each of you in the eyes as you tell me what happened to my poor brother, Carlos."

On the outside chance that he might need Simon after all, Shaw said to Sepreano, "I need to bring my friend with me." He glared at the Barrows, then said, "I might need him to tell us what he saw."

Sepreano looked Simon up and down, then focused on his soiled and ragged clothes and the look on his haggard face. "Bring the drunk with you," he said, "if he knows something about Carlos' death."

Shaw gestured for Simon to follow him. Simon looked as if he'd been struck in the face. "Oh, *por favor*, no, Senor Shaw, I cannot go up there and talk to this man. Look at me. I can barely hold my hands in front of me, I shake so bad!"

"You don't need your hands," said Shaw, reaching

out and grabbing Simon by his ragged serape before he could get away. In a lowered voice he said as he pulled Simon close to him, "Like as not, you won't need to say anything. I want you along just in case." He nodded toward the four Barrows men still standing by their horses. The four stared hard at Simon as if already knowing what he'd seen in Agua Cubo. "Besides, I can't leave you down here now, not with these four looking ready to eat your liver."

Simon swallowed nervously. "If I only had a drink."

"Not right now, amigo," said Shaw, giving a tug on his serape. "Let's go."

Simon resisted. "But my hands, look how they tremble so!"

"Keep them up under your serape," Shaw said, not taking any of his excuses.

Simon made a trembling sign of the cross on his chest and whispered, "I pray that you are not getting me killed. I want to feel better than this when I die."

"You're not going to die. I've got you covered, Simon," Shaw said with a wry smile. "Don't forget, I am the fastest gun alive."

Chapter 26

Dawson and Caldwell had been riding alongside Captain Agosto and Corporal Duego moments earlier, just inside the narrow rock corridor. When they'd heard the rapid shots from Shaw's big Colt resounding in a long echo across the harsh terrain, the two lawmen looked at each other in surprise. "Shaw?" Dawson asked. But he already knew the answer. Of course it was Shaw, he told himself. Who else would have been capable of that kind of shooting?

"He's beaten us here?" Caldwell said.

"But how?" Dawson said, staring with a puzzled expression across the land, toward the sound of the gunshots. Then he sighed and shook his head. "It doesn't matter. He did it somehow."

"That figures," Caldwell murmured.

"What was that?" Corporal Duego asked. "Was it one shot or several?"

"Take your pick," said Dawson, a slight smile

coming to his face. He was glad to know his friend was still alive and taking care of himself. "That was our friend, Lawrence Shaw," he added.

"The one you asked our soldiers to watch for on the trail behind us?" Duego asked.

"Yep," said Dawson, "but he's managed to circle ahead of us some way. From the sound of things, I'd say he's already taken care of any account he came here to settle."

"I hope he did not kill Luis Sepreano," the captain said. "That is one hombre I myself want to kill."

"I'd say those shots weren't meant for Sepreano, Captain," Dawson said. "They had Titus Boland written all over them." They hurried their horses forward across the rough rolling land, the castle ruins rising slowly ahead of them in the morning light.

Five hundred yards from the gates of the stronghold, two of Sepreano's lookouts spotted the column of *federales* riding toward them. They jumped atop their horses, batted their heels to the animals' sides and raced toward the shelter of the thick stone walls. But just before they disappeared over a low rise, a sharpshooter's bullet nailed one of them in the center of his back, knocking him forward and out of his saddle.

The other lookout only glanced back long enough to see what had happened. Then without even slowing, he slapped his reins back and forth on the horse's neck and raced on. When he spotted the men along the top of the stronghold walls looking out to see what the shot was about, he jerked his hat from his head and waved it back and forth, shouting, "*Fed-*

erales are coming! *Federales* are coming! Open the gates!"

Atop the wall, one of the men looked far across the land behind the lookout rider. He saw the body of the other lookout and his horse standing a few yards away. Farther away he saw the dust rising behind the column of *federales* as they rode more clearly into sight. Turning, he quickly waved a hand and called down to the men on the ground, "Open the gates for Miguel! Quickly! Alert the general! Soldiers are coming!"

As two men began opening the gates and others grabbed rifles and ammunition, one raced across the courtyard on foot and up the stone stairs to the second floor. Having heard his running footsteps, the two bodyguards stepped out of the room and met him at the door. One guard grabbed him by the front of his shirt.

"You cannot go in there," the big guard said gruffly to him. "What was the shot we heard outside the walls?"

"There are *federales* coming!" the man repeated. "I came to warn the general!"

"Don't worry, we will tell the general," the guard said. "Go find Captain Rhineholt and Manko. Tell them what you told us! *Vámanos!* Hurry!"

The man raced back down the stone stairs and started along the building toward where he knew Rhineholt and Manko both had rooms. But before he'd gone fifty feet, he saw Manko running toward him. "The general's bodyguards sent me for you and

Rhineholt," he said, speaking fast. "There are *federales* coming. We are being attacked!"

"I already know this, you fool," said Manko, shoving the man away. "Go tell Rhineholt. He knows what to do. I'm on my way to the general." He looked upward toward the empty balcony as he hurried on.

Inside the general's room, Shaw stood to one side, Simon right beside him. A few feet away stood both Barrows. Across the wide room Sepreano sat upon a large stone chair covered with cushions and blankets, the very throne where the original warlord had sat in years long past. Beside the cushioned throne stood a bodyguard with a rifle held at port arms.

The Barrows had just finished giving Sepreano their take on what had happened to his brother when the other two bodyguards stepped inside the room and walked over to the throne. One bent slightly and said to Sepreano close to his ear, "We have soldiers coming. We are under attack."

Sepreano nodded. "Let the rider inside. Then close the gates and prepare for battle. I will be right along. They cannot take this place from us. They will only die foolishly if they try."

Shaw listened intently, making out some of the conversation. He'd heard the rifle shot and some of the commotion on the street below. It was time to get this over with and get Simon out of here. He glanced to his side and saw the poor man trembling, his hands quaking beneath the ragged serape. Yeah, enough was enough, he told himself. Simon was kind and brave enough to come here with him, in spite of his drunken, unstable condition. This was no way to treat him.

As the two bodyguards turned to leave, Manko rushed into the room. The two stopped him; but Sepreano said, "Let him come to my side. This is one man I know who will never betray me. We have been together too long and seen too much, eh, Manko?"

"*Si*, General," said the big Mexican, giving Shaw a frown as he spoke. "I come to make sure your orders are followed, the way we have always done at a time such as this." He glared at Shaw again and said, "And also to kill anybody you want killed."

"Keep that thought in mind, my good friend, Manko," said Sepreano. He turned to Shaw and said, "I hear what these two say about the two lawdogs killing my brother. Now, it is your turn to tell me what you have to say about it."

"These men are lying, General," Shaw said, staring at both Barrows brothers. "The two lawmen weren't in Agua Cubo the night your brother was killed. They're blaming the lawmen for what they're guilty of doing."

"That's a damned lie!" Redlow shouted. Yet, even in his rage he made no move for the gun on his hip, not against Shaw, not after what he'd seen in the street.

"Shut up, Red!" Sepreano shouted, slapping his palm down on the thick stone arm of the throne. Turning to Shaw, he said, "Were you there? Did you see who killed my brother, Carlos?"

Shaw considered it. He sensed the intense fear going

on inside Simon standing beside him. He stared first at Redlow, then at Eddie. Then he made his decision, let out a breath and said, "No, General, I didn't see them kill your brother."

"There, you see?" said Redlow. "He didn't see us do it because it didn't happen."

Sepreano raised a hand to shut him up. To Shaw he said, "Then why do you blame them?"

Shaw let it go. He wasn't going to put Simon on the spot. "I just had a hunch, General, that's all." He stared at Redlow and Eddie with a look that let them know he could have gotten them killed if he'd chosen to.

"You had a hunch?" Sepreano stared at him, looking him up and down, knowing that something was going on here, but uncertain what it could be. After a pause he said, "Did you really come here to ride for me, Shaw?"

"No," Shaw replied, even though he knew honesty could cost him his life. "The truth is I came here to kill Titus Boland, the man lying dead in the street." He looked at Sepreano. "He killed a woman I thought I loved at the time."

"Oh, are you saying it turns out that you did not love her?" Sepreano asked, finding himself interested in the strange man who wielded such authority with a six gun.

"I don't know," said Shaw, "but whether I loved her or not, she didn't deserve to die." He looked off through the open balcony doors. "Boland killed her thinking he was killing me."

"Then he did not kill her with malice? He killed her by mistake?" Sepreano asked.

"That's one way of looking at it," Shaw said, turning back to him.

"What other way is there to look at it?" Sepreano asked. "There are only two kinds of vengeance. There is the vengeance of vengeance of the angels, and the vengeance of the devil. You are at Hell's Gate. Which vengeance is yours?"

Beside the cushioned throne, Manko gave a flat, curious grin, as if he had no idea on what level Sepreano and Shaw were talking.

"I've been at the gates of hell long before I got here," said Shaw. "I suppose I wanted the vengeance of angels. But I took what I could get." He thought about the badge, the one he held a claim to, but had never worn.

Another silent pause engulfed the room. Outside, gunshots began to fill the air from the direction of the column of *federales*. But Sepreano seemed unconcerned. "You are a strange man, Fast Larry Shaw," he said. Looking at Simon he said, "Who is this drunkard who is shaking too badly to show us his hands?"

"This is Simon," said Shaw. "He's on his way home." He gave Simon a look, then said to Sepreano, "With your permission I hope?"

"We will see," said Sepreano.

Outside, a roar of cannon fire resounded, seeming to jar the earth. Sepreano didn't flinch; neither did Shaw.

"Perhaps it is time for us to leave, General," Manko said.

Sepreano nodded, but made no effort to stand up

from his throne. "I have never seen any human being draw a gun and fire as rapidly or as accurately as you did today," he said to Shaw. "Are you sure you won't ride with me?"

"No, I expect that would be a bad idea, General," said Shaw.

"A pity," Sepreano said with a shrug. Another round of cannon fire pealed through the air and landed with a heavy, jarring thud against the wall beside the gates. "May I see the gun that you shoot so well? May I hold it in my hand?"

"Ordinarily I trust no man enough to hand over my gun," Shaw said. Yet he raised his Colt from his holster slowly, reversed it in his hand and stepped forward.

"No!" said Manko, stepping in between him and Sepreano.

"Easy, Manko," the general said. Looking around the big Mexican he said to Shaw, "Give it to your shaky friend. He will bring it to me."

Shaw kept his eyes fixed on Manko as he held the Colt sideways for Simon. "Keep your finger off the trigger. Don't shoot yourself in the foot," he cautioned.

But as Simon started forward, Manko stopped him too, with a hand held out for the gun. "The bullets," he said bluntly.

"Oh, of course," said Simon, giving Shaw a frightened look for approval.

"It's a good idea, as bad as you're shaking," Shaw said.

Gunfire grew more intense outside the window,

back and forth from both sides of the wall. Simon opened the Colt and let the bullets fall into Manko's big hand.

"All right, go ahead," Manko said, stepping aside and staring back at Shaw as Simon walked past him to the throne and handed Sepreano the Colt, butt first.

Sepreano looked at the gun closely, turning it back and forth in his hands. "Giving me his gun tells me that your friend does not care if he lives or dies." He looked at Simon and said, "Even a drunkard like you must see that. If I ordered these men to kill him right now, what would stop them?"

"Noth—nothing?" Simon said, hesitantly.

"*Si*, that is right, nothing," said Sepreano. He tapped a finger to his forehead. "Even though you are a drunkard and a vagrant, I tell you this. A man who does not protect his power and his life is a man soon to die." He handed the gun, butt first, back to Simon. But as Simon took it, Sepreano held on to it for a second longer and said, "Do you believe what I said?"

"Will knowing this inspire you? Will it do you some good someday?" He gave Simon a condescending grin that said he knew better. He turned loose of the gun butt.

"Oh, *si*, General, it will indeed," Simon said quietly, his voice no longer weak and timid, his hand no longer trembling as it came from under the ragged serape. "It already has."

Shaw stared in disbelief as a tall knife appeared from under Simon's serape and drew a straight, deep line across Sepreano's throat. "Damn it, Simon!" he shouted, not knowing what else to say.

"Oh no, General!" Manko bellowed, turning and seeing the long curtain of blood fall from beneath Sepreano's chin and spread down his chest.

Knowing what was about to happen to Simon, Shaw leaped forward, seeing the big Mexican draw his gun as Simon moved around the wall toward the door, the bloody knife in hand. Jerking Redlow around backward, Shaw reached around him, grabbed Luna's shotgun and aimed it at Manko as he cocked the ornate hammer. When the hammer fell, Manko caught only a glimpse of the fire as the scrap-iron shot exploded from the short barrel.

The eight-gauge blast hit the big Mexican all over, turning him into a block of chopped red meat. The brunt of the shot took out most of his midsection as it slung chunks of him across the room and all over the wall.

Eddie turned and drew his gun, seeing Shaw shove his brother away as he snatched Redlow's gun from his holster and shot him.

"You son of—" Eddie's words stopped as two bullets from his brother's gun nailed him in the chest.

As Eddie hit the floor, Shaw looked around in time to see the two bodyguards running through the door. But Simon, as quick as a snake, tripped the first one and snatched his rifle from his hands as he fell. As the second one tried to keep from falling over the first, Simon knocked him cold with a quick swipe of the rifle barrel. Before the one on the floor could get his legs under him, Simon drove the rifle butt down solidly on the back of his head, then stepped back and looked toward Shaw.

"I'm the help the Mexican government sent," he said in a confident, no-nonsense tone.

"I can't wait to tell Dawson and Caldwell about this," Shaw said, stepping over to where his Colt lay on the stone floor. He picked it up, reloaded it with bullets from his belt and, eyeing it closely, spun it on his finger. "I watched you throw back an awful lot of whiskey," he said. "Where was you putting it?" Outside, the battle raged, growing more intense.

Simon shrugged and picked up the knife from where he'd dropped it in order to snatch the guard's rifle. "I drank a lot of it, but not as much as I led everybody to believe." He wiped the knife blade across the belly of one of the knocked-out guards. "You see, I knew it would be a waste of time tracking Sepreano down unless I could get close enough to kill him. I had hoped to get in with Carlos and slip in here. When the Barrows killed him, there went that idea. But then you came along, and I decided it was my best shot. So, here we are." He smiled.

Shaw noted the difference in him: His voice, his demeanor, even his eyes were more clear, now that he kept them open a bit wider. "I have to admit, I fell for it. You fooled me, Simon, if that's even your name?"

"Yes, it is my name," he replied. "I hope there's no hard feelings. After all, we were all after the same thing." He gestured a hand toward the bodies of the Barrows and Sepreano. "We got the job done."

Shaw looked all around, then shook his head and

stepped over toward the door, the cannon and Gatling gunfire having lessened. He picked up a white linen cloth from a table and carried it with him. "Yep," he said, "I can't wait to tell them. . . ."

Outside the walls, Dawson and Caldwell had first seen Fairday and the other three riders go racing off across the flatlands as one of the broken gates fell to the ground after a direct hit from the cannon. Anticipating their run for the hills to the west, the two lawmen cut away from Captain Agosto's column and rode hard. Circling out of sight, they waited until two of the four rode up over a rise; then they opened fire without warning.

Dawson fired three times, each bullet hitting Vincent Tomes in the chest, flipping him backward out of his saddle before Tomes could get off a shot. A few feet away, Caldwell brought McClinton down with one shot, but the outlaw scrambled across the ground, clawing with one hand while his other hand clutched his chest. In a few yards his strength ran down slowly as the blood trail behind him widened. Caldwell stood watching with a detached expression as he dropped the spent cartridge and replaced it. Walking forward to where McClinton stopped and rolled over his back, he looked down at him and said, "Where are the other two?"

"They got . . . the hell away . . . I hope," the dying outlaw said.

"Who are they?" Caldwell asked.

Instead of answering, McClinton said, "Why don't you take . . . that smoking gun . . . and stick—"

Caldwell watched his words stop in his throat. His

eyes stared straight up. Stepping back, Caldwell said to Dawson, "Want to take our rifles and get after them?"

Dawson looked all around. "If they slipped around us, they're in the hills now. I saw them close enough to know it wasn't Eddie or Redlow Barrows. We've done our jobs here."

The two looked over toward the castle ruins, seeing the *federales* swing around it and go after a band of fleeing riders who had left through a hidden gate on the far side of the wall. "Looks like Sepreano's army didn't put up near the fight we expected," said Caldwell, slipping his gun into his holster. "What do you suppose went on inside there?"

"I can't wait to hear," said Dawson, reloading his gun now, glad that the job was over, glad to see things winding down.

"Look at this," said Caldwell. "Somebody's trying to surrender."

Above the thick wall they saw an arm slowly waving a white cloth back and forth. "They couldn't have picked a better time," Dawson said, looking at the busted gate and the black smoke rising above the battered stone walls. A body, its bloody arms hanging lifeless, lay stretched over the wall.

Seeing that all the action had ceased along the wall and upon the flatlands, Caldwell watched the white cloth wave for a moment. "It wouldn't surprise me if that's Shaw waving surrender."

Dawson stared alongside him for a moment in quiet contemplation. Then he said, "It would surprise me if it's *not*."

The two lawmen stepped up into their saddles and turned their horses toward the ruins at an easy gallop. Atop the wall, Shaw stood up with the white cloth hanging from his hand. He watched the two ride closer until he recognized both their faces. "*Mi amigos* . . . ," he murmured. Then he let the cloth fall from his hand and flutter away on a warm desert breeze.

Read on for a special preview
of Ralph Cotton's next novel,

SHOWDOWN AT HOLE-IN-THE-WALL

Coming from Signet in March 2009

Utah Territory

Time to go . . .

Arizona Ranger Sam Burrack stood at the window of his second-floor room. He had wintered as long as he could afford to in the river valley south of Cedar Ridge. Most of the damage from the gunshot wound in his lower back had healed. He wasn't as good as new, but he'd been off his feet long enough.

With his gun belt draped over his shoulder, he lowered the hammer on his freshly cleaned Colt and slipped it loosely into its slim-jim holster. He gazed out the window. The rocky passes in the distance had shed their thick blankets of snow, and the trail had begun to reveal itself. It snaked upward into the mountains toward Wyoming Territory. That's where he'd been headed before a dry gulcher's bullet had stopped him short.

But he was healed now, and it was time to load

the pack mule, saddle the brown and white paint horse awaiting him at the livery barn and ride on. "And that's that," he said as he pondered the street below.

"And you are quite certain I can't talk you out of leaving us, Ranger Burrack?" the Englishwoman, Beatrice Prine, asked quietly. She stood beside him, a tall stately woman dressed in a clean-smelling, plaid gingham dress.

She'd watched him check the big Colt and put it away. She shook her head slightly and gazed with him across the wide basin, where only patches of snow still clung along the edges of rock and dry grassland. Tops of cedar and pine swayed in the raw morning wind.

"I'm certain," the ranger replied after a long moment of silence. "I won't feel right until I get up to Hole-in-the-wall and get my stallion back."

She sighed. "You're fresh over a gunshot wound in the back, yet you insist on riding through a country filled with outlaws just for a *horse*?"

Sam gave a thin, wry smile. "Not just *any* horse I wouldn't," he replied. "But for my stallion, you bet I will." He paused, then added quietly, "I should have been there long before now. Like I told you, the animal was banged up bad in a dynamite blast."

"Yes, so you said . . ." Beatrice Prine considered what she knew of the ranger's situation. He had told her his story over the long winter nights he'd spent with her. "You told me you entrusted Memphis Warren Beck to take care of the stallion for you until you can make your way to Hole-in-the-wall and reclaim the animal. I expect the rest of the gang had a hard time understanding that one."

"Like I told you, I had no other choice," Sam said, noting the doubtful tone to her voice. "Beck gave me his word. I never thought I'd say this about a man like Memphis Beck, but he's proven himself to be good for his word."

"I could have told you that about Memphis Beck," said Beatrice Prine. "I dare say I've known him a good while longer than you have. His word has always stood well with me."

"He's still an outlaw, but I have to say he's a cut above the rest," Sam said grudgingly, recalling how Memphis Beck had saved his life in Mexico when a madman and his cult of murderers had tried to kill him. *Shadow Valley . . .* , Sam thought to himself, recalling the incident all too clearly.

"That being the case, what is your hurry?" Beatrice Prine asked. "A few more days of rest would be good for you."

"It's been all winter since I saw the stallion, and I'm still not there," Sam said. "I won't feel right until I've got Black Pot's reins in my hands."

Knowing the futility of trying to talk him out of riding into the outlaw stronghold, Beatrice Prine patted his arm and said with a sigh, "Well, the girls and I are all going to miss you."

"That's most kind of you to say so, Mrs. Prine. I'll miss you and the girls as well," Sam replied. He could feel her free hand on his foreram.

"We're alone. You may call me Miss Beatrice," she said softly, gesturing with a nod, indicating their privacy.

Sam knew that Beatrice Prine did not easily share her first name with guests. "Much obliged, *Miss Beatrice,*" Sam said quietly. "In turn, I'd be honored if you'd call me Sam."

The Englishwoman smiled to herself. "Sam, then," she said without taking her eyes from the endless rugged terrain beyond the window.

The two stood in silence for a moment, and then the ranger patted her hand, which still rested on his forearm. "I must look a sight better than I did riding in. I have you and your doves to thank for that, Miss Beatrice."

"Go on with you, now," she said softly in her British accent. "It was our pleasure having you here." She smiled and said quietly, "How many of us can say we actually wintered with the Ranger?"

Sam felt himself blush. It wasn't his way to speak loosely of such things, even if only in a light, suggestive manner. "Not many," he said. Then to hurriedly change the subject, he said, "Your hospitality has not only healed my back wound, I believe my hearing has cleared up some, after that dynamite blast."

"Wonderful," said the Englishwoman. "In that case I do hope you'll keep an ear perked for those two along your trail." She nodded at the rough-looking man and woman who had appeared out of a ragged tent saloon on the street below and walked toward their horses, which were tied to hitch rail.

"Stanley and Shala Lowden . . . ," the ranger said

under his breath. He'd observed the couple throughout the weeks he'd spent healing here above the muddy street. He'd also seen them in some of the towns he'd passed through before his ambush. "You can bet I will."

" 'The lovebirds,' we called them when they first arrived here last year," Beatrice Prine said. She tightened her hand on his forearm. "I'm still convinced it was they who shot you."

The lovebirds . . .

"No proof," he said flatly, his tone indicating that he too was convinced these two had been the ones who ambushed him. He'd thought hard about the circumstances of his shooting all through the long winter days and nights he'd lain here, his lower back throbbing in pain, his strength depleted from loss of blood.

"No proof?" Beatrice Prine cocked her head with a curious look. "There was no one else for miles around. You saw them only hours beforehand . . . watching you from a trail above you. That is more proof than most people need. You have every right to—"

"I'm not most people," Sam said, cutting her off with a wry smile. He tightened his hand over hers and added, "That's the cost of wearing a badge. If I start bending justice, shaping it to fit myself, it's time I begin looking for another occupation."

"Come now, Sam," Beatrice Prine said playfully, yet with her cordial air of sophistication. "Would you have me believe you have never bent the law—'justice,' as you put it?" She raised a skeptical brow.

"Please, don't disappoint me . . . don't turn out to be another hypocrite."

"Hypocrite? I can't say," he replied. "I expect we're most all of us hypocrites in some way or another. I don't claim to be perfect. I'm far from it."

He thought about it as he watched another man step out of the ragged tent and join the Lowdens at the hitch rail. The man shifted his eyes back and forth warily. His breath steamed in the cold air; he wore a thick bearskin coat and a wide-brimmed hat cocked jauntily above long, glistening black hair. "Besides," Sam continued, "I didn't say I never bent justice. I admit I have played loosely with justice at times, but never to serve myself—not to suit my own needs."

They stood in silence for a moment; then Beatrice Prine said, "So, what does this mean? Will these two go unpunished for what we both know they did to you? That hardly seems fair."

"None of us go unpunished, Miss Beatrice," Sam said contemplatively, watching the man in the bearskin coat stand and talk privately with the Lowdens. "Everything we do in life has a price. We all pay as we go."

"I have found that to be the case," Beatrice Prine said in agreement.

"Who is that fellow?" Sam asked, nodding toward the man in the bearskin coat.

"He's Conning Glick," said the Englishwoman. "Have you heard of him?"

"Conning Glick . . . also known as the Dutchman." The ranger nodded, running the name though his mind. He stared more intently at the man through the wavy glass windowpane. "So, that's Conning Glick?"

"Yes, that's him," said Beatrice. "Not exactly a name that rolls easily off the tongue, is it?" She smiled thinly. "No wonder so many people prefer calling him the Dutchman."

"He's a paid assassin from years back," said Sam, summoning up his stored information about the man. "Did most of his killing for railroads and big mining companies. Also worked on the sly for any wealthy, powerful man who needed his services."

"As far as I know, he still does," Beatrice said. "I can't see a man like Glick ever giving up his profession. I suspect he loves killing too much to ever retire."

Sam studied the older man's pasty white face, noting the long, shiny black hair hanging past Glick's shoulders. The hair was far too young and far too black for Glick's aged, pale skin coloring. *A woman's hair,* Sam thought to himself. Then he asked, "Is he wearing a wig?"

"You don't miss a thing, Sam. Yes, he is," Beatrice said with a dry smile. She wrinkled her nose a bit in a gesture of distaste and added, "Conning Glick is as bald as a stump. Word has it he was born hairless. No eyebrows, no body hair . . . nothing *anywhere.*" She gave him a look that said her information was reliable.

Sam gave her a questioning look.

"Not that I have seen for myself firsthand," she said as if in her own defense, "but two of my doves,

Fannie and Darlene, have told me as much. Fannie also said the long black hair is a cured human scalp. Fannie said the smell is terrible up close."

"I bet," Sam replied.

"She told me he frequently douses it with perfume and witch hazel, but it only makes the smell worse. It got so bad that Fannie said she refused him service unless he took it off." Beatrice shook her head, contemplating the matter. "Apparently he discards the scalp after a certain amount of wear and tear and procures himself another. God only knows how or where he finds them," she mused grimly.

"I can guess." Sam shook his head slowly, watching Conning Glick and the Lowdens speaking intently at the hitch rail.

"Why doesn't the law do something about a man like Glick?" she asked. "He makes it no secret that he's a killer. I've heard him brag openly to the girls how he uses poisons, fire, does anything it takes to kill men in all sorts of gruesome ways."

"Again, it takes proof," Sam said patiently. "The same thing it would take to accuse the Lowdens of shooting me in the back. It doesn't matter what he says unless he mentions names of people he's killed and there's a way to tie them to him. Otherwise it's all just saloon talk."

Beatrice gave him a sigh and shook her head. "If you ask me, you are entirely too fixed on this proof issue you keep bringing up."

"I admit, it's often a drawback of mine," the ranger replied, going along with her dry style of humor.

Then, dismissing the subject, he asked, "What do you suppose these three have to talk about?"

"Heaven only knows," said Beatrice. As an afterthought she said, "Sam, watch your back out there. Proof or no proof, I don't like the looks of this."

"I always watch my back," Sam replied, staring down at the Lowdens as Glick stepped closer to them, appearing to berate the ragged couple.

"I know you do, of course," said Beatrice, patting his hand. "But I feel better telling you to anyway."

At the hitch rail, Stanley Lowden turned a wary glance upward toward the ranger's window. But the Dutchman jostled him rougly, saying through clenched teeth, "That's it, you *damned idiot*! Be sure and look up there, make sure he knows you're watching his every move, if he doesn't know it already."

Stanley turned his face quickly away from the second-floor window and looked at the Dutchman. "He didn't see me, Mr. Glick," he said in a lowered voice, as if to keep the ranger from hearing him even at such a distance.

"Start using your head, Stanley!" Glick demanded, like an overbearing father. He palmed the bigger, stronger, young man on the forehead. "Do you understand me?" His other hand held firmly onto Stanley's lapel. Shala stared in stunned disbelief. She'd never seen her husband take this sort of treatment from anybody. He certainly didn't have to take it, she knew. Stanley stood over a head taller than Glick. He was young, broad-shouldered and land-hardened from the life they led. Yet he appeared to have let this old man buffalo him somehow.

"I—Yes, I understand, Mr. Glick," Stanley stammered, taken off guard by the quickness of Glick's action. He cut a glance toward Shala and saw the look on her face. He should have done something right then and there; he shouldn't haved allowed Glick to treat him in such a manner. But now it was too late; the moment has passed him by. He started to say something, but before he could, Glick turned him loose, smiled flatly and patted his lapel.

"Good, young man," Glick said in a wet, gravely voice. "If I seem a little harsh, it's for your own good." He grinned at Shala, including her. "You both have grown on me over these weeks. In spite of the trouble you've caused me, I've come to think of you as a couple of innocent children—like family, so to speak." He stared pointedly into Stanley's eyes and added, "You do know that, *don't you*, young man?"

Like children? His *children . . . ?* Stanley swallowed an uncomfortable tightness in his throat and avoided Shala's eyes. "Yes, I know that. We both know that." He paused, then said, "I realize I didn't do things exactly the way I was supposed to. Things didn't go just the way we had them planned—"

"Stanley," Glick said, cutting him off, his voice turning more harsh again, "you shot the *wrong* man."

"I know I messed up bad, but it wasn't all my fault, Mr. Glick," Stanley said, the very same words he'd used all winter when Glick brought up the subject. "I kept watch on the high pass—the one you said he'd be using."

"You shot the *wrong* man, Stanley," Glick repeated in a stronger tone.

"I know that, Mr. Glick," said Stanley. "And I'm sorry as hell I did. But I'll make it right. I swear I will."

"Oh, I know you will." Glick gave flat, sly grin, reached up with his pale, cold hand and patted the young man's jaw. "I'll be right by your side to make sure you get it done right. This Ranger Burrack has to die *now*. The only thing worse than shooting the wrong man is shooting the wrong man and not killing him." He pinched Stanley's jaw roughly. "Eh? Am I right?"

"Yes, you're right," Stanley said, feeling himself shrink smaller and smaller in his wife's eyes.

Glick turned loose the young man's cheek and pointed his blue-veined finger in warning. "Mind you, any more mistakes and I'll have to sternly correct you, just as if you were my own children." From beneath his hairless brow, his yellow eyes moved from Stanley to Shala, looking her up and down. "That goes for the both of you."

From the window above, Sam observed the interaction between Glick and the Lowdens. "It looks like the Dutchman is trying to teach these lovebirds to eat out of his hand," he said to Beatrice Prine.

"I'd say it's more like he's training them to jump through his hoops, if I know the Dutchman," said Beatrice. She paused in consideration, then said in a wary tone, "Now that I see Glick with these lovebirds, I'm even more concerned for you riding up along the high trail alone. I've known my share of gunmen and assassins, but there's something about Conning Glick that makes my skin crawl." She rubbed her forearm. "Maybe I should send No Toes along to watch about you—you know, just until you reach Hole-in-the-wall?"

"I'm obliged for your concern," Sam said, "but No Toes' job is here, looking after you." He gave a wry smile. "How could I live with myself if something happened to you while your bodyguard is off watching me?"

"But, Sam—"

The ranger held up a hand. "I'll be all right," he said. He nodded toward the door. "Come on now, walk me downstairs. "I want to thank all your doves before I leave."